Night Train
to
ODESSA

Praise for
Night Train to Odessa

In this historical novel of love and lore, idealism and corruption, and, always, hope, Mary L. Grow writes with grace and conviction about a young widow searching for her missing children in the beautiful but beleaguered city of Odessa during the upheaval of the Bolshevik revolution. *Night Train to Odessa* is gripping and unforgettable, with writing so transporting I could feel the cold winter wind blowing across the Black Sea.

—JUDITH CLAIRE MITCHELL
author of *A Reunion of Ghosts*

Night Train to Odessa sweeps readers across an explosive wartime landscape, following a brave young woman whose unexpected loss thrusts her into the political upheaval that surrounds her. Mary L. Grow has created heartfelt, compelling, and breathing characters. With passion and eloquence, she brings the past back to clamorous, detailed life. She is a remarkable author to be avidly followed and admired.

—JANE GUILL
author of *Nectar From A Stone*

Night Train to Odessa is a heartfelt, warm, and moving story … one of my most enjoyable reads of the year.

—READERS' FAVORITE
FIVE STAR Review

Deeply informed and highly engaging, *Night Train to Odessa* relates the story of Elvira Maria as she searches for her lost children during the brutal upheaval of the Russian Civil War. The mother's tenacious struggle becomes increasingly difficult due to her poverty and loneliness—until she finds unexpected kindness from an itinerant puppeteer and a woman with an unsavory past. Mary L. Grow visits a tumultuous era with insight and the well-crafted impact of an accomplished author.

—SARA RATH
author of *The Waters of Star Lake* .

Mary L. Grow's beautifully rendered story is set 100 years ago, yet the events then and events now in war-torn Ukraine are frighteningly a story of today. Fleeing horror overnight and the loss of all that is good and familiar, Elvira Maria searches the once-exquisite port city for her precious children as the brutal winter encroaches. *Night Train to Odessa* is immersive, suspenseful, intimate and tender, a page-turner that captures your heart and soul.

—CARLY NEWFELD
producer and host, *The Last Word* on KSFR

A beautifully written protrayal of a Ukrainian family that perhaps resonates now more than ever.

—KIRKUS REVIEWS

Night Train to Odessa is both page-turner and *cri de coeur* that transports the reader to the war-torn seaport, Odessa. The novel's buoyant, well-plotted journey crosses paths with a cast of unforgettable characters. Though snow often whips against the reader's face, the scent of lilacs also stir the soul. I recommend this book to anyone curious enough to be swept into a rich, well-told tale—with an astonishing outcome.

—ALISON LESLIE GOLD
author of *Anne Frank Remembered* by Miep Gies & Alison Leslie Gold

ALSO BY MARY L. GROW

Children's Literature

Chester Meets The Walker House Ghost
Chester and The Mystery of the Tilted World

Night Train
to
ODESSA

A NOVEL

MARY L. GROW

Studio 17
Santa Fe

Fall, Winter, Spring, Summer sectional epigraphs are from the following sources respectively: *Lenin: A Biography* by David Shub, Penguin Publishers, London, 1948, *On The Steppes* by Maxim Gorky in *The Social Democrat*, Vol V, No. 7, July 1901, *My Disillusionment with Russia* by Emma Goldman, Doubleday, New York, 1923, *Love and Other Stories* by Yuri Oleysha, Washington Square Press, New York, 1967.

ISBN: 979-8-9883982-0-2
Library of Congress Control Number: 2023910539

Book design by Kathleen Dexter – KDInkandImage.net

Images
   Cover
      Peasant women in native dress of Little Russia (detail), Carpenter Collection, Library of Congress

      Odessa – Richelieu Street, Bain News Service photograph collection, Library of Congress
   Interior
      Map of Odessa in Ukraine, 1914, by Wagner & Debes, Leipzig www.discusmedia.com. 'The 1900 Map Collection'

Studio 17
17A County Road 84B
Santa Fe, NM 87506

For
Eleanor and Louis
and
Tanta Elvina

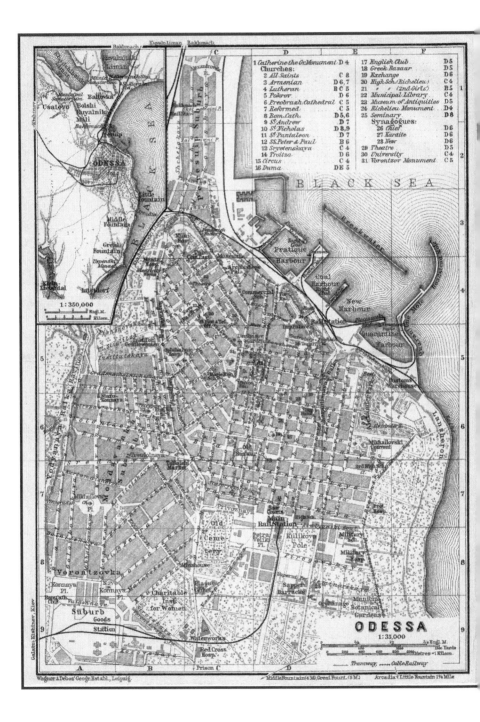

ODESSA

1:35,000

1 *Catherine the 0t Monument* D 4
Churches:
2 *All Saints* C 8
3 *Armenian* D 6,7
4 *Lutheran* B C 5
5 *Pokrov* D 6
6 *Preobrazh. Cathedral* C 5
7 *Reformed* C 5
8 *Rom. Cath.* D 5,6
9 *St Andrew* D 7
10 *St Nicholas* D 8,9
11 *St Pantaleon* D 7
12 *SS. Peter & Paul* B 6
13 *Sretenskaya* C 4
14 *Troitza* D 6
15 *Circus* C 4
16 *Duma* D E 5

17 *English Club* D 5
18 *Greek Bazaar* D 5
19 *Exchange* D 6
20 *High Sch. (Richelieu)* C 4
21 *" " (2nd Girls)* B 5
22 *Municipal Library* C 4
23 *Museum of Antiquities* D 5
24 *Richelieu Monument* D 4
25 *Seminary* D 6
Synagogues:
26 *Chief* D 6
27 *Karaite* D 6
28 *New* D 6
29 *Theatre* D 5
30 *University* C 4
31 *Vorontzov Monument* C 5

B L A C K S E A

Geclatz. Kaschner, Kiew

Wagner & Debes Geogr. Establ., Leipzig.

Middle Fountain (4 M).Great Fount. (5 M).

Arcadia ½. Little Fountain 1¾ Mile

...... Tramway, ----- Cable Railway

PRINCIPAL CHARACTERS

ELVIRA MARIA ANDRUSHKO (Slavic pronunciation, El.veer.ah Maria), a young widow and the mother of Sasha and Ana. The family is from the village of Kos.

MICHAIL LUKASHENKO, an immigrant from Minsk with a puppet theater who performs in the streets and parks of Odessa.

IVAN DASHKEVICH, a life-long friend of Michail's who joins the Bolsheviks in Odessa.

HEDDIE NARYSHKINA, a wealthy art patron who also runs an exclusive brothel in Odessa.

TATIANA KOVALEVA, a street orphan.

DEPUTY VLADIMIR VLADIMIROVICH DUDOROV, a White Army officer who joins the Bolsheviks and becomes General Kotovsky's deputy shortly before Kotovsky takes Odessa for the Reds.

ANATOLY KUZNETSOV FAMILY, are installed in the vestibule of the tenement where Elvira Maria and Michail live. Anatoly, known as Tolya, has a wife, Yagna, and two young sons, Pavlo and Danya.

AUTUMN
1919

There are no morals in politics; there is only
expedience. A scoundrel may be of use to us just
because he is a scoundrel.

—Vladimir Lenin

1

Kos, a village in the Ukraine, near Kyiv

EACH TIME THE ARTILLERY THUNDERED in the east the hurricane lamps hanging from the rafters of the station house flared, illuminating the worried faces of the people trudging out the open door, bundles on their backs, suitcases and canteens in hand. The tickets for the train to Odessa were sold out. Only those who'd lined up hours before and paid their fare would be able to board the Special, a run of freight cars coming from Kyiv and heading to the safety of the city on the Black Sea. The others would have to evacuate on their own before the Red Army arrived in a firestorm of torches and guns.

Elvira Maria Andrushko, twenty-six and two years a widow, fingered the tickets in her pocket. She sat opposite the station house on the trampled grass that stretched beside the tracks. Six-year-old Ana clung to her skirts, while Sasha, her ten year old, turned around her, his wide eyes looking at the faces in the crowd, all these strangers from villages beyond Kos where the Reds had gained ground.

He was particularly intrigued, she could tell, by a group of adolescent boys huddled around a smoldering fire. These were the rail riders and stowaways who traveled from city to city on the trains. They were besting each other with improbable stories of rustling camels in the northern tundra, and riding the beasts along the tracks to overtake the trains bound for Vladivostok. An old man, his white hair disheveled, strands falling across his face, sat with them. He plucked a bandura and sang a lament, his hoarse voice drifting on the smoke-filled wind. "Sasha," she said, "you need to eat," and she pulled the napkin of boiled potatoes from her satchel. But while Ana dutifully nibbled, Sasha was too distracted to bother.

Earlier that morning, before they left for the station, she had scoured the fields, one last time, for the few tubers that remained. In the distant wood, birch trees stood like sentinels, majestic reminders of the golden seasons that had passed. She wondered how long they would last. But any nostalgia, any pull toward staying in Kos, disappeared when she saw the strange wolf tracks in the wet field. They were not in straight lines as usual, but circled the tracks of the horses that, the day before, had staggered across the fields, bony and forlorn as the retreating Volunteer Army soldiers who beat them. The wolf tracks were an ominous sign. She had crossed herself to invoke the Virgin's protection, and hurrying back to the farmhouse had found Sasha and Ana, dressed in all their clothes, in the yard, saying goodbye to a neighbor.

Now a Cossack battalion, rounding the station house, their horses snorting into the cold night, galloped up and down the line to clear the rails. They charged at the urchins who sat on the signal gate and snapped their nagaikas, raising welts on the arms and faces of boys who failed to get out of the way. The urchins hooted and pitched sharp stones at the horses. Then out of the north Elvira Maria heard the engine bell clang. A beam of light blazed, revealing hundreds of men and women running across the nearby fields to the tracks. The train barreled into the station and spit out steam and black ash as it lurched to a stop. The Cossacks shouted and reined in their startled horses. Elvira Maria, jolted to her feet, men pushing past her, felt Ana's hands grab her legs and heard Sasha cry out, but when she bent down to gather them up she found herself staring into the tearful eyes of a stranger's child—Ana was gone and Sasha too. She called for them, her voice lost in the deafening noise. Sweeping the ground with outstretched arms, her hands struck only moving feet, not a familiar coat or the skirt of a woolen jumper. The children were nowhere near her. She scanned the wave of shawls, scarves, hats, rakes, and rifles silhouetted in the harsh light. "Mother of God," she whispered. The engine bell sounded again and again.

In minutes, the five freight cars filled. Refugees and soldiers crammed in the cars, pulled the steel doors shut, the screech of the metal raising alarm among those yet to board. A cloud of smoke and cinders spewed from the engine's chimney and settled over the platform, the train, and the field. Struggling through the crowd, she found an opening. She gathered up her long skirts and ran close behind a cadet who was determined to jump on board. Breathless, she reached the tracks.

A freight car covered in coal dust emerged from the haze and loomed before her, men and women beating on the double doors. Cadets, yelling to each other as they passed her, headed to a side ladder. Her eyes burning, she fanned the air and frantically looked up and down the platform. The children were not there. Steam, billowing from the cylinders, swept along the tracks, as if it had carried them away. She was suddenly alone. The voices surrounding her, drowning hers out, seemed to have vanished. She stood for a moment in that impossible silence, stunned—until the noise of the people on top of the cars, their cries of excitement and despair, returned to her, and she came back to herself and turned in the opposite direction and hurried to the engine where the Stationmaster, standing beside the cab, looked on, impervious to the commotion.

"Impossible," he said when he made sense of her words. "Impossible and dangerous to search overloaded freight cars for two children." She grabbed his arm and implored him again, but he pushed her aside. He blew his whistle. The shrill, piercing sound burned in her ears, forcing her to cover them at once with her hands. He turned to the engineer and waved his signal flag, moving a crisis down the line. At first the train moved slowly and belched cinders into the black sky. She ran beside it, trying to keep pace, futilely shouting. Then with a gush of steam and a clatter the train streaked forward, drowning out her screams, leaving her running madly along the empty track, sparks disappearing before her in the freezing air.

She collapsed in the station house. When she could sit again, she accepted a cup of water from the Stationmaster's wife, but not the babushka's consolation. "Be grateful the children are on a train headed for Odessa," the old

woman said. "They'll be spared death and starvation."
Elvira Maria went outside to check the surrounding area,
praying to find Ana and Sasha. Broken luggage was strewn
along the tracks as far as she could see. A cracked pair of
spectacles, several shoes, and a battered canteen lay beside
her toppled suitcase and her satchel.

The Stationmaster, his forehead flecked with soot, his
wrinkled face weary, assured her the train would travel
straight through to the city. Orders were orders and the
engineer was not foolish enough to invite more trouble.
The Stationmaster and his frail wife, who needed a good
doctor, were taking the last train to Odessa, before the line
was cut for a spell. She could ride with them in the engine
room, he said. It was the only offer he could make.

For the next two days, Elvira Maria waited in the
station house. She was surrounded by refugees camped
on the floor and stretched out on benches near hers. She
could not sleep. As she clutched her knees to her aching
chest, she felt the minutes and hours slipping away, taking
Sasha and Ana toward a danger she was afraid to imagine.
They had always been by her side, never among a shuffle
of strangers or alone on city streets. Like her, they had
lived their entire lives in Kos, a clutter of whitewashed
houses and barns tied to the rich black soil of the Ukraine;
a village of barely three hundred souls where each child
that survived its birth was known and protected by everyone. Sasha had walked to distant estates to repair fences
and barns in exchange for food, but had always come
home by dusk with stories about families they knew. Ana,
a shy, quiet child, had hardly ventured beyond the village
without her brother.

At dawn Elvira Maria surrendered her bench to an old man bent over his cane. Outside, the hoarfrost glistened in the dawn, each pink clump broken from the night's stampede. She walked up and down the tracks. The bitter taste of coal dust was still in her throat. She held her stomach and retched, a stream of black spittle darkening the grass.

Unable to eat the potatoes she'd prepared for the trip, she gave them to a new group of rail riders. Sitting with her on the platform, the boys described the underbelly of a boxcar and how to open the secret compartments in first class. They wanted to get to Odessa and ride with the Wind Shark, a boy who performed handstands on the rooftops of speeding freight cars. While she listened to their exploits she wondered if hunger and desperation had made them so bold and reckless.

The train from Kyiv arrived at two in the morning. She gathered her meager belongings and climbed to the engine room at once, not wanting to see the faces of those left behind. The four freight cars, filled with grain, were followed by two flatbeds loaded with armored trucks. She sat on a bench beside the stoker, a skinny young fellow with tattooed arms and a cheerful smile, a wet bandana at his neck. Each time he shoveled fuel from the tender into the firebox the flames raged and licked the metal edge, the heat so intense she felt cold.

They rattled through the countryside, fields and villages abandoned, lonely. By dawn they passed Uman, where the Jews lined the track and waved their arms and hats in a plea for the train to stop. She closed her eyes as the engineer picked up speed. They were stranded, the

Jews, their shtetl an orange glow on the horizon. The Stationmaster pointed to the fire. "The Whites," he shouted to her. "It's the Whites' Volunteer Army—Denikin." Elvira Maria had heard the name. Yudenich, Kolchak, Denikin. The field commanders with their political promises of land distribution and help for the people. It made her angry. No one had asked her what she wanted or why she'd worked every day tending the fields and livestock. She'd done it for her children. Ana and Sasha were all that mattered. And now the fields were destroyed, the livestock stolen. The children lost.

It was night when the train rolled into Odessa. Tired and weak, her legs shaking, she stepped down from the engine room, the metal railing still hot to her touch. The Stationmaster and his wife urged her to rent a room in a tenement house where their cousin, a docker, lived with his family. After saying goodbye to the couple, she lingered outside the station house. It was dark and closed until morning. A hand to the glass, she squinted through the tall windows into the enormous hall with its vaulted ceiling and tiled floors. It was eerily silent, the counters of the tea pavilion stacked with empty cups. Trailed by the rail urchins she'd met in Kos, she searched the platforms and circled the yard. She found dozens of lost children, but not her own. Once in the street, she hailed a droshky, and sitting beside strangers, headed across the city to the tenement.

2

Odessa

HOURS AFTER ELVIRA MARIA ARRIVED in Odessa an explosion destroyed a garment factory in Peresuip Suburb, a working-class neighborhood north of the city's center. She had been asleep, exhausted from the eighteen-hour train ride, and first thought the distant rumble that woke her was thunder. She got out of bed and went to the small window in her tenement room and searched the sky. It was full of stars. She wondered if it was cannon fire. The sound had echoed like the guns she'd heard in the countryside, just before she'd left her village. She listened for a second round, but heard only a drinker singing his way down the alley, his slurred words fading as he walked on. She returned to her bed, her body aching, eyelids heavy, and fell asleep.

The blast, an act of sabotage claimed by the Bolsheviks the next day, rocked Peresuip and shattered the windows of the houses and shops surrounding the gated factory yard. The Black Heron tavern, three tenements, and the tiny

Church of Saint Nicholas suffered cracked foundations. The factory, constructed of thick granite blocks, burned from the inside out, glowing like a demon's forge straight from hell. The fire brigade, sent clanging to the rescue, knew the blaze was beyond their control and worked only to contain it. They pumped water hour after hour and cleared away wreckage. Fascinated bystanders stood at a distance and watched, their feet wet from the black river that flowed down the street. The firemen sweated and cursed long into the following afternoon, their uniforms layered with soot, their tall leather boots destroyed.

The bomb had exploded at eleven-fifteen, after the factory closed and the workers left, but there were still a few casualties. Several homeless children with glass in their eyes were shuttled to the Municipal Hospital, along with three firemen who were badly burned. A coffin maker measured the bodies of two watchmen after their families identified the charred remains.

At daybreak nervous residents stood in line for ration cards and searched for an open market. They read newspapers condemning the perpetrators. Dealers, who recognized an opportunity, ignored the foul air and black ash hovering over the district and asked the factory's owners if any machines could be salvaged, if broken pipes and fixtures could be carted off and sold.

Odessans feared that more sabotage was on the way, but soon set aside the thought. A cold front, sweeping down from the north, was taking everyone by surprise. Residents now worried about fuel.

Three days after the blast, on a Friday morning, the icy wind arrived. It blew through the wide boulevards, bending the plane trees and scattering dry leaves into the dusty air. Torn handbills, marked with the insignia of the health ministry, fluttered in piles of broken bottles and rusted tins flung near the sea wall that ran parallel to Nikolaevskaya Boulevard, a major thoroughfare. Elvira Maria wended her way through the debris, slanting her body and skirts against the gale as she walked to the end of the street. Her once confident and energetic steps now were cautious, slower. In her hand she held a scrap of paper, an address of a place where she hoped her search for Ana and Sasha would shift in a more promising direction.

Red dust stung her eyes as she followed a well-trodden path next to the sea wall. Here she could safely bypass the screeching trams and impatient pushy pedestrians, the traffic clipping along, and the drivers shouting insults and blowing their horns. But the soldiers, camped in makeshift tents on the hill leading down to the harbor, were impossible to avoid. Their hungry eyes and whistles trailed her as she passed. Gaunt and bandaged, dirty blankets thrown over their ragged uniforms, they slumped on crutches or leaned against the wall. They shared cigarettes and bread, coughs punctuating their gossip. Some had fought on the Western Front and faced the Germans' heavy artillery and poisoned gas. Others, recruited or conscripted for the current Civil War, had fought in the Don Cossack region with the Whites or joined the Bolsheviks, committing themselves to a revolution still in the making. Clustered in loyal units their numbers increased each day, filling the promenades, the courtyards, and the parks that once had distinguished Odessa as an elegant city, prosperous and poised to conduct its orderly business with the world.

Elvira Maria was also displaced from home. Despite her life-long attachment to Kos she'd left the countryside as the Red Army advanced westward, claiming territory with a vengeance she could not understand. She had expected peace after the Great War, to plant the fields and harvest a good crop. Instead, refugees begged at her door and said the Bolsheviks were ruthless, godless, and cunning. Month after month the Whites had driven them from the gate, but the Reds were like the devil slipping through the keyhole. It was only a matter of days until the hellions burned everyone out. Why be foolish and guard a tumbling house and patch of land you didn't even own? Anguished, she had finally fled.

As she passed the Odessa Steps she clutched the knife in her pocket and quickened her pace. The massive sandstone slabs cascading to the dockyards below teemed with peddlers and beggars. She pressed her hand against the small packet of rubles hidden in her bodice and felt her heart pound. Finally reaching the mansion district, she left the sea wall path and headed to the street. Lorries and cars sped past. When a droshky loaded with wooden planks came by, the bony horse and grizzled driver stalling the traffic, she stepped onto the cobblestones and crossed.

Refugees, bundled against the sudden cold, lingered in the adjoining loggia of palazzo number 211, where faces of the missing stared out from makeshift bulletin boards nailed to the gilt moldings. The nineteenth-century mansion with its spacious balconies, cast-iron balustrades, and multiple chimneys belonged to a pastel ribbon of classical buildings constructed when grain wealth had flowed into the city. Now the building, headquarters of the People's Welfare Council, was neglected and grimy.

In the upper hallway, Elvira Maria joined the line at the reception desk. She adjusted her headscarf and straightened the pleated bodice of her black woolen dress. Following the example of the woman before her, she pressed her thumb into a soggy inkpad, then against the paper of a thick ledger. A guard with a pained expression ushered her through an enormous arch and into a crowded ballroom.

She sat beside a babushka who clicked her knitting needles through a row of stitches, the ball of red yarn in her lap shrinking as she finished one sweater sleeve and started another. Elvira Maria thought about the sewing she'd left behind in Kos and wished she had it now. And the scarves she'd knit for the children last winter. She'd set them by the door, but hurrying to leave, hadn't put them in her suitcase. She remembered packing a comb, her shawl, an extra pair of leggings for Ana—but the scarves—she should have insisted the children wear them. She fidgeted with her skirts and prayed Ana and Sasha were together, keeping each other warm.

Hours later, a shaft of sunlight turning the crystal drops of the ballroom chandeliers into prisms, she realized it was late afternoon. The woman next to her was almost finished with her sweater. People who'd been sitting on the parquet floor, strewn with spent cigarettes, had now found chairs. She was counting the empty chairs when the guard called her name. Pulling her papers from her pocket, she hurried to the back of the ballroom and took a seat before the Commissar.

The middle-aged bureaucrat, her short black hair cut bluntly in the latest fashion, sat behind a banquet table, files at her elbows. She checked Elvira Maria's identity card and reviewed the published train schedules that contradicted Elvira Maria's own experience.

"You were the only adult traveling with Aleksander Lyova Andrushko and his sister, Antonina. Is that correct?" the Commissar asked. Elvira Maria nodded and placed a photograph of her children on the table. The Commissar frowned and refused to pick it up. She could not look at another face of a lost child. Russia was in chaos. The Germans' wartime advance and political factions fighting in the countryside had destroyed countless families, leaving thousands of children to fend for themselves. "This department can record the names of your children," the Commissar said, "but our primary focus at this time is identifying missing soldiers who have fought on our behalf." She tapped her pen on the table. "You, of all people, know the destruction that's disrupted your village and brought you here."

Elvira Maria struggled to think of something to say. An image of her children begging in the doorway of a streetside shop passed through her mind. She gripped the edge of the table. "Commissar, please. What do you recommend?" she asked. "What should I do?"

The Commissar directed her to an orphanage she had already visited the day before. She told her to check the train station. Since her arrival, earlier in the week, Elvira Maria had been to the station every day. She'd searched the railyard and the surrounding sheds, talked to those in charge, and waited for hours on a bench out front. The place was overrun with packs of abandoned children who squatted there and knew each other well. Sasha and Ana were not among them.

The interview was almost over, the knot in her stomach tightened. "Where else can they be?" she asked.

"How should I know?" the Commissar said. She had sat at the table for days and listened to the pleas and cries of village women who couldn't keep their young ones safe. Their stories grated on her nerves. The problem of missing children was not hers to solve. She signed the interview dossier and dated it with a stamp that echoed through the hushed room. Raising her pen, she signaled the next in line to come forward.

Elvira Maria stared at the folder that identified Sasha and Ana. It now joined a stack of hundreds. She rose from her chair and walked through the ballroom and down the stairs. In the palazzo's courtyard, hooligans who'd settled in for the night catcalled and propositioned her. She made her way through the rabble and headed for Nikolaevskaya Boulevard. Now nine o'clock, it was quiet, the trams gone, the lorries parked beneath the plane trees. Pedestrians, afraid of a nighttime attack in the city's center, had disappeared. Three peddlers grinding their pushcarts home, their quilts and blankets piled high, claimed the thoroughfare. They reminded her of the merchants from Kyiv who came to Kos with their exotic goods, war reports, and tall tales. She leaned against a lamppost to retie her undone bootlace, then stood still to listen to the murmur of the city. Feverish, she heard children's laughter coming from a courtyard, several buildings away, but as she walked toward the sound she realized what she was hearing was only the wind.

3

IT WAS A COLD AFTERNOON AT THE BEGINNING of October when Elvira Maria, walking back to the tenement along Gogolya Street, saw the dressmaker's sign. Posted high above the door and swinging gently to the rhythm of the traffic passing by, it depicted a golden needle strung with dark green thread that spelled out the name of the shop, the cursive letters ending at the blade of a delicate silver scissors. The façade of the brick building was plain, and unlike the other streetside shops that had display windows, it was impossible to see what was happening inside. Elvira Maria had spent all her rubles, and with only a few coins left in her purse, needed employment. Taking a deep breath and summoning her courage, she opened the door.

The jingling bell announcing her was absorbed by the chatter of five women examining bolts of woolen fabric draped across a long table to the right of the entrance.

"It would have to be lined in the same color," one woman said. She ran her hand over a bolt of navy twill, her garnet rings flashing in the light spilling down from the clerestory windows.

"No, no," replied the proprietor. This was a man with a French accent. He towered over the women, his trim torso framed by stooping shoulders. Dressed in a black flannel three-piece suit, a burgundy silk handkerchief at his throat, he wore the latest in European attire. He sniffed, his thin dark moustache bristling. "I suggest a complementary color, a gold or dark orange. It's much more fashionable. Like the winter coats in Paris."

"If you choose one of those colors, I will too," another woman coaxed her friend. "Monsieur Oury." She looked up at the man's confident face. "We'll trust your judgment and good taste."

"You are too kind, Madame," he said. He took her arm, and stroking it, escorted her to a rack of colorful swatches.

Twenty-three years ago, determined to escape another gloomy winter in Paris, where he'd lived all his life, Monsieur Benoit Oury had vacationed in Odessa. He fell in love with the entrepreneurial spirit of the city and its sunshine. He never left. Now in his early fifties he sold his fashions to women who valued his sense of style. An innovator, always seeking to enhance his reputation, he promoted the forward-thinking trends of modernism and selected bold colors and geometrical patterns that moved effortlessly with the body, creating a sensation on the streets. Though he had an apartment above the shop, where he lived alone, he spent long days in what he preferred to call his 'atelier,' hovering over his shop girls and sketching designs.

When he realized Elvira Maria was standing by the door, he gestured to a chair on the opposite side of the room where girls sat behind a row of whirring sewing machines. "Please," he nodded. He adjusted the tape measure hanging at his neck and turned back to the women.

Elvira Maria looked around the room. Glass cases built into the apricot-colored walls held bolts of fabric, spools of colorful ribbon, skeins of thread, and pincushions pricked by needles of different sizes. Mannequins, each dressed in a stylish coat, one with a cape attached, stood near a round table where fashion catalogs were placed before the chairs, all of which were upholstered in gold velvet. The bleached linen the girls were sewing smelled clean and luxurious. Elvira Maria tucked her dusty shoes beneath her skirt, and opening her mantle, arranged the front panels over her shoulders to hide an old stain she hadn't yet removed. She heard a faint tapping. The girl, working at the sewing machine closest to her, leaned forward. "He needs hand stitching, embroidery," she whispered.

Elvira Maria smiled as Monsieur Oury shook her hand, his customers having left in a flurry.

"You are here for work," he said, as if he'd already hired her.

"Hand sewing. I can also embroider, if you like."

"This is your needle?" He pointed to the pleats in her skirt and then, stared at her bosom where more were displayed. "May I?" he knelt down to measure a pleat on the edge of her skirt and examined the stitches, turning over the fabric to check the other side. As he reached for the hem of her petticoat she shifted her legs, forcing him to stand.

The girls at the sewing machines looked up. The whirring noise stopped. Something other than surging seams caught their attention. They exchanged glances and smiled knowingly. Someone coughed, scattering the lint collected on the table. The other girls shifted in their chairs. He cleared his throat and glared at them. They bowed their heads and the sound of treadles pumping up and down filled the room.

He counted out twenty blouses with unfinished plackets. "Five buttonholes run down the left side," he said, marking the place with tailor's chalk. "They must match the ivory buttons exactly—if you want to be paid." He looked at her with a stern eye. Then writing '20 Pieces' after her name in a ledger, he told her to return with the completed work in two days.

Once in the street she still felt his hand on her back, guiding her out the door. Never before had a man stared so intensely at her bosom, much less handled her petticoat. Didn't he know how to conduct himself? Everything about the city—the soaring apartments and endless crowded boulevards, the constant wind flinging dust in her eyes, the hustling merchants and black marketeers, and now her employer—seemed intimidating, aggressive, and waiting to harm her if she let down her guard. She hurried to the tenement house.

It was perched on the cliffs above Pratique Harbor. Her tiny room was on the third floor of the building's four stories. Painted pale blue and yellow, the colors chipping along the cracks in the plaster, it had once been a bedroom cupboard, tucked beneath a dormer, jutting out toward the sea. It now contained a bed, and a wooden chair beneath the single window from which she could see the harbor, gulls coasting on the north wind, crying into the sun. Their shadows flickered on the slanted rooftops of the neighborhood before they flew out over the choppy water.

She placed the blouses at the foot of her bed and sat on its edge to remove her shoes. She stretched out her aching legs and rubbed them until they tingled, then tugged off her woolen stockings, bloody at the toes. Her feet were swollen, red blisters on both heels, a cut she hadn't noticed before, on her right ankle, just below the boot line. Elvira Maria could not get up.

Immobility was a blessing. For the past three weeks she had walked through twisted lanes that stretched from one neighborhood to the next looking for Ana and Sasha. The flash of a yellow ribbon, the tilt of a knit cap, strands of blond hair—she'd stop and peer at the small faces. Children wandered everywhere in Odessa. Alone or in gangs, they rummaged through trash bins and ate discarded food, wiped their runny eyes and noses with filthy hands, begged, and snatched parcels from shoppers at the daily market. All had bewildered expressions, as if wondering how had this happened.

She asked herself the same question. How had it happened? Since that night at the station she'd thought through the events a hundred times, never understanding exactly how the children had vanished. Had Sasha run to the freight cars with the advancing crowd? No. He was sitting next to her, with Ana. Then again, he was fascinated by the rail riders, listening to their stories, their laughter. Had he inched his way closer to the circle of boys while she was giving Ana something to eat? Her confusion was tinged with horror. How could she have been so neglectful, so oblivious to danger? When she bought her tickets at the station house she was told to hand them to the conductor, who would help her board the train with the children. How could she have been so trusting? What was she thinking?

She closed her eyes and, drained, leaned against the headboard. In the yard below, the voices of women tending to their children mingled with the droning traffic on nearby Gogolya Street. Suddenly a lorry, the driver blasting his horn, raced down the alley, passing them. The women shouted for him to slow down, but he continued, speeding on to the port. Elvira Maria glanced at the window, expecting to see pebbles cast against the glass.

After a while, the pain in her legs subsiding, she looked through her suitcase for a clean pair of stockings. As she lifted the folds of her shawl, she discovered a piece of cardboard; a postcard of the Odessa Harbor. She and the children had bought it from a peddler in Kos. The image of gleaming tall ships anchored in the pristine water, along with colorful dories sailing beyond Voenni Pier, was magical, a guarantee of grand travel and adventure. The harbor now was clogged with rusted steamers floating in pools of greasy water. It hardly looked like the photo. Nadia, a talkative woman living in the apartment down the hall, said the larger vessels were chained to the port, their ownership in dispute since the latest pogrom against the Jews. Sasha had treasured the postcard, and so excited to be going to Odessa, must have slipped it into her luggage. Overcome with guilt, she placed the card in the niche beside her door.

She picked up her needle and reached for the first blouse. As she sewed, footsteps stomped up the staircase that rose through the house. Overhead, the rafters creaked as men shuffled about, their animated voice rising and falling as the afternoon turned into evening.

4

Ivan Dashkevich warmed his hands at the grate in Michail Lukashenko's attic garret. He inhaled deeply, glad to be out of the cold wind sweeping across the port. Fair-haired, middle-aged, tall, and wiry, he wore an oversized greatcoat draped around his shoulders, cavalier and theatrical. "Michail, my friend, you've got a good fire going here," he said, rubbing his palms together. "You're the only man in this city with a cozy attic." He scanned the narrow room atop the tenement. The low rafters, supporting a water-stained ridgepole, were shoved between a chimney and a small square window. Colorful puppets and sacks of cloth lined the splintered walls, a wooden box of chisels, hammers, and saws on the floor. "Careful you don't attract too many vagrants, like me."

Michail, forty years old, stood at his workbench, the firelight accenting his high cheekbones. He was strikingly handsome, his chin dimpled, his black hair still thick, his body lean and muscular. He laughed. "You think this place is cozy?" The walls were paper-thin, held together by mice nesting in the cracks. Heat seeped out from the rooftop and disappeared into the wind. By midnight he'd be scavenging in the alley for more fuel, fighting over a rotten fence post with a carter who had six hungry mouths to feed. "It's good to have you here," he said. "Your hot air is filling the room." He poured two glasses of vodka and handed one to Ivan. "Na zdrovye!" He raised his glass.

Childhood friends, they had grown up together in Minsk, and left that city four years before, escaping the war and poverty and violence that had followed a railway strike affecting the Moscow-Brest line. They headed for Odessa, the jewel on the sea, the golden city of merchants, artists, and poets.

The destination offered promise and a chance for Michail, assisted by Ivan, to present his family's puppet theater to a new and generous audience. In Odessa well-heeled bankers and ship captains, ambitious bureaucrats and their fashionable wives, supported a range of art forms. Grand opera flourished in baroque theaters. Organ grinders played on the main streets. Literary swells in bookshops and private salons recited the classic verses of Alexander Pushkin, while agitated students in tearooms praised the war stories of new writers living in the Moldavanka, the colorful and crowded Jewish district.

Yet despite the exciting cultural landscape, Michail and Ivan knew that the ultimate success of their puppet theater depended on the responses of children. Since arriving in the city's parks and markets they had delighted Odessa's youngsters. Michail added new characters to their repertoire of old Russian folktales and wrote his own songs. For the parents in the audience, he joked about politics. It had all been going well, even as the turmoil in the city escalated. But then Ivan grew tired of performing make-believe stories, of telling foolish jokes in silly voices. Inspired by the Bolshevik Revolution, he had joined their ranks and now spent his time behind a flatbed press, cranking out propaganda, proud of his ink-stained fingers.

"To a warm fire." Ivan tilted his glass toward the grate. He whistled softly. "How did you get vodka this smooth? I thought you were broke."

"She likes to give presents," Michail said. He smiled at Ivan's surprise.

"I don't know how you do it." Ivan studied Michail. "With her husband back from the Front? I thought it was over."

"How can I turn down such a beauty?" Michail asked. "You should have a woman in your life. She might make you happy, steal you away from your stone-faced comrades and manifestos."

Ivan rolled his eyes. The beauty Michail referred to was the wife of a White Army commander, who wanted to be entertained by more than puppet shows while her husband was in the field. Ivan wondered how she'd hoodwinked his best friend, who'd always shown good judgment. He feared that a duel would be inevitable if the commander, an excellent shot, discovered the tryst. "Unfortunately, I don't have your charm or your patience," he said. "Is her husband still moving the family to Kharkov?"

"At the end of the month. He's being transferred to a new regiment and wants her to prepare the apartment." Michail picked up a handful of straw from his workbench and tossed it on the fire. The flames crackled, lighting up his somber face. "The children and governess will go with her. Everyone installed in their proper place."

"It's about time. She's a spoiled aristocrat."

"That's not completely true." Michail frowned while he poured another round of drinks. He was fond of the woman, enjoyed her company more than most who came and went from his life. But Ivan was right, she was from a wealthy family and if their dalliance lasted much longer it would likely bring him trouble.

"She's playing games with you. I'm glad it's ending." Ivan turned to the workbench and examined the curly brown fleece that covered a large puppet with a lion's face, long whiskers attached to its bright red mouth. "What's all this?"

"I'm making the Beast for The Scarlet Flower," Michail said. "If I finish the other puppets I'll be set for the winter season. Want to join me? We could have two shows— alternate Scarlet Flower with Father Frost. What do you say?"

Ivan shook his head. "I'm waiting on a shipment. I'm too busy for this kind of thing." He tapped the wooden teeth lining the puppet's mouth. "Anyway, I'm rusty. I haven't held a puppet in months."

"It'll come back to you," Michail said. "I'll write out your lines, tack them up backstage. The children love your voices and you're funnier than I am. Come on, let's work together again." He held out his hands, hoping for Ivan's enthusiastic response. But there was none. He lit a cigarette from the grate. He paced the attic and blew smoke toward the ridgepole. Ivan had recently joined a clandestine operation that shipped guns from Constanța to Odessa. A novice to such illegal activity, he was eager to prove his worth and be recognized by the Party as a comrade who took risks that others would not. "You don't have to be involved with such madness," Michail said. "Just print their propaganda and paste it to the walls." Ivan wrapped a finger-full of coarse tobacco in a scrap of newsprint. Michail lowered his voice. "Which guns are coming this time?"

"Nagant Ms. Double-action revolvers. They're new."

"God save us, you're a damn fool!" Michail said. "Leave it to somebody else." Ivan was quiet. "Can you walk out of the deal?"

"I don't want to."

Michail turned away. As the Civil War dragged on the Bolsheviks were getting bolder. A factory explosion in the middle of the night was bad enough, but armed conflict in Odessa's streets would be deadlier. He could not support either one.

"The bribes we paid are finally getting results," Ivan said. "I can't pull out now. We need the guns."

"Aren't there enough already? The countryside's awash with weapons."

"How can we support the current regime? Corruption is everywhere. Workers abused, peasants taxed to death, and what happens? Your darling waltzes to the opera decked out in jewels."

"Watch what you say." Michail was tired of arguing, tired of violence. Since they'd come to Odessa Ivan had changed. The once soft-spoken, reserved man now was passionate about a cause. He was ready to die for it and Michail worried that he actually might. Did Ivan have the

good sense to know when he was being used? It was difficult to tell and impossible to discuss.

"Don't you understand, Michail? We're going to win."

"Speak for yourself, Comrade. I'm not involved. I
didn't leave Minsk to fight in a Civil War."

"You think you can play it safe with your puppets and sit on the sidelines while the world is turning
upside-down?"

"Don't push me, Ivan. Someday when you're sick of
the violence you'll be thankful I'm a pacifist and performing for your hungry masses."

"Someday because people like me risked our necks,
the masses in your audience won't be hungry."

Sleet pelted the darkened windowpane. The fire
dwindled. Ivan tossed his cigarette butt into the grate. He
selected a piece of red taffeta lying on the workbench and
pleated around an unfinished puppet.

"Stay here tonight," Michail said. "It's too cold for you
to return to the docks." He handed Ivan several tacks. "If
the shipment arrives they'll send a courier to find you."

5

DESPITE WEEKS OF FREEZING TEMPERATURES and biting wind, the clouds had stubbornly refused to release the snow and hide the ugliness that followed the gray rains of autumn. But now here it was, in late November, powdering Odessa, turning the muddy tracks, naked chestnut trees, and sooty limestone villas a glittering white, and crunching beneath Michail Lukashenko's felt boots.

Dressed in a sheepskin coat and woolen cap, he walked to the shed at the back of the tenement yard and turned his key in the rusted lock on the wooden doors. The colorful panels of his puppet theater were propped against a wall, next to two horse stalls, empty except for a tangle of worn leather bridles. He hoisted the painted boards over his shoulder, then bent to collect two sacks filled with puppets and props. He straightened his back to balance the lot, and headed down the alley.

As a child he'd been honored to carry puppets for his grandfather, the first puppeteer in the family, and had helped his father assemble the stage. Boys at school, saddled with book bags, envied him and followed him to the markets and town square where the sparkling theater stood as a beacon of joy and excitement. When he was ten, and had practiced for days, he held his first puppet on stage, a flea-ridden mouse that flew on Baba Yaga's broom while the witch snored herself to sleep. He was completely entranced by the experience. Seeing his grandfather was tired and ready to stay home, he begged his father to take him on tour. His three older sisters laughed, but his mother encouraged him. As her only son, she knew he would carry on the show long after her husband retired. Abandoning school, Michail sat with his grandfather and memorized epic poems and folktales. He often struggled to remember the lines. Improvise, spin a tale, the patient old man recommended, that was the art of storytelling—and the only way to shake coins from a dumbstruck audience.

Summers of dust, strange beds, and boisterous crowds followed, introducing Michail to a life full of improvisation that intensified for him in the winter of 1891 when he and his father came home to a new family member. Ivan Dashkevich, a friend who'd always lived next door, was curled up in Michail's bed, crying. His parents and two younger brothers had died the week before of influenza. Busy relatives, who'd known Ivan since birth, ignored him, and looked to Michail's parents to take him in. Within months, the two boys shared not only a bed, but also apples, secrets, wooden pistols, sweets, and an intense dislike for bullies who sometimes came their way. When Michail was fifteen and Ivan twelve, they cut their forearms and exchanged drops of each other's blood. Reciting an oath of solidarity, they became blood brothers. Though they argued and sometimes came to blows, the affection they maintained for each other only grew stronger when they took the puppet show on the road, and survived windstorms and robberies and losing loved ones at home, this time to scarlet fever.

Now after months of preparation, Michail looked forward to performing again in Odessa, but was sorry Ivan was not by his side. They'd been a great team. They'd traveled for sixteen years, built a circuit of reliable patrons, and earned enough money to stay afloat—even won awards at the mid-summer fairs in Lutsk, where their names and repertoire appeared on posters and in a special broadside.

Streaks of blue cut through the slate-colored sky promising sun by midday. Michail walked along the back lanes to Bazarnaya Street. A breeze from the northwest had blown away the usual reek of outhouses, rubbish, and tar that hung in the air. He followed the frosted windows and white fairytale turrets to the Old Bazaar where the daily market was opening. Vendors, red-faced from the cold and muffled in scarves, shuffled in their boots and hovered over steaming samovars, their scant produce and abundant bric-a-brac set before the public.

Volodya, a vendor for many years, stood beside his dented kettles, washbasins, pails, pitchers, and baskets of chipped Limoges. Gray-haired, short and stocky, he wore a denim worker's cap and a quilted coat of the same material that was frayed at the collar and cuffs. The long ties of his leather apron swaddled his round belly. He greeted Michail and offered him a cigarette.

"Have you heard about the new fees?" he asked. "The police captain came 'round earlier. Two hundred rubles, starting next week."

Michail considered the news. "Just enough to give him tea-money and pay the commerce bureau. Pretty smart. I thought he worked for the People."

"That's what they say." Volodya picked a flake of tobacco from his stained lip. "I work for the People too. Stand here all day dickering with war widows and babushkas who don't have a kopek. What kind of revolution is this?"

"Good question," Michail said. "Sticky palms all around. Nothing's to be done. Too many people fighting for their patriotic share."

"You're right about that." Volodya pointed to the sacks resting at Michail's feet. "What's the show today?"

"*The Golden Reindeer.* I performed it last year—for the holidays."

"Where's Ivan?"

"He's busy. Might be back in the spring."

"You'll play all the parts yourself?" Volodya was skeptical, but willing to give Michail the benefit of the doubt. He knew nothing about juggling puppets, only that Michail could make an audience laugh and help the market vendors sell their scrappy war-time merchandise.

"I'll manage," Michail said. He picked up the sacks of puppets and props. "Just play the major parts. Keep everyone happy."

A young couple, hand in hand, interrupted them. The woman took a copper kettle from Volodya's stall, and offered a price that even Michail knew was insultingly low. Volodya scoffed and put on a performance of his own. He laughed derisively, polished the metal with his handkerchief, but made it clear he was ready to haggle. Michail headed to the opposite side of the square.

"I'll send over Yuryi to help you set up," Volodya called after him. He waved to his son, a strapping boy, soon to be a man.

The chimes from Saint Gregory's bell tower began to toll. The Patriarch, standing at the door of the nearby cathedral, ignored the revolution. He greeted a handful of aging worshipers who kissed his ring and received his blessing before he entered the sanctuary to celebrate his mass.

Michail pounded the iron stakes through the frozen ground while Yuryi unfolded the red stage and attached the golden castles that decorated each side. Children circled the area, their coats and pants covered in snow from sliding through the drifts. They poked and teased each other and watched the set-up. Performing troupes in Odessa had become rare due to war and civil unrest. But Michail still performed, proud to be the third generation in his family to do so. He handed Yuryi the fire-spitting dragons that topped each castle and planted a crimson banner above the stage. The banner unfurled, its gold letters shining brightly with his family's name. A group of little girls cheered, and then giggled bashfully into their mittens.

Backstage Michail lit a charcoal brazier to keep his feet warm. He pulled the puppet, Kolavanya, over his right hand and shouted into the crowd.

Welcome comrades . . . ladies and gentlemen . . . children of all ages . . . protestors and jailers . . . revolutionaries and priests. Yes, the priests, who remain for my confession. I, Kolavanya, am here to entertain you. To celebrate our beautiful snow with your favorite story from the Arctic, 'The Golden Reindeer.'

Michail blew his pishchik whistle to signal the start of the performance. He slid the wrinkled and doddering Kolavanya back and forth, until the old hunter, costumed in a fur parka, a harpoon and pair of skis tied to his shoulder, stood huffing and puffing in the center of the stage. The girls twittered like small birds. Patrons shouted and clapped. Kolavanya bowed to acknowledge their greeting and began the story.

Ah, my fair and lovely daughter, Kara—my adopted darling who blesses my humble lodge in this wild tundra—take your place at the hearth with your charming kitten. Let us sit before the fire and begin this mysterious tale.

A murmur spread through the audience as Michail swept Kara on stage. Her blue velvet gown, trimmed with silver fox fur was sumptuous, showing off both her beauty and his artistry. He'd spent hours beading her towering headdress, making sure the figure could be appreciated from a distance.

Always moving from one location to the next, avoiding political demonstrations that might turn hostile, Michail had not performed in the square adjoining the Old Bazaar for many months. But this morning calm prevailed and his show was drawing an eager audience. Children wrapped in wool and felt stood spellbound before the stage, along with the noisy street urchins who pushed to the front. Older girls and boys flirted and huddled together. Even his new neighbor, a quiet woman he'd seen at the tenement, was there. He'd nodded to her moments before, but hadn't caught her eye. Sledge drivers and dockers, soldiers and sailors, merchants, shop girls, nannies, couriers, and idlers gathered in the frosty air. People with other business

enjoyed a glimpse of the show as they skirted the edge
of the crowd and hurried on. They ignored the drinkers
leaning against the bare trees along snowy walkways and
steered away from the beggars heading in their direction.

Davnym-davno, long ago, Kolavanya said, there was a
magical golden reindeer that lived deep in the alpine tundra.
Although he was rarely seen, the grandfathers, the wise dedushki
of the village knew he was special, different from all the other
reindeer in the herd.

Oh Kolavanya, why was he special? Kara asked.

My darling, he was born when the night sky was shimmering with rainbows. A dancing ray of light touched his pelt and
turned it to gold. And when he ran across the tundra, under the
full moon, beautiful gemstones appeared in his wake: rubies,
emeralds, pearls, and diamonds.

Oh Kolavanya, how wonderful. Is the story true?

The wise dedushki never lie, my child. But alas, the story is
very old. The reindeer has not been seen for many years.

Oh, what a pity, Kara cried. The Golden Reindeer has gone
away. She pointed to the empty shelves painted on the
scenery and lamented. Dear Father, our cupboard is bare. We
have no food. I cannot make you supper, and I too, am hungry.

My child, we are poor—not rich, like some who live on the
grand boulevards in Odessa! Alas, I do not have money, not even
a kopek. I, a noble woodsman, am fated to hunt for our precious
food.

You are so brave and steadfast, Kara exclaimed.

Yes, I'm a brave hunter, Kolavanya boasted. Not handsome, but brave. I know the fierce tigers, slippery seals, and wild
bears of the Arctic. My sweet Kara, I must leave you now to hunt.
Do not be sad. I will return . . . I will return.

Michail slid Kolavanya beneath the curtain and placed the puppet over the backstage spindles. Pitching his voice higher, he sang Kara's lullaby:

> Alone all the daytime I wait for my father,
> Tending the fireside, keeping the house.
> Alone in the nighttime I pray for my father,
> Koska, my kitten, she watches the mouse.
> So gently I'm sleeping,
> So sweetly I'm dreaming,
> Sleeping and dreaming,
> Ah, ah, ah. Ah, ah, ah.

"Hey, princess, sing it again." An unexpected shout broke through the crowd. "Think she's here just for you, you spoiled brats?" It was a ragged boy, stumbling from drink, pointing at the group of little girls. "This here's for the People and any worker who can stand in the damn cold." His arm was wrapped around the neck of another boy, equally rough-looking. The two of them were small and lean from neglect, their heads exposed and scabby. They wore torn jackets and grimy trousers and over-sized military boots, girded with baling wire for a better fit. They clung to each other and laughed.

"Behave yourselves!" an elderly man said. He stood near the boys, dressed in a full-length fur coat and a Persian lamb astrakhan, his hands gloved in leather with more fur at the cuffs.

The boy smirked. "Vaslav and me was just helping the maestro."

"I'm warning you both, I won't put up with your rudeness." The man shook a fist at the urchins. "If you can't keep a respectable distance and control your tongues, I'll have you removed from the square."

"Oh yeah?" the boy said. "You think you're a big shot, but you ain't got no gun." He scrambled to hide behind his accomplice, who threw up both hands, feigning innocence.

"Go back to the gutter where you came from." The man, lunging to collar the troublemakers, slipped on the ice and stumbled into a docker. The stubble-faced worker glared. For a moment Michail, watching between the curtains, thought the two older men were about to take swings at each other.

On stage, Kara swayed to and fro, her gown and headdress sparkling. *Dear me, the noises of the tundra are so loud tonight*, she cried. *The bears and chipmunks are making a terrible, terrible ruckus. I cannot sleep!* She patted her kitten and yawned. Laughter rippled through the audience. The docker turned his attention back to the stage, while the elderly fellow adjusted his hat and straightened his shoulders, proud of keeping order. The boys, colliding with onlookers, ran helter-skelter across the square toward the church.

Michail sang the last lines of Kara's lullaby several times to engage the audience again. Then he quickly trotted the Golden Reindeer across the stage. The puppet, wide-eyed, curious, and shy, hid behind the alpine forest and pranced back and forth to peek at the sleeping Kara. The reindeer did not speak, but cavorted between the trees, and sniffed the empty cupboard and the kitten. He stopped next to Kara, shook his antlers, and batted his long eyelashes.

She awoke, and seeing the reindeer, threw her arms around him. Overjoyed, the Golden Reindeer ran back and forth across the stage. Michail, a hand in each puppet, pulled the red cord hanging next to the spindles with his teeth. Colorful gemstones popped up through the stage floor. The Golden Reindeer bowed. He pranced to Kara and nuzzled her cheek, then waved a hoof and trotted off stage.

Oh Kolavanya, Kolavanya, Kara cried as the old hunter returned. The story is true. The Golden Reindeer has come!

Yes, yes, the old hunter shouted. We are rich, my child. Imagine that? I, brave and steadfast Kolavanya, am surrounded by rubies, emeralds, pearls, and diamonds. There is always hope, always surprise, always joy in our humble home. Let us celebrate and sing our thanks to the Golden Reindeer and the wise, wise dedushki:

> Deep in the forest he hides from our view
> We wait and we hope for dreams to come true.
> Sleep little darlings he draws very near
> Gemstones are yours when you listen and hear
> His hoofs on the tundra
> When he runs with the winds.
> His hoofs on the tundra,
> Your new life begins.

Fresh snowflakes whirled through the square as Michail closed his stage curtain. A flurry of snowballs crisscrossed the sidelines. Gleeful boys laughed and dodged behind the stark frozen trees. Ready to hurry on, adults tossed their coins into Michail's cap as he approached them, his sheepskin coat and black hair gathering snow as the thick gray clouds expanded, swallowing the blue sky and dusting the city anew.

The street children gathered around him, tugging at his sleeves and coat as they begged for the coins he'd collected from the crowd. He laughed good-naturedly and kept moving. Some held out their palms, others reached into his pockets, surprised to find the stash of cloves he chewed to freshen his breath. They all followed him as he packed up his theater and puppets, their dirty, hollow faces still bright and excited from the show.

The orphan, Tatiana, stood to the side, watching. A skinny girl, she had a heart-shaped face, big blue eyes, and wavy blonde hair flowing down her back. Her summer cape, burnt orange and torn at one seam, billowed behind her in the harsh wind. She was fifteen years old and had lived on the streets since she was seven and her mother, a gambler, had failed to come home from Vito's Imperiale Casino.

Tatiana waited for Michail, her jaw set, the snow stinging her red cheeks. She held a rusty bucket, her hands wrapped in woolen rags to keep them warm. Setting the bucket at Michail's feet, she stepped back while he bent down and poured the remaining live coals from his brazier into it. They steamed as they hit the cold metal.

"Careful," he said. He lifted the handle and put the bucket in her hand.

Tatiana hurried off. She knew the coals would last through the night if she added kindling the moment she reached the abandoned horse shed where she was living. As she turned to wave goodbye, four small girls ran toward her, and together they headed to the snowy streets where horse-drawn sledges trundled along to the steady rhythm of cracking whips.

6

Elvira Maria opened the rickety gate to the
tenement yard and stepped aside as Michail muscled
his scenery through the narrow entrance. He grunted
thanks, and continued along the snowy path between
the outhouse and storage shed. Now late afternoon it was
bitterly cold and dark. The factory smoke, spiraling ash
to the heavy clouds, hurt her lungs and made her think
about the countryside where the sweet scent of pine filled
the air. She drew her mantle around her throat and hurried into the vestibule. Small clusters of dust and dried
leaves, caught up in the sudden draft, spun along the
cracked baseboards as they drifted to the back of the vaulted room. She picked up her skirts and avoided touching
the greasy railing as she mounted the steep stairs.

"You were at the performance this morning," Michail
called to her, closing the front door after he'd entered.
He jogged up the stairs. "Did you stay till the end? It was
freezing." He reached the landing where she stood, the
smell of snow and charcoal lingering between them.

"Yes. It was wonderful." She was surprised he'd spotted her in the crowd. "I've never seen the story performed. I used to tell it to my children."

"It's one of my favorites. I'm glad you know it."

From the corner of her eye she noticed the snowflakes melting on her woolen mantle. She was embarrassed to be talking so casually with a strange man. It was inappropriate, contrary to the way she'd been raised. But when he extended his hand and said, "It's a pleasure to meet you, Madame," she shook it. They exchanged names and she told him she was new to Odessa, that she'd come from Kos, near Kyiv.

"I performed in Kos years ago," he said. "It was summertime. Beautiful region. They say the current fighting has destroyed the village. It's a terrible loss." Her deep blue eyes, sunken into her round face, were sad. He searched for consolation. "Odessa may be crowded and chaotic these days, but at least you're safer here."

"Yes, that's what everyone tells me."

She looked past him to the frosted window on the next landing. The sound of Nadia's children quarreling and crying in their rooms above drifted through the hallway. They climbed the stairs without talking, grit on the soles of their shoes scraping each step. When they reached the third floor, she went to her door and fumbled with her key.

Michail, the sacks of puppets thrown over his shoulder, paused. "Good night, Elvira Maria," he said and continued up to the attic.

A pale light from down the street cast shadows on the slanted walls of her room. She lay on the bed, closed her eyes. Summertime in Kos. When her kitchen garden was fragrant with roses and the winter beets, swollen in the ground, broke through the soil in purple rows leading to the back gate, and the wheat fields stretched forever, a landlocked sea rolling with the wind. Her house swept, smelling of soap and cedar. Ana and Sasha running from the nearby woods, their baskets of freshly picked chanterelles mixed with smooth flat stones, oddly twisted pinecones, a blue butterfly with only one wing.

Summertime with her children and Lev, her husband. She'd married him when she was sixteen. With her parents dead, she had honored her brother's wishes and pledged obedience to this older man she barely knew. He managed the estate of a military commander stationed in the Crimea. She moved to his thatched house at the edge of the village and, as time passed, adapted to being a wife and mother. Unlike other women who suffered beatings from their husbands, she had been spared that humiliation. Lev treated her well, recognized her work in the commander's dacha and fields. One Easter he tied flowers to her apron strings and serenaded her to make her laugh. He was passionate about singing, especially when drunk. Faithful, he'd been a good husband and had given her children she adored.

During those early years with Lev she never imagined their simple life together would be disrupted, but the Civil War upended their family, and all the others in the region. Men who worked the fields and kept the estates running were rounded up with rifles at their backs, first by the Imperial Army, later by the Whites, finally by the advancing Reds. Undisciplined and hungry, the troops ransacked houses and barns, stole whatever they could:

harvests and livestock, even quilts and fine dishes. The villagers organized themselves into a fighting force. They held secret meetings and sent couriers throughout the countryside to recruit help and take revenge, but they were outnumbered. Forced to abandon the fields, everyone hid in the forest, days at a time. Crouched behind a narrow ravine that ran parallel to the creek, they heard rough voices and gunfire echo through the trees.

One summer, when cannon pounded the road leading to the church, great clouds of smoke settled on the poplar, oak, and beech and turned the shiny green leaves black. A babushka who read omens said they resembled crows eager to fly and predicted the soldiers would soon move on. But another woman, known to foretell the future with greater skill, declared the leaves were vultures and that death roosted in the trees. When the fighting stopped, and a foreboding silence invaded the forest, the villagers cautiously returned to their shattered homes. They picked through debris and stamped out embers and carried hidden stores of food back to the ravine, knowing the departing soldiers would be replaced a week or so later with different soldiers roaming the fields with bayonets, rifles, and ill intent.

A Cossack regiment, frenzied by their losses, captured Lev as he'd been running home to warn her they were coming. Three soldiers dragged him to the gate and beat him, while others set fire to the barn. Hidden in a copse of trees with Ana and Sasha, she watched, stifling the children's cries. His face bloodied, his hands bound, Lev was taken away on their neighbor's workhorse. She'd been left with stubbled fields, frightened children, and mounting taxes she could not pay. Two weeks later, Lev was killed while fighting at the Don River, near Tsaritsyn. Only his sword would come home, a scratched blade of sharp steel, returned by a cadet of the Imperial Army who tried to hide his shame as he stammered the death announcement in her doorway. It had been windy that morning and a falcon had circled the empty field three times as she stood and listened, frozen by the news. She was twenty-four.

Distant shouts outside interrupted her memories. She reached for her shawl, her fingers gripping the tangled fringe. The voices grew harsher and more urgent as several men rounded Gogolya Street and ran down the alley beneath her window. The curses and scuffling continued—then stopped abruptly. She held her breath and waited. In seconds a deafening volley of gunshots filled the air, ricocheting against the clapboard shed in the yard. A flare of light instantly lit her room, throwing her shadow against the cracked wall.

She crouched next to her bed, crossed herself, and grasped her pendant of the Blessed Theotokos. "Oh, Mother of God, am I to die here? Forgive me, forgive me for losing my children!" She repeated the Virgin's name over and over until she heard the creak of Michail's boots on the stairs. Cautious, she opened her door and stood trembling on the threshold.

"I think they're gone," he whispered. He stepped away from the window that overlooked the yard.

"What's happening?"

"I can't tell. It's too dark."

Her thin frame, now without her headscarf and mantle, barely filled the doorway. Strands of blonde hair

escaping the braids coiled on top of her head, curled across
her cheeks and narrow shoulders. She seemed vulnerable.
It was clear she was from the countryside. Few women
in Odessa had such an open face. He wondered how she
survived from day to day. Did she have friends nearby?
Did she know what was happening in the city? "There'll
be a manifestation tomorrow," he said. "The machinists,
factory workers from Peresuip, the suburb up north, will
be marching."

"Could the gunfire be part of that?"

"Perhaps," he said. The workers hadn't been paid in
months. Many had been dismissed without cause. If their
delegate meeting went badly, he knew it would be a rough
day. "Steer clear of the streets, if you can."

She wiped away a trickle of sweat sliding down the
side of her face. "I didn't know. I thought I might—"

A cold draft swept up the stairs and the shuffle of
footsteps drew their attention. She felt for the knife in
her pocket. Michail, his face taut, moved to the center of
the landing and motioned for her to return to her room.
But she remained, unable to move, a chill rushing through
her.

Ivan Dashkevich mounted the stairs. "My God, I
thought I heard you out there," Michail said, his voice
hushed. Breathless, Ivan staggered into his arms. Blood
seeped through the sleeve of his greatcoat. His hair was
disheveled, his cap missing. Michail pulled him away from
the window. "Come upstairs!" he said.

Drops of blood spattered to the floor as Ivan, holding
his wounded forearm, followed Michail. He paused before
Elvira Maria, his face grimaced with fear.

NIGHT TRAIN TO ODESSA

She watched them disappear. Her hand shaking, she struggled to open the jammed latch on her door and entered her room. She leaned against the wall, flakes of plaster collecting on her back. The house was still, as if the dust was suspended in space, waiting for another barrage of bullets to scatter it throughout the house. She took a shallow breath.

Far from the Front, Odessa was reported to be a safe city, and yet, since she'd arrived street fights and unexpected explosions happened almost every day. She thought violence like that belonged to the countryside, where soldiers wreaked havoc. But here, even vagrants and prostitutes stalked her neighborhood, forcing her to carefully consider her need to leave the tenement. The hours she spent crossing the city to explore a new district, where she might find the children in a park, a marketplace, or school yard, were filled with glances over her shoulder and a painful tightening in her chest as she hurried along. Worried for Ana and Sasha, she prayed they were with other boys and girls who knew how to handle living on the dangerous streets. Perhaps the Virgin had heard her pleas and been merciful, and a generous family had taken them in. It was possible. Lev's brother and his wife had sheltered lost children in their home, a boy and girl displaced by the war. Her mind would not stop, not when she was frightened, close to despair. And who was this man who'd been shot in the alley, right beneath her window? With a start, she remembered the blood on the floor outside her door. She searched for a cloth, and stealing out to the hallway, wiped away the trail of drops.

Michail locked the door to his room and handed Ivan the flask of vodka. They listened for more voices in the alley, but heard only the wind battering the shutters and a lorry, rolling down the distant boulevard, shifting into high gear, then groaning on.

Ivan tossed back a drink. He removed his greatcoat and tunic and collapsed on a crate near the fire, his chest heaving.

Michail examined the wound. "The bullet grazed you. Gave you a bad nick and passed through your coat sleeve. You're a lucky man. You could have been killed!" He cut a strip of muslin and wrapped it around Ivan's arm. "Stay still till I finish this—the bleeding will stop soon." In the fire's light he could see Ivan's exhausted face. "Tell me, what happened?"

"The shipment came in from Constanţa." Ivan took another drink. "Three comrades and I went to meet the dealers at a draper's shop in the Moldavanka." He fingered the folded layers of the bandage, wiped specks of blood off the metal flask with his thumb and set it on the floor. He was hesitant to tell Michail the details of what had happened, afraid of what he would think, and of the argument that would follow. But he was badly shaken, needed to talk, and knew Michail would keep what he heard to himself. "They expected us to pay on delivery," he said, "just like always."

Michail listened anxiously while Ivan explained he'd inspected the shipment and discovered that a quarter of the guns had defects, triggers that wouldn't engage. The dealers still wanted their money. They claimed they'd risked their lives to deliver on time. In ten crates of five hundred guns, you had to expect a few defects; that's the way it worked. Quality, if there was such a thing, was out of their control. But Ivan refused to pay, and much to everyone's surprise, hadn't even brought the money. Suspicious from the start, he'd left the cash with a comrade at the dockyards, who was waiting for his signal to deliver it.

He held his ground. The shipment was not what they'd bargained for. Outraged, the dealers had shoved him and his three comrades in a back room, barred the door, and taken them hostage.

The dingy shop, dank and smelling of paraffin oil, was in a rough section of the Moldavanka district, where petty criminals and notorious gangsters operated. Those who claimed that quality *was* their business peddled shredded gold, Greek vodka, and marafet—the highly addictive cocaine that robbed its user blind, then threw away their souls. Other racketeers forged documents, ran gambling rings, shoplifted and resold high-end goods, and trained street urchins in the aerial art of second floor robberies. The back room of the shop was filled with haggard-looking girls, who coughed and spat while they packed crates with ammunition or polished handguns with kerosene.

Ivan reached for the flask. "They told us to give them the money or they'd break our legs."

"I can't believe you're involved in this," Michail said. "How did you escape?"

"A boy came with a delivery that needed attention and three of us bolted out. Their men trailed us all the way over here. The others veered off to the dockyards. As far as I know, one fellow's still a hostage, poor bastard."

Michail threw the bloody tunic in Ivan's lap. In all the years they'd been friends, he'd never known Ivan to engage in such reckless behavior. "Do you realize you're in real danger? How could you take such a chance?"

"Listen to me. This city's going to fall. It's only a matter of months, maybe weeks." Ivan began explaining with an earnestness Michail had rarely seen in him that things were happening faster than anyone had thought possible. The Whites were changing sides, joining the Bolsheviks. Propaganda was no longer enough. It was time for guns.

"Stay out of it," Michail said. "Let the devil finish the transaction."

"Ha! The devil's already involved. And the longer that shipment stays in that shop, the more hell we'll pay." Ivan pushed the tunic aside. "They know we're desperate for reliable weapons, so they keep upping the price. What they're asking for now . . ." He stopped. Michail could tell he was calculating the costs, trying to make a painful decision. "Well," he said at last. "It's a lot."

7

EARLY THE NEXT MORNING, the students from the nearby Nicholas I Commercial School gathered in the tenement yard. They called to their friends coming down the alley and pulled them through the gate, eager to increase their numbers for the factory workers' march. The school, an institution since the 1800s, was closed temporarily because of financial problems caused by the war. The students needed another place to assemble, and Nadia's daughter, Lydia, had offered the yard. Now thirty people milled among the acacia trees, taking advantage of the outhouse and water pump. Some painted large square signs and long banners in bold red letters: UNITE FOR WORKERS' RIGHTS, ALL POWER TO THE WORKERS, and ABOLISH SLAVERY AT THE WORKBENCH. They wore winter coats or layered jackets, thick scarves, kerchiefs, caps, and boots, an effort to protect themselves from the damp, cold wind breaking through the fog that enshrouded the harbor.

A middle-aged woman dressed in a dark green coat, a flowered scarf tied around her black hair, moved from one student to the next and served hot tea. She filled a communal cup from a steaming kettle she held in one hand. The students chatted with her and she laughed loudly, her wide mouth traced with red lipstick. Several girls, bobbed hair beneath their knit hats, stacked the finished signs against the fence. They lit each other's cigarettes and smoked. Elvira Maria, watching from her window, remembered a woman in Kos who'd tried to smoke. Her husband had beaten her.

At a shout from a slender fellow with wire-rimmed glasses, the students collected their signs. One by one, the placards rose, transforming the dull gray sky into a red wave of protest. The students trooped out of the yard, falling in step behind two tall boys who held a crimson banner that stretched across the alley and identified their school. Elvira Maria saw Nadia, a baby crying on her shoulder, run to Lydia. The curly headed girl was dressed in multiple sweaters, her leather boots cracked and worn. Nadia handed her a thermos and kissed her on the forehead. The students, some shouting directions, left the alley to march down Nikolaevskaya Boulevard. When they reached Cathedral Square next to the grand Opera House, they would join the strikers from Peresuip. The students would look out for provocateurs and together would stand strong.

The singing of the marchers faded, stanzas of "Varshavianka" blending into "L'Internationale." Elvira Maria turned from the window. She put on her mantle, but quickly removed it. She felt claustrophobic, anxious. The thought of remaining confined for the day in the tiny space was intolerable. Ana and Sasha needed her. She could not stay here all day like a silly girl, worrying and expecting things to change for the better.

Yet she was afraid to leave her room, to face the thousands of demonstrators crowding the streets. They were so loud. She could hear they'd claimed the steps of the Opera House where they were chanting the slogan, Power To The Workers—Pay Us Now. Cheers followed, rippling across the lanes. Runners with bullhorns shared the developments in the meeting between the union bosses and factory owners. Their muffled announcements were answered by elated cries or angry booing. It was the booing that intimidated her.

But after a while she picked up her mantle and straightened it on her shoulders. Ashamed of her provincial behavior, she defiantly forced her hands into her gloves and steeling her nerves, left her room.

She met Nadia hurrying up the stairs. The door to her apartment was open and children in the front room were making grunting animal sounds and laughing. The baby in her arms was quiet, its face wrinkled and flushed. Elvira Maria guessed it was a few months old.

"Are you marching?" Nadia asked. A brown linen apron covered the front of her dark blue dress. Her house slippers were wet. Her thick brown hair, shoulder length and wind-blown, framed her angular face. She didn't wait for Elvira Maria's reply. One foot on the next step, she said she wanted to march with her husband, but couldn't because she was nursing. He was one of the factory workers who'd been laid off. A member of the machinist union, he wanted higher wages and inspections on the shop floor. But the bosses had sabotaged every meeting. They arrived late, hemmed-and-hawed, changed the agenda items, contacted their bankers, and postponed signing a deal. Worst of all, they tried to divide the workers, levied fines on some and increased the hours of others. Nadia, her eyebrows knit together, rattled on. Her husband was angry, and she was tired and frustrated, sad for her four girls who were always hungry and wanting one thing or another.

Elvira Maria reached out to stroke the sleepy infant's cheek. As she did, her mantle fell open and Nadia pointed to her pendant of the Blessed Theotokos. "I used to have one of those," she said. "I sold mine. She didn't help me and I needed the money."

Elvira Maria was speechless. She tucked the pendant inside her blouse and buttoned her mantle. The Mother of God protected everyone, especially the needy. How could Nadia sell something so precious?

"The church should stand by the workers," Nadia said. "It should say something to make things right, but it doesn't." She turned and ran up the stairs. Elvira Maria watched her go, but couldn't tell if she was ashamed of what she'd said or was simply in a hurry, as always. Nadia swung the door shut with her foot, children's voices answering her arrival.

Elvira Maria headed for a square adjoining Grecheskaya Street. Once there she hoped to ask the children who sold matches to passersby if they'd ever seen Ana and Sasha. But within minutes of reaching the square, she was swept along with the marchers, forced to keep pace with the workers and activists walking urgently beneath their huge red banners. As more marchers poured down the steep incline, separating Peresuip Suburb from the city center, the crowd swelled, pushing her onto Deribasovskaya Street.

Once a prosperous thoroughfare, where high society had enjoyed fine cuisine and elegant fashion, the street now was an obstacle course of loose cobblestones and mud. She struggled to maintain her place on the edge of the walkway next to the shops, looted and empty, their broken and boarded windows marked with graffiti exhorting the Jews to leave. She'd heard about the pogrom from refugees in Kos, but had never seen city buildings destroyed. These were constructed of stone, bricks, and stucco, ornamented with carved flowers, vines, and birds, even mermaids. She wondered how such a wealthy neighborhood could be burned and viciously sacked like a common country village. Bewildered, she moved down the long street with the aggressive crowd, passing shattered stained glass, burnt-out rooms, broken balconies, chipped ceramic tiles, splintered doors, signs bearing family names defaced. Distracted by the wreckage of the vandalized shops and gutted apartments she tripped on a slab of cement that had fallen from a building onto the walkway. She grabbed hold of an iron railing to restore her footing, but the near tumble unnerved her, and she refocused her attention, determined to avoid the additional rubble that littered the neglected walkway. As she took a deep breath, the stench of rancid wool, tobacco, and sweat filled her lungs. She coughed into the crowd jostling and pushing her along.

At Deribasov Garden the marchers stopped. Unable to continue any farther, they stood and listened to the demands of union bosses and workers. A terrible cold gripped the crowd. Men and women closed their eyes and struggled to breathe. A frosty cloud hung over their heads.

Sleet began to rain down, turning jackets, scarves, and hats to ice. Numb, Elvira Maria tucked her face into her mantle and looked out over her knit cowl at the heaving mass of quilted coats and weather-beaten faces surrounding her. An elderly couple standing next to her leaned against each other. The woman, dressed in a long gray coat and matching felt hat, her face thin and exhausted, put a hand in the pocket of her husband's frockcoat. Grim and stoic, he held a large sign, the red and blue crest of The Bund, the secular Jewish socialist party whose members supported the strikers. Glazed in ice, the sign shook in the wind.

Finally, Elvira Maria saw an opening in the dense crowd. She elbowed her way to the small square where she found a gang of boys selling cigarettes and begging. She bought a box of matches from one of them and showed him the photograph of her children. The boy pocketed the coin. He examined the image, shook his head, and pointed to the trees.

"Take a look, Comrade," he said. "There's a bunch of them up there watching the show."

She shifted her gaze to the bare chestnut trees lining the square. Groups of children perched in the treetops clung to each other and the massive limbs that stretched above the crowd. As she pushed through the demonstrators, moving from one tree to the next, she was stunned by what she saw. She'd followed her intuition and desperation, taking to the perilous streets, and here she was, looking up at hundreds of street urchins beyond her reach.

Cheers erupted from the crowd. People pushed and shoved and surged toward her, one excited group following the next. She flinched as three men ran into her, almost knocking her down. Seconds later, Michail Lukashenko pulled her out of the crush of bodies. She slid across a snowy lane, running to keep up with his long strides. Clear of the marchers, they stopped at an open intersection. He let go of her arm.

"You can get trampled in a crowd that size," he said, shouting above the cheers of the workers. "What are you doing daydreaming out here?"

Elvira Maria bent over and gasped for air. She looked at him through her gloved fingers, tears streaming down her face. "I'm sorry, I'm sorry, I'm so sorry."

"Come on, let's go. The crowd is coming."

He guided her along a slippery path toward a tavern, a chorus of "L'Internationale" rousing in the distance.

Elvira Maria sat on the edge of her chair and took small bites of her bread. Ashamed of her outburst and feeling awkward, she was thankful the tavern was poorly lit with tallow lamps and that they had the table to themselves. She stared at the wooden boards. They were thick and worn, crumbs stuck in the crack next to her bowl.

Michail ate his watery soup with relish. He looked at her, hunched over, avoiding his gaze. "The workers did well," he said. "Most of their demands were met. It's quite a reward after struggling for months."

"Yes, I'm sure they're happy," she said, her voice faint. "But hard working people don't always triumph in the end."

He waited for an explanation.

"What I mean is—" she looked across the room, "—sometimes when we try to improve our lot, it brings unforeseen problems, and we realize we should have just learned to live with the difficulties."

For someone who seemed so naïve, her insight and candor astonished him. She intrigued him. She was not pretentious, didn't even flirt like the women he met at his puppet shows, or the chatty shop girls who wanted to promenade the boulevards clinging to his arm. The waiter came by with hot tea. She held her glass with both hands, warming her fingers. She was aware Michail was watching her, that he wanted to say something.

"What is it?" she asked.

"It isn't my business," he said, "but I noticed you showed a photograph to the match boy. Are you looking for someone? Perhaps your husband?"

She set aside her glass and slipped her hand in her pocket. She paused. Was it wise to show him the photo? The shooting in the alley, his bloodied friend, and the hushed voices she'd heard in the attic until dawn made her think twice. She wondered if she could trust him. Would he complicate her life, make her regret that she'd greeted him in the vestibule? Yet despite her apprehension, she wanted to tell him about Ana and Sasha. He knew the city better than she did. Perhaps he could be helpful. She placed the sepia-colored photograph on the table. Her eyes followed his hand as he picked it up.

He held it to the light and examined the boy and girl dressed for Easter in their best clothes. It was a picture like many others he'd seen, children standing next to a tall vase of lilies, the boy always holding a big book, looking proud and serious, the girl, hands clasped behind her back. But this time as he looked at the innocent faces that resembled hers, his heart was heavy, and he knew why she was alone. "They're missing?" he asked.

"Since September."

Nearly three months, he thought. "So many children are lost these days. It makes me angry just to think about it." He looked at her anxious face, the lamplight wavering across her pale cheeks. "It's a beautiful photo."

"Yes." She placed her hands beneath the table. "My husband took us to Kyiv to have it taken." It had been spring, a family adventure for business and sightseeing. Kyiv was known as the City of Four Hundred Churches and the children wanted to count them all. But after an hour, and unable to remember the higher numbers, they'd given up. Lev had taken them to the botanical gardens to see a large greenhouse he'd heard about. They marveled at the lush plants that towered above their heads, the sunlight streaming in through the domed glass ceiling. It was the first time she'd ever left the countryside.

Michail handed the photograph back to her. "I have an idea," he said. "Can you help me tomorrow morning with my Christmas show? I could pay you. Not much, but tomorrow's a holiday and people will be generous. We could look for your children in the afternoon. I know a girl who might help us."

She searched his face. It was welcoming, in a quiet way, and his request seemed genuine. She'd spent hours wandering alone through neighborhoods she didn't know, enduring the rude lorry drivers, beggars, and strange men who brushed against her in the narrow lanes. And the money, even a small amount, would be better than nothing. As inflation rose, her rubles disappeared overnight. When she'd returned a second batch of blouses to Monsieur Oury and was paid, he'd told her the shop would be closed for the holidays and to come back in a few weeks for more work. She had worried about what to do next. She stood, holding her gloves, and agreed to meet him in the tenement yard the next morning.

Before he realized she was leaving, she was out the door. He had wanted to order something else to eat, to talk for a while, and walk back to the tenement together. Had he offended her? Been too pushy? He drank the last of his tea, then studied the leaves in the bottom of his glass.

Elvira Maria exhaled into the cold evening air. She was relieved to be by herself. He had asked about Lev, said he was sorry to hear he'd been killed. She didn't want to answer more questions he surely would have asked, if she'd stayed. Lev would have been furious if he'd known she was in a tavern telling an itinerant performer her troubles. Whenever performers came to the village he had warned her to lock the doors, keep an eye on the children, and watch the show from a safe distance with friends. Minstrels and puppeteers with their gaudy banners and clever folktales were not like villagers or peasants tied to the land. They traveled from town to town, the authorities checking their papers, pockets, and reputations. They were smooth talkers. Elvira Maria stopped at the street corner. As far as she could remember Lev had never attended a performance, but always headed off to the fields instead. She doubted he'd ever met a performer. And yet—he must have known what he was talking about, heard the rumors.

When she reached Gogolya Street, full of jubilant marchers heading home, she paused before the window of a shop where matryoshka dolls were displayed on the shelves. They looked like Michail's puppets. She wondered if the ones she'd seen dancing on his stage were crafted from wood or from papier-maché, like these dolls. She would know tomorrow and find out if his offer to help her was sincere, or was just a show he knew would impress her.

8

Red ink was messy. It smudged easily and took more time to set than black or brown, especially when the printing paper was cheap and flecked with sawdust. It wasn't Ivan Dashkevich's favorite color, but he knew that was irrelevant. Personal preferences were not important and belonged to a bygone era. Now was the time for solidarity, change, and bold choices—like red—the color of blood, the blood of the workers.

Late afternoon light filtered through the upper windows of the printshop. Tucked down a blind alley off Grecheskaya Street, it was a good location. Ivan could hear the cheers of the demonstrators as they left Deribasov Garden. He smiled. Members of the machinist union had demanded higher wages and a seat at the table when shop rules were set. It sounded like they had succeeded.

He pushed up his sleeves to check the type locked on the bed of the press and blew a bit of dust to the floor. Then inking the rollers a bloody red, he stepped back to inhale the sweet odor. Instantly, he was in Mińsk cranking out broadsides for Michail's uncle that advertised wash boards, laundry soap, scrub brushes, and bleach. Nine years old, he had worn a printer's hat fashioned from folded newspapers and pretended he belonged to the printers' guild, a group of spirited men who prowled around their clanking presses in long black aprons, puffing on their cigarettes. Generous, the men praised his work and ignored the fact that he skipped school too often. After all, they said, the boy was adrift, still in shock from the sudden death of his parents and younger brothers the year before. Though he was grateful to be taken in by Michail's parents, long-standing neighbors who delighted everyone with their puppet theater, Ivan found refuge in the print shop. Here the men, bored with their bread and butter advertisements, drew scandalous cartoons of the Tsar he knew were illegal and talked about crooked politicians. The atmosphere was charged with humor, strong opinions, and the smell of oil, paper, and ink.

Little did he know, after touring with Michail and the puppets for years, that he'd be operating an underground press in Odessa for the All-Russian Publishing House, a central branch of the Soviet Executive Committee, where workers and soldiers called the shots. It was exhilarating. Educating a down-trodden public with political handbills and posters gave his life purpose. And now he was dealing guns, a dangerous and unpleasant business, but indispensable to the liberation of Odessa. It was all part of a bigger plan orchestrated by comrades who'd swept through a decaying empire with the promise of a new beginning.

He set the press rolling, shaking the floorboards, rotten from water that seeped through a damaged roof whenever it rained or snowed. The poster, with the banner, RISE UP!

THE TIME IS NOW, depicted a fierce-looking metal worker, an enormous rifle cartridge under his arm, forcefully
pointing at the viewer. The red earth at his feet included
the mandatory warning in black letters: THOSE WHO TAKE
DOWN THIS POSTER COMMIT COUNTERREVOLUTION.
He wondered if it was designed by Mayakovsky, the young
poet and firebrand who'd joined the cause in 1917 and to
date had turned out thousands of different revolutionary
posters. Ivan had seen him in Odessa months before and
could not forget the poet. Mayakovsky, his voice booming
across the crowds that gathered to hear him, inspired the
workers by calling them glorious heroes. Answering their
cheers with his fist in the air, he insulted their bosses and
bellowed that the Philistines were taking everyone for a
ride.

In the alley and streets near the printshop, people
were singing, ready to carry the enthusiasm to the taverns
and celebrate into the night. Ivan's fellow comrades were
certainly toasting each other. They had even marched,
leaving the shop with red placards under their arms. But
he had stayed behind to complete a print run of 250 posters that would be plastered to the city walls at midnight.
Ivan believed in discipline and sacrifice. Michail's aging
father had uttered those words repeatedly when Michail
had taken over the theater and Ivan joined him. If the
right props weren't set in the right place backstage a well-
timed scene could be ruined. And if they were determined
to stay close to home, where a soft bed and a hot meal
waited, they would never make a living. They had to
travel—go on tour. It was the only way to find wealthy
patrons to finance a beautiful show and keep them from

joining the ranks of poverty-stricken performers who roamed the country like beggars.

The puppet theater had been a good training ground for practicing discipline and sacrifice. He and Michail, following the old man's advice, had exceeded their expectations, gathering a lucrative audience that respected and loved them. They'd also seen a countryside where illiterate, malnourished peasants toiled in the fields day after day, and lived in hovels where the only thing that promised them hope were capricious household spirits, ancestors long gone to the grave. He wasn't surprised when revolution stormed the country. Lenin had the mandate for change — and he had the ink.

"Ivan," a boy shouted on the other side of the door. He pounded three times. "You in there?"

Ivan recognized the voice. "Coming," he yelled. He adjusted the stack of sheets and stopped the press. The floorboards settled in place. "Are you alone?"

"I got my friend who's gonna help me. He was here last week."

Ivan unlocked the door and let in two young boys, grubby-faced and thin as blades. Street urchins, they knew every corner of the city and where the posters would attract the most attention.

"They're almost ready," Ivan said. He threw a glance at the press. Then giving the boys two jars, he directed them to a sticky canister and fresh brushes laid out on newsprint. "Stir the glue before you pour it," he said, "it's lumpy." He turned back to the press and lifted off the last poster. The red ink was damp, but hadn't smudged. He divided the stack of printed posters into two piles, then felt the ones on the bottom. They were dry enough. They would survive the wind and rain for at least five days, if they weren't ripped down—long enough for him to print more.

The boys tied the bundles with twine and stood near the door, anxious to leave.

"Take it easy," Ivan said. "You've got to wait a couple of hours or the cops will be on your back. Timing is everything." He handed them a few coins.

"Whatever you say," the boy he knew answered. The two sat on the floor and examined the poster. "My friend here, draws cartoons. Can he use some of your paper?"

"Sure." Ivan set a sheet of newsprint and a piece of graphite in front of the boy. "Let's see what you can do, Comrade."

9

THAT NIGHT, THE BROTHEL on Ekaterinskaya Street was lit from top to bottom, each stained glass window in the red brick façade glowing in the twilight. Garlands of icicles and snow wrapped the rooftops of the three-story turrets that climbed each side and ended with wrought iron spires that pointed to the stars. With its six small balconies glittering with frost, the house looked like a jeweled holiday cake—expensive, but worth the price.

Heddie Naryshkina loved the house. She had been born in it and, upon her mother's death, inherited it. She ran it as her mother had, filling the spacious rooms with gifts from her admirers and clients, maintaining its elegance, taking pride that it remained a destination for the city's powerful, wealthy, and striving elite.

Her mother, Tsilia, had been a stunning beauty with ivory skin, green eyes, and a radiant smile. Raised in the Jewish community of Petersburg, she adored ballet and studied at the Imperial School of Ballet at the Mariinsky Theater. But her life changed when, at nineteen, she caught the eye of a wealthy, aging general with ties to

Tsar Alexander I. A grasping love affair followed, as did family disgrace and a pregnancy that was hidden from her parents and the general's wife of twenty-five years. Tsilia's desire to pursue a career in dance ended.

The couple, escaping the insults of gossiping balleto-manes, went to Odessa where they occupied the house on Ekaterinskaya Street, one of several the general had built in the western frontier of the Russian Empire, known as the Pale of Settlement. Arriving in the spring of 1865, they joined a thriving population of over 100,000 residents. The dusty streets were noisy and rag-tag, a sharp contrast to the orderly imperial capital. Greeks, Italians, Turks, and Jews. Romanians, Germans, Bulgarians, and nomadic herders from the Levant. All lived together in the city, its status as a free port encouraging foreign and local entre-preneurs. Cultural institutions, municipal improvements, and shipping opportunities unfolded each day in the growing city where residents were determined to live well.

The general, however, was not happy. Three months after moving in with his new love, he was overwhelmed with regret for leaving his family and friends in Petersburg. One day Tsilia woke, big-bellied and plagued with morning sickness, to find a large envelope on the side of the bed where she slept. It contained a remorseful love letter, a packet of rubles tied with a black satin ribbon, and the deed to the house bearing her name.

Despite being alone, or perhaps because of it, Tsilia had been a good mother. Her greatest pleasure was doting on Heddie. But a string of lovers, indifferent to family, gradually depleted her finances and reputation. When Heddie was twelve, Tsilia feared losing the roof over their heads. She schemed and planned, and favoring spring-time, opened her exclusive brothel, using the house to her advantage. Bureaucrats, businessmen, and commanders from the Imperial Army paid a hefty fee to enjoy musi-cal entertainment on the first floor and sexual pleasure on the second. After Tsilia died, Heddie, uninterested in the troublesome institution of marriage, followed in her mother's enterprising footsteps.

Ekaterinskaya Street was quiet when Michail Lukashenko approached Heddie's house. After squeezing through the noisy throngs of drunken marchers celebrat-ing on Lanzheronovskaya Street, he was relieved to be there. A sack of paints and brushes slung over his shoul-der, his cold face peered out from an up-turned collar. He stopped in the alley to light a cigarette and looked up at the second floor. He wondered if the mural he'd been hired to paint in the upstairs lounge would be visible from the street when the curtains were opened. The mural filled the room; it had been a good commission. He hoped to finish the details in a few hours. The paint had to be dry and the fumes gone by St. Basil's Eve, the date of Heddie's lavish salon. He imagined it would be grand, with plenty of liquor and beautiful women to seduce the honored guests into spending a fortune. Heddie's house was a far cry from Mimi's, the seedy little brothel he frequented, where the skinny girls were sad and the rooms smelled of cheap cologne.

He could see Boris, sitting in the kitchen window, swirl the last of his cognac as he read a newspaper. Boris wore a crisp white shirt and black suspenders attached to his usual pinstriped trousers. A tall, broad-shouldered man with silver hair, he was Heddie's strongman, confidant, and silent business partner, but also happy to play the role of valet when she had large gatherings. He kept the men in order with a firm hand and watchful eye. Michail knew him from Mimi's, where Boris was known to line up the prostitutes and pick a new one each week. Boris had joked about Heddie's strict house rules that forbade him from engaging with the women living and working under his own roof.

Michail tossed his cigarette stub in the snow and popped a clove in his mouth to freshen his breath. He climbed the back porch steps. Before he was able to knock, Boris opened the door and hustled him inside.

"It's cold enough to freeze the hair off a dog," he said. He was the one who'd hired Michail based on his puppet show's scenery, particularly the rolling canvas that depicted a sinister forest of wild animals. He took Michail's coat and hung it on a rack. "It's slow tonight, only two fellows. Everyone's home with family or drinking in the taverns with the marchers."

He led Michail up the back staircase and down the hallway to the lounge, where the girls relaxed between clients. Piano music floated through the house, joined by laughter coming from the green salon downstairs. He unlocked the door and opened it. The smell of fresh paint greeted them. They stood on the threshold and admired the mural, six buxom nudes clustered around a waterfall in a forest of palm trees and parrots. Several monkeys scampered through a tangle of exotic vines and red passionflowers, their paws and tails brushing the enormous leaves that twined around the room and ended at the white marble fireplace. Heddie, who dreamed of faraway places like Martinique, had furnished Michail with the lid of a cigar box and a deck of racy cards as inspiration.

"You've hit the mark," Boris said. "She loves it. Couldn't be more excited."

Michail laughed. He enjoyed being in the house. The girls were off limits to him, but he met them while taking breaks in the kitchen. They gossiped and complained about their clients, flirted with him, and ate their supper in the afternoon.

"I'll finish the parrot feathers tonight and give the ladies some rouge to liven them up," Michail said. He walked across the canvas that covered the floor and set his tubes of paint on the hearth where a small fire blazed. Stiff from the cold, they had to be warmer before he could trace the charcoal lines he'd drawn last week.

"It's up to you," Boris said, "but they look feisty enough for me." He knew the mural would create a stir on the streets. Heddie hoped it would generate new business, something Boris wasn't sure he wanted. Newcomers were the most demanding clients, especially those who couldn't hold their liquor. He'd have to winnow out the troublemakers and deal with the complaints from their regulars. It was just more work for him.

Heddie arrived then, the scent of her gardenia perfume challenging the sharp odor of turpentine. "I knew that laugh was yours," she said to Michail. Past middle age and heavy, she wore a deep purple evening dress, trimmed with silver thread at the cuffs and plunging neckline. Her wavy hair, accented with silver and ivory combs that matched her carved floral necklace, was dyed jet-black and swept high atop her head. The hairstyle added several inches to her average height and made her look regal and assertive. Her intense dark eyes, musical voice, and teasing smile that broke through the deep lines on either side of her mouth, hinted at the beauty that had defined her youth. She kissed Michail on the cheeks and slipped her arm in his. They looked at the mural. "I'm thrilled," she said. "If I can't go to the islands at least I can sit here and conjure up warmer weather. I wish I had the nerve to do the entire house."

"Tell me whenever you're ready," Michail said. He winked at Boris, who looked alarmed.

"What do you think? Dry by next week?"

"If you keep a low fire going."

"Stay as late as you like, dear," she said. She kissed him again before descending the main staircase, imagining the fun she'd have showing the mural to her older, stodgiest clients.

"I'll leave you to it," Boris said. "When I get these young fellows paired off I'll be in the kitchen. How about a drink when you're done? We can celebrate your tropical paradise with a little rum."

Michail selected a brush and felt the fine bristles as he studied the wings of a parrot flying over the waterfall. He picked up his palette, filled his brush with emerald green, and slowly traced the fine lines. Martinique was far away, but tonight he'd close that distance, and bring Heddie's tropical island to her house in Odessa.

10

WHEN MICHAIL'S CHRISTMAS SHOW was over at noon the small boys ran backstage to help him pack-up his puppets. Elvira Maria watched them pass around Father Frost and examine how it was made. She could see their demeanors change. Honored to be entrusted to hold the puppet, they put aside their street habit of wheedling and begging and stood on their best behavior.

Their eager hands stroked Father Frost's curly beard and pet his fur robes. "He's still warm inside," the youngest said. He snuggled his hand into the puppet's long robes and pushed his fingers to the wooden neck that poked through the layers of quilted cotton and velvet.

"He looks heavy, but he's not," another said. "Michail, how heavy is Father Frost?"

"Michail, does this one have a heart too?"

Michail folded-up the last scenery panel and handed a silver banner to Elvira Maria. He walked over to the boys and parted Father Frost's robes. "Of course he's got a heart," he said. "See, it's right here." The boys leaned forward to inspect the red satin heart sewn to the puppet's chest. "Father Frost can't perform without it. Now cover him up and remember, it's a secret just between us." He put his finger to his lips and looked sternly at the scruffy boys.

Elvira Maria wished Sasha and Ana were with her, and knew they'd have loved being backstage with Father Frost. Three years ago, at summer's end, she and the children had seen a puppet show; nothing as elaborate as Michail's, but entertaining nonetheless. Sasha, wanting the fun to continue, mimicked the squeaky voices of the puppets for days after — until Lev, who'd refused to join them because he thought it was a waste of time, told him to stop.

She held out a piece of muslin and helped wrap Father Frost. Carefully tucking his robes and cape into the bundle, she handed him to the oldest boy and opened a large gunnysack. Together they placed the puppet inside while the others watched quietly.

Their mood was wistful despite the excitement of the performance. Holiday presents, food, and miracles belonged to another time and place. Few of them believed in fairy tales that granted wishes out of nowhere. Across the city cathedral bells rang out carols celebrating the savior's birth. Elvira Maria listened to the music and collected the stage props, trying to be useful. Earlier in the day she had attended the mass at Preobrazhensky Cathedral and placed her candle next to the miracle-working icon of Theotokos, Mother of God. She prayed for one blessing only.

An hour later, the puppets deposited in Michail's attic room, they boarded the horse-drawn droshky that bumped along, careening around the ruts in the muddy road. Elvira Maria and Michail sat on a blanket, shoulder to shoulder, among the cartload of peasants laden with baskets and satchels. Their little boys and girls were pale and wide-eyed as they bounced on the laps of older siblings and stared at the strange couple. Two Armenians sitting across from each other, dressed in dark woolen coats, red and yellow scarves wrapped around their waists, talked excitedly in their language, their voices rising over the cries of a waking infant. As the cart reached the top of a hill, they shouted to the driver, whom they seemed to know. The droshky stopped. One of them got up from the rough planks and jumped down, the cart listing to the side. He stood on the snowy embankment and paid his fare. The other fellow opened his coat, and leaning down from the cart, handed over a speckled hen. Startled by the sudden change of hands and freezing air, the scraggly bird pecked at its new owner as the swarthy fellow slipped it into the pocket of his heavy tunic and headed off.

The droshky continued. It turned down a winding lane where ramshackle huts cluttered a vast and foul-smelling neighborhood of unrelenting poverty. The spacious boulevards and tree-lined parks that distinguished Odessa's central district were gone, replaced by a shantytown where Ukrainians, Poles, Jews, and Armenians plied their trades, both legal and otherwise.

Elvira Maria had never dared to walk in these far-flung lanes. She had combed the city squares and adjoining streets, braved the dockyards, and gone time and again to the train station in search of Ana and Sasha, but she'd been too afraid to come here. She'd resisted imagining her children in such a sinister place. And yet, here were these children, as innocent as her own, who lived in this god-forsaken slum. She gripped the bench and glanced at Michail. He was scanning the next field, his hands shoved inside his sleeves.

At the end of the lane, the remaining passengers climbed down from the cart, balancing their bundles and little ones as they stepped in the snow and dispersed over the paths that led to shophouses, lean-tos, and crumbling shanties. She rolled the blanket under her arm and picked up her skirts to keep the hems dry. Following the footprints frozen in the deep snow, Michail led her toward railroad tracks that crossed a distant field full of rubbish and icy piles of human waste. After trudging along for almost half an hour, they arrived at a derelict shed built into the hillside below the tracks.

"Tatiana?" Michail shouted through the door. "Open up, we're here."

"She's gone," a scratchy voice said.

"What do you mean, she's gone?" Michail asked. "I told her we were coming this afternoon. Open the door, it's Michail."

"I can't," the voice said. "She told me not to open for nobody. Go away!"

"Luka," Michail said. "I know it's you." He looked at Elvira Maria and put his ear to the door. They waited. "I've got a big blanket to keep you warm. Now, open the door. I'm Tatiana's friend, the man with the puppets. You know me."

Moments passed until a board scraped across the inside wall and Luka, a sick and spindly four year old Tatiana had rescued from the dockyards, cracked open the door. He squinted at Michail and Elvira Maria, and rubbed his scabby eyes as he stepped aside to let them pass. Once inside Michail secured the crossbar and took the blanket from Elvira Maria. The boy ran to an older girl coming forward from the shadows.

A dim light seeped through the boards of the flat roof, the smell of ashes in the air. Piles of straw, rusty buckets, soiled sheets, and chipped crockery were scattered on the ground. As Elvira Maria stepped away from the door eight more girls appeared from behind a horse stall. Unkempt and poorly clothed for the weather, their faces were white as chalk, their eyes slanted with suspicion as they waited to see what she and Michail wanted. They were the same age as her children. She felt afraid. Her imagination ran ahead of her to other abandoned sheds and barns she'd seen in the back streets of Odessa—places where Ana and Sasha might be curled together in the dirty straw, struggling to keep warm each night, like these girls.

"We had the fever," the oldest in the group said. "Luka still coughs." She pulled him in front of her and put her hands on his sunken shoulders.

Michail knelt and spread the blanket on a mound of straw. He gestured for Luka to lie down. "Where's Tatiana?" he asked.

"Went to the city with your friend."

"What friend?" He looked up at the girl. "What are you talking about?"

"You know, your friend." She cocked her head to the side, annoyed. "He worked with you last summer. He knows puppets too."

"You mean Ivan?" Michail got to his feet. He glanced at the other children, who were silent and unresponsive. "Was he wearing a greatcoat?" he asked the girl.

"Yes, and a long scarf wrapped around his neck."

"Why was he here?"

"I dunno. He got angry with Tatiana. Pushed her out the door. She didn't want to go." The girl coughed and wiped her mouth on her sleeve.

Michail stared into space. What was Ivan up to? Why would he bother with Tatiana, a girl he'd ignored whenever she came backstage looking for a handout? He walked to a boarded-up window and examined a thin line of tar running the length of the panel. Abruptly, he turned to Elvira Maria. "It's freezing in here already and it's not even night."

The girls milled around her and pawed her skirts as they sought her attention. She crouched on the straw and gathered Luka in her arms. The others watched her stroke his forehead, whispering and fidgeting as they moved closer.

"You'd better show them now," he said. "The last droshky of the afternoon will be leaving soon. We can't miss it."

She took out the photograph and smoothed the cardboard frame, now creased in one corner. The girls leaned over it. She could feel their cold breath on her cheek. The oldest pushed the others away and held out her hand. Elvira Maria hesitated, then gave her the photo. Her heart beat faster as she watched her examine it.

"Those are my children," she said. "Have you seen them anywhere? They've been missing for several months." She put her hand to her pendant and held it.

"I've never seen these two," the girl said, "but maybe Tatiana has." A smile crossed her chapped lips. "It's a smart picture, with the flowers and all. I'd like to get dressed up like them. Can your boy read that book he's got?"

"Yes, Sasha can read a little," she said. "He was learning—"

"All of you, look at the picture," Michail interrupted. The older girl handed it to someone else and stepped back. The girls passed it around, running their fingers across the smooth image. "If you see them, tell Tatiana or me right away," he said. "This lady will give you a reward. You understand?"

Quiet, they watched Elvira Maria put the photograph in her pocket.

Wisps of smoke rose from the dark shanties silhouetted against the orange sky. Daylight faded fast as Elvira Maria and Michail crossed the field and navigated their way to the nearest lane. Unable to find the footprints that had guided them to the shed, they now plodded through drifts of snow. Brooding, both were distressed by the visit, and anxious about missing the last droshky heading to the city.

Elvira Maria heard a low and persistent rumbling in the distance. She stopped instinctively and let Michail continue on. The menacing sound swallowed the silence as it came closer and broke into a shaking beam of light bearing down on the nearby tracks. Transfixed, she stood in the deafening roar as the shadowy cars of the night train streaked past her, spraying coal dust and sparks into the field. The line of cars wound across the horizon and shook the ground where she stood stranded in the snow. She watched it disappear, then closed her burning eyes. It was the train she had missed in Kos months ago, the train bound for Odessa.

Michail, shouting above the noise, called to her from across the field. "Elvira Maria, come now. For God's sake, don't stop."

She struggled through the drift and joined him in the lane. Short of breath, she eagerly took his outstretched hand.

Together they hurried to a shophouse tilted between a stack of railway ties and a roofless shanty, now abandoned. Upon opening the door they confronted a large and scowling woman who stood behind a counter. She ignored them and continued to siphon her homebrew of samogan into the bottle of her customer, a consumptive who leaned against the far wall. The half-starved man waited and coughed.

The woman counted her rubles and handed over the smudged bottle. She wiped her hands on her filthy smock and looked up with contempt at Michail and Elvira Maria. "If you ain't buyin' none, you best move on," she said, "unless you want a mattress up top." She pointed to the loft and grinned, her thin lips stretching across her brown teeth.

Elvira Maria headed for the door, but Michail let the insult pass, knowing that in a rough district like this putting the woman in her place would start a quarrel. He and Elvira Maria were strangers here and could easily stumble into trouble. Better to hold his tongue and leave as soon as possible.

"We're looking for transport back to the city," he said.

"Busy day, ain't it?" the woman said. She turned her back to him and proceeded to arrange a crate of bottles behind the counter. "He'll be 'round soon enough. Go outside. Can't catch a horse in here, Comrade."

Once in the lane they waited, their breath turning into steam as it rose in the icy air.

He looked at her vacant face. "You mustn't lose heart," he said.

She put her cold hands in her pockets and shivering, swayed back and forth on her stiff feet.

They stood in the dark and listened to the muffled voices from the shanties drift on the sweeping wind, an arc of stars overhead.

"Can you trust Ivan?" she asked.

"I'm not certain I know what trust is these days, do you?"

She did not answer, but turned toward the jingling bells of the horse and cart jolting down the lane.

11

VOLODYA RAKED THE ROASTED CHESTNUTS to the edge of his circular metal pan and added the last of the lot to the pile that steamed over the dwindling coals. "Move along," he said to the pack of urchins gathered in front of his market stall. "Not today. I'm doing business and don't need your company." He shook his heavy spatula at the hungry children. "Go pick somebody's pocket. Standing around here won't help you."

A boy with a gash on his chin stepped forward. "If you give us some cones we can sell them in the square for you," he said.

"I know what that's all about. Hand over the money first and we can talk about your grand plan. If you're hungry go to the detdom. It's Christmas time. They've got food."

"Nah," the boy said. "It's all gone." He eyed a box of spoiled turnips and kicked it with his torn boot. "We were at the orphanage earlier."

"I can't help you," Volodya said. "Go beg at the church. This is a market and I have to make a living with the little I've got." He turned to Michail and Elvira Maria as they approached his corner stall. "What can I do? Last week these homeless besprizorniki tipped over my brazier and ran off with everything. Little criminals—they're every-where—well organized too."

"Keep your wits about you, Volodya," Michail said. "The war's not over yet."

"Doors are open for trouble, isn't that the old saying? These military commanders better come to terms before spring or we'll all be starving." Volodya looked with disgust at the children. "This market used to be respectable, remember? Fine produce for a paying public." He fanned the steam rising from his pan. "Now I'm standing here with a bunch of wormy chestnuts I picked up last fall and guarding them from a pack of thieves."

Michail balanced his theater panels across his back and tipped his cap. "I'll stop by after I finish the show and we can settle this trouble once and for all," he joked.

Volodya laughed and brandished his spatula.

Elvira Maria, carrying a sack of props for the morning's performance, followed Michail to the square. Swarms of raggedy street children were stationed at every market stall. They begged aggressively from holiday shoppers, or peddled newspapers, candy, cigarettes, matches, train tickets, stolen baggage, wooden toys, trinkets, and assorted odds and ends that could fetch a kopek. The cacophony of their voices, crying out their wares and pleas above the usual clamor of the market, heightened her anxiety as she walked along. She passed a hand-clapping boy hawking butcher knives and paused. His gray eyes and blond hair, matted beneath his soiled fur cap, reminded her of Sasha. But the boy, now urging her to buy, was not her son.

Her anguished searching stopped when she recognized Luka, the little boy from the shed. He was straddling the waist of an older girl she assumed was Tatiana. The girl, her eyes set on Michail, struggled through the crowd. When she reached him, she grabbed his sheepskin coat and lashed out. "Where are they?" she cried. She hit his shoulder again and again with her fist. "Tell me, tell me where they are, you traitor!"

Michail dropped his theater panels and turned around. He seized her wrist. "What are you doing? Stop that—right now."

"You tricked me, you stole them," Tatiana raged, drawing the attention of by-standers. "I know it was you. Her too." She spat at Elvira Maria. "I'll get my hands on a knife and kill you both!"

"Tatiana, that's enough," Michail said.

"You were *there* yesterday." She wrenched her hand from his grip.

"And where were you?" he asked. "We planned to meet at the shed."

"I don't have to answer that," she snapped. She jostled Luka, who now was crying. As he squirmed to get down, Elvira Maria held out her arms to take him. "Get your hands off him," Tatiana screamed. "Don't come near us." She turned back to Michail, her face pinched and streaked with tears. "What did you do with the girls? Where are they?"

"They weren't at the shed when you returned?" Michail asked.

Tatiana sobbed. "Nobody was there, just Luka." She wiped his wet cheeks with her cape. "He was out begging at the tavern when everybody left."

Michail cursed under his breath. He turned to Elvira Maria and looked into her wild eyes. The shoppers surrounding them muttered to each other. Ready to leave the square, he collected the theater panels at his feet and handed Elvira Maria the sack of props. She stood beside him confused, unable to comprehend the startling interaction or to help Tatiana. He nodded, and pushing through the crowd, they hurried to the boulevard.

Tatiana, clinging to Luka, wrestled past a gang of street boys. They shouted insults and hooted in unison. She snatched a bottle of kerosene from a market stall and hurled it at them. The sound of shattering glass and screams filled the corner of the marketplace as she ran toward the church across from the square.

In the distance the drone of a hurdy-gurdy drifted through the streets; a lone gypsy sang the mournful song of the homeless besprizorniki:

> Forsaken, ever hungry
> My cries you ignore
> I forever live
> With misery at the door.

12

I N ODESSA'S COAL HARBOR, where ships waited for
commerce and transport to resume, a half-loaded collier at the Voenni Pier stoically endured the bitter wind
blowing across its flat deck. Once part of a fleet that
steamed along the prestigious Black Sea Route between
Odessa, Constanţa, and Alexandria, the rusting collier
now was stranded and neglected, its ownership tied up in
the courts. While the distant factions argued their cases,
a group of Bolsheviks squatted in its poorly ventilated
chambers.

Michail stood on the third landing of the Odessa Steps
and considered boarding the collier to search for Ivan,
but the memory of visiting him there once, listening with
increasing impatience to his comrades' schemes for has-
tening the end of the Civil War, convinced him to instead
begin his search in one of the night shelters that cluttered
the dockyards.

Inside the first shelter, dockers waiting for work sat at
long tables where they drank heavily and talked of union
deals, wages, war, and portside intrigues. The sinewy men,

toughened by seasons of backbreaking work, regarded Michail, a stranger, with interest as he stood inside the entrance. When his eyes adjusted to the half-light, he circled the smoke-filled room, and Ivan Dashkevich called out from a far corner where he played cards with a cluster of his Bolshevik friends.

Ivan kicked out a stool for Michail. "Want in? The game just started."

Michail declined and leaned against a nearby shelf piled high with tarps. He reached for his tobacco and methodically rolled a cigarette as he watched the young men slide their cards across the table and nervously finger their coins. Though unshaven and dressed in dirty sailcloth, Ivan's band did not look like the day workers they pretended to be. Their hands, for one thing, were smooth, not like the hands of the men who hauled heavy loads through the busy port.

Ivan stretched his legs beneath the table and watched the dealer circle the cards. As his turn came around he folded his hand and bowed out of the game. "Fate is unkind," he said. He looked up at Michail. "Isn't that what your father said the day we left Mińsk?"

"The old man was right."

Ivan left the table. He struck a match with his thumbnail and lit a cigarette. Both men watched the smoke rise and curl into the thick air.

"What was your show this morning?" Ivan asked.

"Tatiana."

"Ah, Tatiana. The girl with the big blue eyes. She likes you, Michail."

"Don't get clever with me. What's going on?"

"She's a little hungry these days. I wanted to help her out."

"You're lying," Michail said. He clenched his jaw. "What the hell are you up to and where are those girls?"

"Michail, not so loud." Ivan glanced at the men playing cards. "Calm down. It's a little deal, nothing serious. Don't get involved."

"Did you finally get your bloody shipment?"

"Those guns are more important than a bunch of scrappy street girls. Any day now Kotovsky's Red Brigade will sweep through this city and our world will change for the better."

"You're becoming a gangster," Michail said. "You're a member of a glorified cult that sells children for weapons."

"We didn't sell anybody. We didn't make any money. It was just a trade, part of a hard bargain. We had no choice."

"Good God, you're in worse shape than I thought." Michail grabbed Ivan by his coat lapels. "Are they in the Moldavanka? Tell me before I lose my temper all together."

"They went to Stamboul early this morning. They're gone."

"You swear this on your mother's grave?"

"I swear."

Snow clouds hovered over the city. It was dark, the dockyards quiet, except for the husky voices of men coming and going from the night shelters. Michail slowly climbed the Odessa Steps that led to Nikolaevskaya Boulevard at the top of the steep incline. Each step, exhausting and painful, took him farther away from Ivan, a man he loved. He thought about the girls at the shed. Ivan had conned Tatiana. He'd taken her to town on some pretext, allowing his comrades to arrive at the shed after dark and herd the girls into the hands of gun dealers who traded them like chattel. Michail's anger and despair mounted, taking away any peace of mind he thought he ever had. Street orphans and vagrants who prowled the landings emerged from the shadows and begged for coins and cigarettes as he passed. The smoke from their small fires on the hillside trailed up the stairs behind him. He reached the street and sat on a stone bench facing the sea. His legs ached.

Far beyond the breakwater, ribbons of amber light glistened in the black water. These came from the armed vessels of the French occupying forces that supported the Whites' Volunteer Army and kept the Bolsheviks at bay. Though he couldn't see their flags, he knew they flew their tri-colored banners. Somewhere aboard these ships, their seasoned admirals, patriotic and proud, played the old war games. He laughed bitterly at the futility of it all. If Ivan was right, the French would be gone in a matter of weeks, replaced by a new round of Bolshevik commanders who shouted for change, and fired their heavy guns in an effort to get it. A foghorn echoed across the water. By midnight the ships and harbor would be swallowed up in a chilling mist.

In her room, Elvira Maria waited for Michail to return to the tenement. She unbuttoned and pulled off her damp shoes. The leather was cracking, the soles too thin for everyday wear, but she hadn't been able to leave them behind in Kos. A present from Lev, he'd purchased them in Kyiv the same day the children's photos were taken in the fancy studio with shining lights and striped wallpaper. She'd worn the shoes only on Sundays. Though the family walked along a country lane, the shoes made her feel sophisticated and worldly. She had put them on at the last moment before fleeing, certain she would need to wear them in the city. But now they were sadly impractical and uncomfortable. She sat on her bed and rubbed her cold feet, longing for her felt boots, the ones she'd hastily given away to a destitute woman stranded in the village.

She regretted many of the decisions she'd made those last days in Kos, alone and under duress. Naïve, and not as worldly as her shoes suggested, she did not know how to travel on a train, how to conduct herself in an unruly crowd, how to protect those she loved. She had layered the clothes Ana and Sasha wore to keep them warm, but never thought to sew their names into their coats, never gave them any form of identification. This oversight, this carelessness, this peasant ignorance was pointed out to her repeatedly by those at the detdom who were overwhelmed and irritated with their orphanage duties. A photograph, they said, was not enough to find a child in a city this size. How foolish could she be, they asked, wiping the nose of a sniveling toddler and pushing it away.

Although she was haunted by this terrifying oversight and berated herself each day as she prayed for forgiveness and divine assistance, she firmly stood by her decision to leave Kos. There had been nothing else to do. The constant sound of artillery in the east, signaling the seizure of nearby villages and estates, meant it was only a matter of days, possibly hours, until the Bolsheviks, their ranks augmented by deserters from the Imperial Army, arrived to pillage and burn her home to the ground.

She put her shoes beneath the window and paused to look at herself in the dark glass. She was white, gaunt, and morbidly serious, the softness gone from her round face, along with her once gentle smile. Leaning forward to study this stranger, she traced her fingers along her eyebrows, pressed her sharp cheekbones, and rested both hands under her chin. "Will the children recognize me?" she wondered aloud. Afraid to answer her question, she turned away. She unpinned her thick blonde hair and combed out her long braids. She replaited them, fastened them to the top of her head, and tied her scarf in place. "Of course they will know me," she whispered. "I'm their mother." She picked up her shawl and went down to the vestibule.

Twilight was slipping off the horizon into the sea. Slurred voices of drunken men rose over the lewd propositions of prostitutes, hustlers, and urchins seeking business for the night. Michail walked past them as he made his way to the door. Elvira Maria greeted him.

"I'm afraid the girls are gone," he said. He leaned against the railing next to her and avoided her gaze. "They've left the city."

She gripped his arm. "Are you sure? How could that be? We just saw them." She waited for his reply, but he was silent. "Perhaps they went to the orphanage, to the detdom."

He shook his head. "Elvira Maria, don't you see what's taking place in this street tonight? Look outside that window. Look!" He pointed toward the noisy crowd he'd just passed through. "Those wretched people are selling themselves just for a scrap of bread, for a drink. Open your eyes. This is not Kos."

Shrieks of laughter from the street flooded the vestibule. She would not let go of his arm. "How do you know the girls have vanished?" she asked.

He could not tell her. She would think he was involved, dismiss him as a thug, never speak to him again.

"What about your friend, Ivan? Did you find him?"

Outside, men argued and scuffled near the door. After a long pause he took her hand from his arm and held it. "Forgive me," he said. "I don't want to make your life more difficult."

"Do you think other children could be—"

"—I don't know." He turned and slowly climbed the stairs.

She rewrapped her shawl around her shoulders, and walking to the window, watched the snowflakes flurry against the frosted pane.

WINTER
1920

I know that in our highly civilized days people are becoming more and more tender-hearted, and that when one seizes his neighbor by the throat with the object of strangling him, it is done with every possible kindness and the decorum appropriate for the occasion.

—Maxim Gorky

13

Odessa

WEEKS AFTER SAINT BASIL'S EVE, on an overcast morning in February, Elvira Maria boarded the tram and handed her fare to the conductor's assistant, a young boy who wore a red cap and waved a handful of tickets. He greeted her, the strong scent of onions on his breath, and stepped aside to let her pass through the crowded aisle. She reached for an overhead strap and leaned against a group of older women. The coach lurched along Preobrazhenskaya Street, one of the city's longest thoroughfares. Subdued by the cold, passengers huddled together, shifting silently from side to side whenever the tram stopped and someone stepped down to the street.

She strained to remember the passing landmarks that would guide her back to the tenement. Short of money, and waiting for Monsieur Oury to give her more piece-work, she would walk home, following the tracks that wound through the southern edge of the Moldavanka Suburb. The tram clattered along, spitting blue sparks into the dull sky. As passengers disembarked, she took a seat on a vacant bench and looked out onto the street. Three women in fur-lined shubas and cloche hats stood in the doorway of a shuttered bakery. Farther along the route, a group of men, dressed in black, newspapers tucked under their arms, walked toward Privoz Market.

The tram turned a sharp corner, bells clanging, and reached the end of the line. It jolted to a stop in front of the Old Jewish Cemetery. Elvira Maria disembarked. Several babushkas with children and parcels trundled past her.

Avoiding the dirty snow near the track, she stepped onto a shoveled walkway that ran beside the cemetery wall. Urchins sat on top of the slender pilasters, panhandling. She stopped, took the chunk of bread from her pocket, and handed it to a ruddy-faced boy who leaned down from his perch. He snatched the bread with a bare hand, his thumb and index finger missing. Careful of the icy path she hurried on, the memory of that boy replaced by the next one begging at the cemetery gates.

The Old Jewish Cemetery, established in 1793, a year before Empress Catherine II officially founded the city, stretched across a grid of lanes that were dotted with modest headstones and elegant family vaults. Etched in Hebrew with the names of merchants, lawyers, and bankers, dockers, factory workers, artists, and writers, they memorialized the Jews who'd helped transform a once remote and wild terrain into a vibrant, cosmopolitan city.

Elvira Maria had never before seen so many graves in one place. The headstones stood side by side in long rows that claimed several city blocks. Glistening with frost, they emerged from the snow, somber and mysterious. Most were simple, with a Star of David carved at the top, but some were more ornate and decorated with urns, flowers, a miniature library of books, a ruler and compass, a lamb. At the far end of the cemetery two men stooped over shovels at a freshly dug grave, mounds of snow and earth piled nearby. The gnarled branches of an ancient yew hosted sparrows that waited for the sun.

At the end of the cemetery, the Jewish Hospital, a large two-story building with a giant clock, stood on the corner of Gospitalnaya Street. This was Elvira Maria's destination. Nadia said that its medical students brought street children with typhus there for treatment. Perhaps Sasha or Ana were patients.

The reception area was hushed. People read old magazines and newspapers. A nurse in a starched white apron and cap pushed the wheelchair of a veteran who wore a copper medal pinned to his coat. She leaned over so they could talk to each other quietly as they crossed the room. They left through a set of doors marked with Hebrew letters.

Elvira Maria waited in line behind two young girls carrying a basket of freshly ironed sheets. She studied the photograph of doctors and nurses that hung behind the reception desk. Two of the doctors were women. They stood in their lab coats at the end of the top row, their faces serious. Elvira Maria had never known a woman doctor, and had met a nurse only once when one visited the estate years ago. The villagers joked about her cap, said she wore wings. But they lined-up at the dacha and displayed their rashes, sores, and runny eyes. They called their children in from the fields. They'd eagerly taken her medicine and begged her to come again.

When it was Elvira Maria's turn, the matron, portly and middle-aged, wrote the children's names and ages in a notebook. Elvira Maria watched her hold her pen at an angle, so the ink flowed effortlessly across the lines provided. Her penmanship was beautiful, each letter curved and attached to the next, yet distinct. Any literate person occupying the desk could easily read the names. If I knew how to write, Elvira Maria thought, I'd want my letters and numbers to look like hers. The matron turned to the patient roster, her fingers scrolling down three long pages lined with purple ink. Elvira Maria inched closer to the desk and listened to the names the matron muttered.

"They're not logged-in here," she said. "But go to the second floor and check the blue room on your left. The children without families are there. They're off the critical list and recovering. Take a look." The sharp voices of a man and woman quarreling came from the hallway. The matron shook her head. "Winter takes its toll, doesn't it?"

At the second floor landing Elvira Maria recognized the sweet sickly smell of sweat and blood. It was a smell she remembered from the time when she, thirteen years old, had nursed her mother dying of consumption. Her mother was forty-one when she'd passed. Elvira Maria wasn't married then. Ana and Sasha hadn't been born. War had been only a rumor.

A sour taste flooded her mouth. She stopped on the threshold of the blue room and swallowed. She wiped her wet lips with her cold fingers. The room was dimly lit, heavy curtains partially drawn across the tall windows. It would have been restful had it not been for the labored breathing of the children. There were at least forty occupied beds in the ward, far more than she'd have guessed. She walked down the center aisle slowly. A feeling of dread filled her body as she paused and examined the waxy face of a little girl, her black curls tangled and stuck to her forehead. Next, a boy, fair-haired, like Sasha, and almost the same age. His face reminded her of Lev's, the strong jaw, thick eyebrows. Drool slid from the boy's mouth onto his stained pillow. She looked again, more closely, but no, it was someone else, someone with a brown birthmark on the side of his face. Another bed. Then another, where a child's head had been shaved and covered with yellow salve. She couldn't tell if it was a boy or a girl.

She forced herself to continue, to linger at each bed until she was certain she could move on. Most of the children were too sick to register her presence. Feverish and dazed, their spotted arms folded over their quilts, their thin bodies were almost invisible.

She reached the end of the long row and turned around to look at the children once more. "Ana and Sasha are not here," she whispered. "Oh, Holy Mother, thank you." She kissed her pendant of Blessed Theotokos. She closed her eyes at the sight before her, relieved and ashamed of her thoughts.

As she turned to leave, the little girl with black curls cried out and sat up in bed, tears streaming down her blotchy face. Elvira Maria, startled by the piercing sound, rushed to the top of the row and picked her up. Her body was burning, her nightgown soaked. She tried to soothe the child, but the girl's crying intensified. The other children grew restless. Several started to whimper. Soon a nurse was standing next to her. She handed her the child and left the ward. When she reached the street and pulled the hood of her mantle to her head, she realized her cheeks were wet.

Now afternoon, a gray wintry light slanted across the city. Elvira Maria, bracing herself against the cold, followed the path beside the tram tracks. She stomped the snow from her shoes and continued along the deserted street where shops were closed, their windows empty. Haunted by the small faces she'd seen in the ward she sought a distraction—watched the streetcars streaming past, the lorries and horse carts spinning snow from their wheels as they rattled along. She walked faster. How many children in Odessa were stricken with typhus? How many had died? She could not entertain such questions. They were too frightening, too painful. Ana and Sasha had rarely been sick; their stomachaches, worms, coughs, and colds short-lived, ended by doses of linden leaves and peppermint tea. She was a vigilant mother, had fed them as well as she could, and scoured the house weekly to keep it clean. Even Lev had laughed at her buckets of soapy water, told her to forget the housekeeping in favor of gathering wood or tending livestock.

A Volunteer Army convoy rumbled by, shaking her from her thoughts. Bandaged and wrapped in blankets, the soldiers slouched against their rifles and cast their eyes at the floorboards as they jostled along. Elvira Maria watched them disappear down the street in a grinding cloud of black exhaust. Had they fought the Reds or swarmed the villages up north near Kos? She could not tell; the Front was always moving, scattering the wounded in its wake. The soldiers, sitting in motionless rows, seemed dulled by too many battles and too many winters.

Their fatigue was weighted with a fear she knew but could not describe.

She glanced at the windowpane beside her and stopped. A cream-colored puppy bouncing in front of a torn curtain yipped as it played in the window of a streetside shop. She watched it cavort across the sill dragging a shred of green cloth between its tiny teeth. It rolled over and curled-up beside the pane. She tapped on the window. The puppy, nose to the glass, tried to sniff her fingers, and then impishly grabbed the crumpled curtain. Suddenly, it looked to the interior of the shop, jumped to the floor, and was out of sight, leaving the fabric swinging in the smudged window.

She prepared to walk on, but saw a figure inside appear at the edge of the glass. A spark of recognition flickered between them. Tatiana. The young girl quickly slid the curtain across the empty window, leaving Elvira Maria standing before it, bewildered. She approached the shop door and tried the heavy latch. It was locked. As she knocked and waited, she knew Tatiana would not answer.

Hours later, she sat on her bed and stared into the dark sky beyond her window. Like a sleepwalker, forever circling a confusing maze of snow-packed streets, she was too numb and detached from her surroundings to hear the sporadic rifle shots and machine gunfire coming from the streets below. As the shots continued they merged with a persistent rapping on her door.

"It's Michail," he said. "Are you there?"

"Yes, yes," she said, trying to connect with her voice. She braced herself against the wall as she opened the door.

"I'm sorry, I'm not ready yet. What time is the show this afternoon?"

"This afternoon? It's evening. We didn't have a show today."

He'd come with the news. The Bolsheviks were taking the city, occupying government buildings, swiftly establishing their positions. The Whites' Volunteer Army soldiers, joined by Ukrainian irregulars, were overwhelmed. A tram, tipped on its side, was now a barricade on the upper half of Nikolaevskaya Boulevard. Fires raged. In Odessa Harbor the Allied warships of the British, and a U.S. vessel sent to assist stranded diplomats, were evacuating thousands of refugees. Many had pushed on board while Bolshevik snipers fired into the crowd, wounding people, shooting out the tires of cars and trucks, shattering a gilded mirror propped against a mound of luggage. When the Rio Negro, a British vessel overloaded with refugees and wounded officers and cadets, pulled up its gangplank the crowd had shouted wildly, then surged toward another ship.

Michail held a war bulletin he picked up on the street. Dated the seventh of February 1920, the ink still fresh, it announced the liberation of the city. Had Ivan set the type and cranked it out? How many of the guns on the street were the result of his deals? Was he on board the collier, obeying orders to shoot?

"Kotovsky's entering the city tomorrow with his Red Banner Brigade," Michail said. "We won't be performing anywhere."

It was only then he saw she was wearing her wet mantle and cape, both spattered with mud. "Come upstairs," he said. "I've got a fire going."

"I'm fine," she said, straining. "I just need to catch my breath."

"I'm burning a stack of old shingles and don't want to waste them on a drafty attic. Please come."

The room, cluttered as always with tools, fabric, and sacks of puppets, glowed in the firelight. Wood shavings covered the floor surrounding the workbench. She sat near the grate and sipped a steamy glass of water. The charred shingles curled in the flames until they snapped and broke apart.

"I saw Tatiana today," she said. "She was in a shophouse several blocks from the hospital, near the tram line."

"How was she?" He stood beside her and refilled his glass. He glanced nervously at the bright light flashing in the window.

"I have no idea. She never opened the door."

He pulled up a crate and sat down. "Are you sure it was her? Perhaps it was someone else, someone with long hair like hers."

"Do you think so?" Her voice faded to a whisper. She gazed at the fire for a moment, then returned to him. "No. It was her. She recognized me. I know she did. She didn't want any contact with me—wouldn't answer the door when I knocked."

"That's not surprising." He placed a few twigs on the fire. "I hope she's got a decent place to live."

"She's got a puppy. A tiny powder puff."

"She's got a dog?"

Elvira Maria thought about the lively animal, and about Sasha, who'd also had a dog. But his had been a watchdog, a big black hound named Bruno that had adopted Sasha, who fed him crumbs from his pocket and took him to hunt in the woods. One spring the dog had flushed out and killed a fawn hiding in the grass near the creek below the farmhouse. When Sasha brought it home she'd cried all afternoon.

Michail waited for her to say more, but the cannon aimed at the port increased its rounds. The tenement shook. Pebbles and dirt in the rafters sifted down and dusted the attic. In the lower hallway, chucks of plaster could be heard dropping from the ceiling, striking the door of Nadia's apartment. The children's cries grew louder. The blast of the Rio Negro's horn sounded throughout the tenement as the vessel left the harbor. Elvira Maria stood with a jolt. The fatigue she'd felt before was gone; her memories vanished. The shelling intensified, the riveting sound coursing through her round after round. She reached for Michail. Together they stepped around the tools and crates that had shifted to the center of the floor and made their way to the window to watch the gunfire, as if it were a show of fireworks. The shots that exploded over the water sprayed hundreds of sparkling fans into the sky. They fell and glittered fiercely in the black slabs of ice that choked the frozen harbor.

14

HEDDIE NARYSHKINA KISSED MICHAIL three times on the cheeks, welcoming him to her party celebrating the Bolsheviks' victory. A last-minute affair, it was an opportunity to host the new officers who would evaluate her business in the days ahead. In the meantime, she intended to assess them, these potential allies and adversaries.

"Darling, we've got sturgeon tonight and black caviar," she announced. "I've thrown our rotten kasha to the beggars!" She nodded with approval at Michail's tailored jacket, fresh white tunic, and silk cravat, clothes his father had given him when he left Mińsk. She herself wore a red satin gown and garnet-studded combs tucked behind the spitcurls plastered to her cheeks.

"Ah, Heddie," he said, "there's nothing like a military triumph to bring out your best." He laughed and put his arm around her stocky shoulders.

In the reception room Red Army soldiers shouted a drinking song that rang through the brothel. Their heavy boots stomped in unison, shaking the ornate mirrors on the walls. Guests circled a large mahogany table, a brass urn filled with red carnations, pine boughs, and miniature Bolshevik flags in its center. The table was laden with platters of the rapidly disappearing sturgeon and side dishes of caviar, sour cream, and pelmeni dumplings, all bought on the thriving black market. There was more food than anyone had seen in years.

The green salon was crowded as well. Elena, one of Heddie's favorite girls, sat at the piano and played a request by an elderly officer sharing her bench. Her red fingernails flashed across the keyboard as she pounded out "In the Valley of Daghestan," a Bolshevik favorite. Soldiers leaned against the piano and eyed her breasts peeking through her crimson peignoir. The guests toasted each other as girls in satin evening dresses, slit at the sides to reveal their long silky legs, lit cigarettes and flirted. They moved among the men like the seasoned courtesans they were, pausing to compliment one officer on his valor or to whisper a naughty secret in the ear of another.

Heddie coaxed Michail to an alcove in the smoky salon. She raised her voice above the din. "I haven't seen you in ages. All this turmoil's driven away my favorite people."

"What can I do? The mural's completed and your girls are too expensive." He held up empty hands. "I haven't got a kopek."

"No, no, no! Don't talk like that. Not tonight. The worst is over. I don't know about you, but I intend to stay on top."

"You do have that reputation, don't you, my dear."

She slapped Michail's arm. "Boris, Boris," she called out, "for God's sake, fill this man's glass before those thirsty barbarians drink it all."

Boris, his silver hair slicked back with pomade, glided through the throng with crystal coupes of champagne on his sterling tray. His livery of black waistcoat and trousers was impeccable. He shook Michail's hand. "You're looking smart," he said. "Did you bring your brushes to capture this historic occasion?"

"Just my curiosity," Michail said, "and my appetite."

"Indeed." Boris chuckled. He served them both with a gloved hand, then moved on to find the coats and hats of three gentlemen, supporters of the opera, who were heading for the vestibule.

"Thank you, Heddie," Michail said. He raised his glass. "Here's to peace."

"Yes, that's a good one." Pulling him closer, she placed a jeweled hand on his chest and lowered her voice. "Just remember Michail, we've got to keep our eyes open. I've seen it before and so did my mother, God rest her soul. The purer anyone says he is, the more corrupt he'll turn out to be. These Bolsheviks say they're for the workers, but you watch. They'll make a few grand gestures to set up their proletarian government and divvy out favors to their friends. They'll act high and mighty, then come in here and take my best girl for the night, free of charge."

"We need to wait and see what's next."

"Yes. Haste is never a wise counselor."

Young soldiers in drab and ill-fitting uniforms stood in line on the staircase waiting for a room, their arms around sleek, sequined women. The couples slowly rose to the landing and upper hallway. The singing crowd, jovial and drunk, joined arms and swayed, liquor spilling from their glasses onto Heddie's oriental carpets. The heavy smell of hashish drifted across the rooms.

"Good champagne," Michail said. He took another sip.

"The Bolsheviks had enough sense to liberate it from a French ship before she sailed away," Heddie said. She arched her penciled eyebrows and took a step back to look at him. "Now tell me, Michail. You didn't come here for a girl, so what do you want? I'll give it to you if I can, but I have my limits."

"Fair enough."

"Well?" She put down her glass, reached into her bosom, and pulled out two cigarettes. She offered one to Michail. "Turkish tobacco — very smooth. You'll like it."

He lit them both. "Heddie, I'm looking for two children," he said. "I need to know if they're hostages in a brothel."

"You know I don't pander to that sort of nonsense," she scoffed. "My girls are as close to legal age as you can get. I don't want children here."

"But you know people who do."

"Michail, there's a war going on. There must be a million girls and boys selling themselves."

But he knew that deals were made, that money changed hands every day as gangs snatched children from the streets. They were sold or traded for food, work, sex, guns, and marafet. Ivan's transaction was just a fraction of a business that involved hundreds of Odessa's displaced and orphaned children. "Just listen," he said, "and tell me if you hear anything."

"It's dangerous and I don't like it."

The music stopped. Several officers of the Red Cavalry had entered the adjoining salon. Soldiers shouted and raised their glasses. Heddie waved to Boris, who headed in their direction.

"Why do you want these children?" she asked.

"I'm trying to help a woman, the mother. She's my assistant, changes the props and scenery, or she will if I can ever perform again."

"Good Lord! Are you in love?"

"It's nothing like that, Heddie." He paused. "To be honest, I don't know how I feel about her."

"Well, that's a pitiful confession." She dropped her cigarette stub in a crystal ashtray. "Michail, you're too complicated for your own good."

He leaned closer to her and explained where Sasha and Ana were from, that the boy was now eleven years old and the girl six. "The name is Andrushko," he added.

She patted his hand and gave him a sympathetic look. "I'll see what I can find out, but don't expect too much and *don't* pester me. And have something to eat before you leave." She realigned her shoulders to the elegant cut of her gown. "I've got guests to attend to."

15

CATHEDRAL BELLS CHIMED ACROSS ODESSA, herald-ing the Bolsheviks' arrival and summoning the city's war-weary residents to the cold and windy streets. Some people cheered Kotovsky's brigade riding their horses down Nikolaevskaya Boulevard, and children, excited by the parade of swirling red banners, ran beside the horses, calling up to the soldiers, but Elvira Maria, shivering at the entrance of Mendeleyev Lane, was among those who only watched.

Kotovsky was from Bessarabia, but had spent enough time in Odessa to gain notoriety. Some of the locals claimed he'd been a gangster and seized control over the criminal world formerly in the grip of Mishka Yaponchik, a power-ful boss. They didn't trust him. Nonetheless, after robbing a bank and conspiring with the authorities for a prison reprieve, he'd fought on the Romanian Front and distin-guished himself in battle. By 1919 he'd risen in the ranks of the Bolsheviks, and now, as a Red Army general, had taken the city. It was the final prize for the Bolsheviks. They'd waged a revolution across the Russian Empire and won.

The sight of so many soldiers terrified Elvira Maria. Had they come from the north having finally burned Kos to a cinder, murdering the few helpless souls who'd remained in the ravaged village? Or had the Whites beaten them to it? There was enough blame and destruction to go around. She pulled her cowl over her nose and mouth, the freezing air stinging her face. As the brigade reached the windswept bridge, rising over its stone arches, it paused momentarily for all to see, then descending, continued its procession. Workers, dockers, unionists, students, sympathizers, and stragglers followed. They brandished red flags and sang songs of solidarity and revolution.

She walked back to the tenement. Shops along the plundered streets were riddled with bullet holes, their windows filled with broken glass and snow. Inside, display cases were shattered and empty. Shreds of paper, spools of string, masonry, and ceiling tiles covered the scarred floors. A shutter, swinging on a twisted hinge, pounded against the charred wall of a butcher shop. Black clouds hung over the Moldavanka and Peresuip Suburbs.

She headed to Gogolya Street to check Monsieur Oury's shop. It was padlocked, but still standing, his beautiful sign cast in the gutter like a crumpled leaf. In the adjoining alley, water gushed from a broken pipe that jutted out of a muddy whirlpool and flowed toward the building's foundation. The shop would be closed until that was repaired. She would watch her expenses in the days ahead and pass by again to see how he was, and if he could open anytime soon.

Her cape, still damp from yesterday's relentless sleet, was heavy and cold as she moved through the hundreds of

refugees who roamed the streets. Trapped in the city and
fearful of the Bolsheviks they had fought and resisted for
years, many were desperate to leave. Hustlers and oppor-
tunists strategically working the crowd approached her as
she passed. They pressed her with offers of transport for
exorbitant fees.

"You can depart tonight," they whispered. "Boats to
Stamboul are ready." "Or a lorry? Yes? A lorry can take
you to the border. Madame, we can arrange it for a special
price."

Later that afternoon, she passed through a group of
strangers milling about in the tenement vestibule, their
bundles tossed on the floor. Weather-beaten and dressed in
grimy clothes, they looked like they'd been on the streets
for months, and indeed, after leaving their village east of
the Dnieper River, they had walked for weeks, stopping
overnight in a Peresuip courtyard to shelter from the violence before they entered the city center. One of them, the
only man in the group, coughed heavily and struggled to
catch his breath.

"What are you looking at?" he said to her when he
could speak. He was draped in a moth-eaten blanket, his
face glowing and feverish, deep lines of dirt across his
forehead.

She didn't answer, sensing the man was trouble, and
hurried up the stairs to the landing.

"I've asked you a question, Comrade," he insisted.

Nadia padded down the stairs in her house slippers,
her hair tied up in a kerchief, a kitchen towel in her hand.
"She's going to her room," she said. "It's a little corner

that's none of your business." She took Elvira Maria's arm, ready to escort her up the stairs.

"Did you hear that?" the man said. He was addressing the woman standing beside him, her shoulders stooped beneath the weight of a large cast-iron kettle. "She's got her own room."

Elvira Maria stared at two boys tussling with each other near the front door. They appeared to be five and ten years old.

"Danya, Pavlo," the man yelled. "Get over here!" He raised the back of his hand and coughed.

Now an older girl joined the others. Dwarfed in a huge quilted overcoat, she yanked the boys apart and boxed their ears. Danya, the younger boy, whimpered and pushed the girl aside. He scuttled behind Pavlo who mumbled insults under his breath.

The man hacked into his blanket. He shook until the violent spasm stopped. Wheezing, he turned back to Elvira Maria and Nadia and introduced himself. "Anatoly Kuznetsov's the name. Everyone calls me Tolya." He gestured to the woman and children. "These here are my wife and her sister and my boys." The older woman bowed her head deferentially. "We'll be living in this hallway. I got the residency permit, in case you got questions. The officer in charge signed it this morning." He pulled out a document, stamped with three red seals, and limped up the stairs to hand it to Nadia. "See there?" he said. "Don't ask me what his name is. I can't read a word of it."

"What does it say?" Elvira Maria whispered.

"The family's been assigned to the vestibule until further notice."

Tolya hiked-up his blanket, holding onto it with a calloused hand. "That's his signature, ain't it?"

"It is," Nadia said. "It's been signed by the Odessa Commissar of Housing." She squinted to make out the name. "Comrade Ivan Dashkevich."

Nadia pulled Elvira Maria into her apartment and slammed the door. Wet diapers, underwear, shirts, towels, and a baby's blanket were pinned to a clothesline strung across the room. A large portrait of Lenin sitting at his desk, pen in hand, hung on a far wall above a shelf of dishes. A fire sputtered in the stove near the window. Two of her girls, three and four years old, played on the floor with the baby, who waved a metal spoon and drooled.

"Dashkevich!" Nadia said. "I can't believe it. He was Michail's partner for years. Wait till I tell him the news." She shook her head in disbelief. "How did Ivan become a housing commissar?"

"He's a Bolshevik," Elvira Maria said. "A member of the Party." She felt protective of Ivan. He had been so frightened the night he was shot.

"Our house is full," Nadia said. "We don't need a family of five crammed in our vestibule. He should send them to a hotel or a fancy spa." She placed cups on the kitchen table. "Keep your door locked," she said. "Those folks will rob us all."

Elvira Maria laughed. "I don't have much to take."

"Just be careful. They're rough, and if he's as sick as I think he is, they're desperate too."

They drank hot water steeped with pine needles and gossiped about the other occupants of the house. How the family on the first floor, who'd lived there for years, swept their dust and table crumbs to the end of the hall, then left them there in a pile that attracted cockroaches and rats. How their only son got a coveted job at the dockyards, only because he drank with the foreman and staked him at cards. How, down the hall, the husband had called his wife a brute because she'd beaten his favorite daughter who had refused a marriage proposal from a distant cousin who was an interrogator at the jail, and really, Nadia said, who could blame the poor thing?

Nadia explained that the house had always been filled with people who came and went. Like Michail, she said. Her eyes gleamed as she looked at Elvira Maria, knowing they spent time together. When Elvira Maria didn't flinch or blush, she continued. Most people minded their own business, but everyone had their little annoying habits. They sat and smoked on the stairs or left their chamber pots in the yard where the children played. You couldn't control everything. The neighborhood was convenient, especially for her older daughter, Lydia, who was enrolled at the commercial school next door and waiting for classes to resume.

"Could she teach me to read?" Elvira Maria asked.

"Lydia, my girl? Of course." Nadia beamed and grabbed Elvira Maria's hand. "Reading's important."

"When I was in Kos it didn't seem to matter. The priest helped us with letters and papers."

"You don't want to run to a priest. They're counter-revolutionaries. I'll talk to Lydia when she gets home."

In her room, Elvira Maria unfolded a war bulletin she'd left on her chair. She examined the numbers and letters. She knew most of the numbers already, but learning

and assembling the letters to make words would be difficult. Sasha had spent weeks studying a newspaper and a
calendar, trying to decipher bits of text. He'd only begun
to read the summer before they'd left Kos.

She opened her suitcase and took out the scraps of
paper she'd collected from the streets. Paper was scarce.
Everyone complained there was never enough. The
Bolsheviks, who used what little there was for their newspapers and propaganda, rationed it. Fashion magazines
and literary journals, once so popular in Odessa, had
stopped publishing. Shopkeepers, when their stores were
open, no longer wrapped purchases, and notebooks, once
a school necessity, were impossible to buy. She smoothed
the creases from each scrap and placed them across her
bed. They were different shapes and sizes. She stood back
and looked at them. Soon they'd be filled with words she
would read and write. Before dawn, when the fog was still
thick, she'd run down to the alley and steal boards from
the broken-down fence next door. With Nadia's help,
she'd build a small desk beneath her window, one that
looked something like Lenin's.

16

Now the first week in March, Michail and his puppets were stranded, confined to the attic until the storm subsided. It had raged for days. Ice had formed on the window latch. Snow circled the chimneystacks and blew down the alley. Trash bins rattled against a broken lamppost that had crashed to the street during the night. The foghorn at the Vorontsov Pier moaned, as ships at sea also waited for better weather.

The room was cold, despite a struggling fire in the stove. Elvira Maria, wearing her cape, sat before it. She slowly turned the pages of the book he'd given her several weeks ago when she started her lessons. It was the size of her pocket and contained pages trimmed in silver. The spine and covers were red leather, scrolled with gold letters. She was amazed that books could be more ornate than family Bibles, and had never expected such a precious gift. The book, entitled Petrushka, had been part of a folktale collection Michail had inherited from his grandfather. Michail loved the story and had performed it with Ivan many times. An etching opposite the title page depicted the court jester, Petrushka, standing beside a ballerina, his long nose pointing toward her elegant horse and carriage. Now starting the second chapter, Elvira Maria was trying to figure out their relationship, but the words she didn't know made it difficult.

"Is this 'necessary' or 'necessity'?" she asked, pointing.

He looked over her shoulder. "It's 'necessary,'" he said. "'The ballet master told her to wear satin slippers. They were *necessary*, given her profession.' Just keep reading and look at the pictures. You'll get the idea."

He went to the other end of the room to examine his puppets and consider his options, if spring ever arrived. He took down Dedushka, the old Grandfather, who hung on his peg next to Babushka. He frowned. It was easy to hold a puppet in each hand and have them banter as he moved them across the stage, but changing scenery, adding another puppet, or producing sound effects and elaborate props at the same time was impossible. If he continued to perform alone the shows would have to be simpler. He might end up with slapstick jollies that hit each other every two seconds.

Elvira Maria, her voice low and halting, reread the paragraph that described the ballerina. He watched her and listened.

"I want you to perform with me," he said, surprising even himself.

"What?"

"Perform with me—please? You'd be good."

"I can't do that." She closed the book and laughed. "Besides, I'm a woman."

"That doesn't matter. Odessans love novelty. Lots of women perform, but none with puppets." In all the years he'd traveled with the show he'd never seen a woman behind the stage. But his father had. In the Caucuses, where there were at least a dozen troupes, his father said, women puppeteers played the female roles and sang their own poetry.

"Oh Michail," she said. "I'd be too nervous. I can hardly talk to strangers, much less perform."

"I'll teach you." His mind raced as he thought about trying something new. "If we practice now, we'll be ready in a few months."

"You might regret it. Then what would you do? You'd have to fire me!"

"I want you to give it a try." He brought Beauty, her favorite puppet, to her and placed it on her outstretched hand. "Relax," he said, "dance it around the room, hum a little."

The next day, he shoveled his way through the snow to the shed and hauled the theater to the attic. They assembled it together. He showed her the tiny gauze slits in the curtain that allowed her to see the stage, as well as the audience. Scenery and special effects, like gems that seemed to appear out of nowhere, were attached to simple cords. By the end of three weeks she'd learned how to breathe deeply and project her voice, how to manipulate the puppets so they didn't look stiff, and how to stand solidly on two feet so she wouldn't get tired or distracted. She had been surprised at how much she enjoyed it all and how excited she felt when she woke each morning. Michail also seemed happier than usual. He was patient when she fumbled with a puppet, forgot a cue, or laughed nervously.

After she'd practiced with Beauty, he introduced the Beast, a large woolly puppet that filled almost half of the stage. She'd placed Beauty to the side, careful of her sweeping gown, but then realized the puppet was too close to the opened curtain and was hidden from the audience. There was always something that demanded her attention, a detail she hadn't thought of.

"Perhaps you should work with Lydia," she said. "She'd be better than me."

"I wouldn't think of it," he said. "It's just a matter of practice."

"I know. But I'm not good enough to perform for the public."

"Nonsense, you're better than you think. You've already mastered Beauty's voice."

He decided they would perform The Scarlet Flower when the season opened, and that rehearsing only one show would be best for them both. Suddenly, Elvira Maria was busy learning to read and write new sentences with Lydia and practicing most afternoons with Michail. Now that Monsieur Oury's shop was open, she ran to collect collars and plackets that needed finishing touches. It was then that she shared her photo with street vendors, young mothers, and students, and visited the railyard and markets to talk with the children camped there as the snow fell across Odessa.

At last, Michail announced it was time for a dress rehearsal. Though nervous, Elvira Maria was eager to see if she could perform in front of an audience. Nadia and her girls came to the attic to see the show. They chattered all at once as they circled the theater, and Nadia warned them not to touch. The two dragons on top of each castle sparkled in the lamplight. The red banners, freshly ironed, looked crisp and new. The younger girls, wide-eyed, held their dolls and sat on a beach mat before the theater. Nadia and Lydia perched on crates.

Michail blew his pishchik and Elvira Maria swept Beauty onto the stage. The children were rapt. Once or twice they walked to the edge of the stage and pointed to a puppet. Nadia laughed at the Beast and snarled back at him, demonstrating to her girls that he was not so fierce after all. When the curtains closed she stood up and clapped until her hands stung.

"What an exciting show," she said. She held Elvira Maria by the shoulders, her eyes aglow. "Think of how progressive you are, performing like that. If Lenin's wife hears about you she'll want to write an article."

"I hope she'll get us our labor books first," Michail joked. He knew it was impossible, but he'd soon be making the rounds and cajoling bureaucrats selected from the Party who were ready to wield their authority.

"I'm glad you enjoyed it all," Elvira Maria said. She stole a glance at Michail, who stood next to the stage, smiling.

"We're ready to see more," Lydia said. She and Nadia coaxed the little girls to the door while they waved goodnight.

"Well done, my Beauty," Michail said. He bowed to Elvira Maria and took her hand. "I am at your service." Then humming a song from the show, he guided her into a waltz. She was surprised his steps were so certain. Clearly, he'd danced before and enjoyed it. He was lighter on his feet that she was. She lifted her long skirts from the floor and they crossed the room, whirling past the workbench, the gunnysacks, the stove, the stage and castles tilting, the colors of the puppets on the back wall streaming as she twirled beneath his arm. They stopped near a wooden crate, almost tipping it over. Breathless, they held each other and laughed. Her headscarf slipped to her shoulders. She looked into his eyes, then felt his hand on her cheek slowly caress her upturned face. As he brought his lips to hers, she drew him close, feeling the urgency between them.

When he stepped back to look at her, he tucked a stray lock of her hair behind her ear. "You are my Beauty, aren't you?" he asked.

She was shaking, hardly able to speak. "I really must go," she whispered.

He watched her descend the stairs. The pins in her thick braids askew, the tress he'd held in his hand trailing over her shoulder. Her image had passed through his mind time and again, kept him awake at night. Now she had entered his heart. He shook his head, mystified by the intense feeling. Perhaps he would never sleep.

In her room she sank to her bed. A few hairpins scattered to the floor. She placed her hand to her mouth. Her lips were still warm, and her mouth tasted sweet — tasted like honey and cloves.

17

PALE BLUE, TURQUOISE, CORAL, PINK, AND CREAM. The colorful thread was dazzling. Each strand slid through her needle and left a silky trail in her lap as she pierced an organdy placket where a delicate buttonhole was needed. The camisoles she'd collected from Monsieur Oury's shop that morning were pastel, each one lovelier than the next. In line with spring fashions, he had proudly told her. Weeks after the Bolsheviks' victory, he was open for business and doing well.

Elvira Maria, starry-eyed over her dance and kiss with Michail the night before, had eagerly taken the beautiful camisoles, not realizing that Monsieur Oury had added five more pieces to her usual workorder of twenty. She'd seen him write '25 Pieces' in his ledger, but hadn't thought to object. This was a large order to complete in just two days. She'd be stranded in her room for hours.

She finished the buttonholes of a turquoise camisole and fastened the tiny shell buttons in place. The garment was blousy through the midriff, and cinched at the waist with a satin ribbon that matched a delicate ruffle at the neckline. Each capped sleeve was trimmed with a narrower ribbon of the same color. It was exquisite; the fabric soft and smooth, so sheer you could see through it. She held the camisole to the light and laughed.

Her own, a mere shift, was sewn from a flour sack and was a white rectangle with holes, one for her head, two for her arms, and the last and largest for pushing the garment over her torso and settling it under her petticoat. Homespun linen, it absorbed the sweat of a grueling harvest workday, but there was nothing exciting about it. Pastel camisoles of sheer cloth and delicate stitches were for the wealthy, for women who sat at fine tables, walked leisurely along the promenades, or rode in cushioned carriages, looking with disdain through the polished windows at the dirty streets.

Women, like the wife of the commander who owned the large estate where she and Lev had worked, wore camisoles like these. When doing the laundry at the dacha she'd seen the fine clothes the commander's wife discarded in a special wash basket that held organdy blouses and fine stockings that rolled over the knee. Elvira Maria had washed these garments in a porcelain basin, using a fragrant soap that came in a white wicker box and couldn't be used for anything else.

Installed for the summer, and dressed in fashionable clothes, the commander's wife had sat on the veranda of the dacha with her friends who came from the city, their idle conversation lasting for hours. Hours that Elvira Maria spent in the kitchen taming a hot iron while she pressed the delicate garments and listened to the cook complain about the endless meals she had to prepare. It was humiliating to work for a woman who ignored you when you gave her a pile of fresh clothes that had taken you ages to wash and iron. The servants were told to keep to the hallways and kitchen when not scurrying around her, and were rendered invisible when they answered the ring of her little bell.

One day as Elvira Maria pulled nettles from the garden, she had entertained the prospect of slipping a sappy frond into the woman's underwear. But she dismissed the idea, knowing the servants would protect themselves from the woman's fury by pointing a finger in her direction.

In need of work, Elvira Maria was glad Monsieur Oury's shop was busy and that wealthy customers could afford an expensive camisole. Most were the wives and lovers of speculators, men who had profited during the war with Germany and now continued their brisk business, selling everything from caviar and champagne to illegal guns and dynamite.

After she completed seven camisoles and set them in a neat pile, she took a break. She stretched, shook her hands, and rubbed her fingers. She rearranged scraps of paper and the pencil on her desk. From her window she could see Nadia, hurrying along the path to the shed, carrying a broken chair.

"What happened?" she hollered out the window.

Nadia looked up and laughed. "It fell apart when Lydia sat on it. I'm chopping it up to put in the stove."

Elvira Maria returned to the camisoles and counted the ones that still needed buttonholes. There were nineteen. She paused and looked at both piles. Then counting again, she took a short breath. Altogether there were

twenty-six, not twenty-five. Had Monsieur Oury given
her an extra one by mistake? She quickly spread the camisoles across her bed and discovered there were five of each
color, and six that were coral. She ran her fingers over the
shimmering ribbons of the coral camisole. "I'll keep it,"
she said out loud. "I'll keep it and not say a word." She
bit her lip. She'd taken a dish or two of flour from the
dacha, or sometimes bars of laundry soap, but had never
stolen anything like a camisole. Was it right to steal from
Monsieur Oury? Weeks ago she'd peeled his hand from
her waist and told him never to touch her again that way.
Sputtering, he had apologized, and now treated her with
more respect than the other shop girls.

She removed her bodice and tugged her shift over her
head and placed both on the chair. As she slipped her arms
into the sleeves of the coral camisole it floated over her
bosom, gave her shivers. Tying the ribbon in place, she
adjusted the folds that ran down her breasts and flounced
the apron at her hips. The garment was light as a feather.
She thought of Monsieur Oury, fiddling with his tape
measure, jingling the coins in his pocket as he pored over
his latest patterns. She would deliver his order on time,
but would keep the camisole. After all, it was in line with
spring fashions.

18

MONSIEUR OURY, KEYS IN HIS HAND, unlocked the door and escorted her into the shop. Elvira Maria stopped at once. The tables were empty, his prized sewing machines gone. Naked mannequins were pushed in a corner. The shop girls, nowhere in sight.

She handed him the package of finished camisoles while he told her that yesterday morning, on his busiest workday in weeks, the Bolsheviks had loaded his machines into a lorry and taken them to their new sewing cooperative in Peresuip Suburb.

Was the shop closed, her job terminated? Bolts of fabric were still on the shelves, along with his pattern books, but everything else was gone, even the chairs. "What will you do now?" she asked.

"Hand sewing, piecework, special orders." If he was careful and advertised only through word of mouth, he could continue to serve a select clientele. "That is," he said, "if they have any money."

He checked her handiwork, a smile lighting up his worried face. "Parfait! Excellent!" He gave her a few rubles. Then realizing her hand was still extended, he added more. "I know, it was a lot of work," he said. "I'm sorry to be so stingy. I just don't know what's next."

"Should I return?" she asked.

"Of course." He undid the chain and opened the door. "Next week, come next week. I'll see what I can do."

In the street, she thought about the shop, once filled with excited customers, fashion displays, and a line of girls pumping their noisy sewing machines. The Bolsheviks had emptied it overnight. She was lucky, at least she'd been paid and might be able to continue working if Monsieur Oury was clever and determined to stay in business. She felt a bit guilty about keeping the camisole, but pushed the discomfort aside. She had more important things to think about. Earlier that morning a boy had stopped her in the street with news of Sasha. He'd seen her photo weeks before and had remembered it. He was certain her son was at the dockyards. She'd given him a ruble and some bread in exchange for more information, but the boy, suddenly confronted by others who were stalking him, had run off, a gang of at least five yelling urchins at his heels. She had watched him disappear down an alley, worried she'd never see him again.

The Odessa Steps were wet and slippery from the recent thaw. Melting snow, collected on the landings, trickled down the incline. Dockers, beggars, and Red Army soldiers sloshed past her, kicking up water and grit. She watched her step as she made her way down to the last landing.

When she reached the dockyards, an enormous steamer stranded in drydock loomed before her. Covered in scaffolding, it was being repaired, a swarm of welders with sparking torches at its hull. The din of carpenters hammering on the deck competed with the shouts and whistles of carters hauling loads to Voenni Pier.

She looked up and down the harbor. Then walking toward the dinghies resting in the sand, she saw the boy wave. Excited, she waved back and ran along a muddy path leading to the dinghies.

"I thought they got you for good," she said when she caught up to him.

"I run fast," he said. He shook her hand, as if their relationship was professional. Eight or nine years old, he was filthy, his head wrapped in a thick greasy cloth. The coat, hanging on his thin body, was patched and extended to his ankles. "They got the bread," he continued, "but not your ruble." He lifted the string around his neck to reveal a small bag hidden inside his coat.

"Come on." He beckoned her to follow.

In minutes, twenty or thirty boys and girls, appearing from behind the boulders and bushes that scattered the hillside, joined them. They stopped at a dinghy and surrounded it, the children's small hands reaching to the rim where the oar locks, salvage metal, had been removed.

"Take a look," the boy said. "He's in here."

This was not what she'd expected. Her eyes traveled around the circle, searching for Sasha, Ana next to him. They were not among the children. She glanced behind her, but no one was running across the beach to meet her. She'd envisioned their rendezvous all morning, hurried to deliver her order to Monsieur Oury just so she could get to the dockyards as fast as she could.

The boy pulled back the heavy sail that covered the boat.

The stench of dead bodies and rotten flesh filled the air. She gagged and reached for her handkerchief. The children were silent, their hollow eyes watching her. She leaned forward, and white with fear, peered into the boat. The bodies of boys and girls curled around each other like kittens lay in a shrunken mass of tattered clothing. She crossed herself and whispered a prayer. Some of the children, clinging to her skirt, did the same.

It was too cold, the boy explained. His voice was hoarse, straining over the sound of the waves rolling in at high tide. She heard his words as a plea. The world was deaf and dumb to the plight of these children. Most people said they were a nuisance, an inconvenience. What could you expect after years of war?

She touched the rim of the boat, using it to guide her, and walked around the dinghy. She took note of all the faces, pausing at the one the boy pointed out to be Sasha. He was right, they looked alike, could have been brothers. But this boy's eyes were shaped like almonds and his face freckled, unlike her son's. It was the flaxen hair, distinct and seen so well from a distance. She had always looked twice at a child with hair that color.

She sat on a rocky ledge with the boy, her arm around his shoulders, the other children close.

"I told them to stay by the fire I built," he said, "but they wouldn't listen, just wanted to sleep." He leaned against her, his body quivering. He smelled of seaweed, wet sand, and smoke.

Soon the other children grew restless and wandered down the beach to beg at the steps they claimed each day.

"Ask a docker if he's got a shovel we can use," she finally said, pointing toward Voenni Pier.

After a while, the boy returned with an old docker whose thick mustache drooped on his tired face. He carried the shovel over his shoulder, said he couldn't trust the urchins to give it back. She led him to the boat and watched him close his eyes and clench his knuckles around the handle of the shovel. Together they buried the children, topping the grave with stones. Overhead, gulls cried and circled the heavy clouds, only to disappear on the wind.

19

PAVLO AND DANYA, TOLYA KUZNETSOV'S SONS, bickered in the tenement yard, excited to assist Michail and Elvira Maria with their morning show, *The Scarlet Flower*. It was the first performance Michail had been able to schedule since the Bolsheviks had installed themselves in the city. He was ready, but knew Elvira Maria was apprehensive about performing for the public.

Pavlo yelled at his younger brother. "Keep your hands off, Danya. I'm carrying this one by myself." He elbowed Danya aside and heaved a sack of puppets over his shoulder. The contents clacked loudly. Michail winced.

"Mind what you're doing," he said. "You're not hauling bricks."

Pavlo shifted the sack to his other shoulder and pushed back a bushy clump of black hair from his high forehead. He sauntered to the edge of the yard and shoved a fist in his trouser pocket.

Michail turned to Danya, sniveling in front of the shed. "If you're coming with us, you'd better stop fussing," he said. He handed him a banner. "Don't open it until we get to the garden."

Danya wiped his face with the edge of his soiled tunic. He smiled, exposing a few crooked teeth. Elvira Maria took his hand and guided him around the muddy pools of dissolving snow. Weather-beaten from the long harsh winter, the tenement houses leaned into the southern wind, their clapboards drying and creaking. A flock of terns, survivors of the war, streaked across the pale blue sky, calling for spring.

"You've got our labor books?" Michail asked.

Elvira Maria was pleased he trusted her with them. For weeks he had filled out multiple forms, feigned interest in the Party, and flattered a line of stubborn comrades at the Commissariat of Internal Affairs. Finally, he met a well-placed official who remembered his puppet theater and sympathized with all the skomorokhi minstrels who sang of freedom and performed stories steeped in folklore. He issued Michail the papers and sent him on his way. The new rules limited the times and places where he could perform. Michail had fumed. "The Party of the People," he said, "unless the People want to earn a living."

They entered Deribasov Garden and paused to admire the two bronze lions commandeered from a private estate and recently installed near the walkway by the new government. Pavlo and Danya rapped on them to see if they were hollow and ran their fingers along the metal grooves. "The Beast you made looks a lot like this one," Pavlo said, pointing to the lion with prey beneath its paw.

"Yes," Michail said, "but these are magnificent."

He unfolded the theater in a corner of the small garden. Pavlo set down his sack with care, then hurried to the street to drum up an audience. *The Scarlet Flower* would be the first puppet show he and Danya had ever seen.

Elvira Maria attached the rolls of scenery to a set of hooks backstage and tacked up her lines. The sheet was long and her letters a little too large, but she'd managed to write out the dialog for Beauty. Although she'd memorized the lines, reciting them many times at her desk while she held the puppet to the window, the sheet boosted her confidence.

Michail, ready to begin, smiled at her. He was pleased she was standing next to him. She'd learned quickly, and was more enthusiastic than Ivan had ever been. He blew the pishchik whistle. She shifted her feet and ignored her jittery stomach. Danya, standing beside her, clutched a large red flower fashioned from silk.

"Don't crush it," Elvira Maria whispered. "The audience needs to see it when the time comes."

Michail opened the theater curtains. The Merchant, white-bearded and wrinkled, waved his golden purse.

Once upon a time long, long ago (and we all know how long it's been since we've seen each other) I, the Greatest Merchant in Odessa, was well known. I had a harvest of wheat in my granary, ships sailing out of the port, and a feast on my table from morning to night. Comrades, do you remember those days? Ah ha, they're gone. But I'm still a merchant, and now am a proud Party member. I share my wealth, like everyone here in this glorious Public Garden. I work for my three beautiful daughters. They are my prized possessions. Take heed comrades, vagabonds, soldiers, and suitors.

Michail sang the Merchant's song and presented the daughters, one by one:

> My daughters are elegant, regal, and fair
> The oldest is lovely with dark auburn hair.
> The second is tiny with soft sparkling eyes
> The youngest is Beauty, a name of surprise.
> She is the sweetest, known to be true
> With pleasure I now introduce her to you.

Elvira Maria slipped Beauty over her hand, fluffed up the folds of her red gown, and danced her to the Merchant, her Father. She shouted her first line into the audience and began the dialog between the two characters.

Dearest Father, must you travel abroad to seek your livelihood? I cannot live happily without you.

Ah Beauty, do not be sad. I will return soon, for you are my greatest treasure. Tell me, my sweet, what gift shall I bring you? What is your heart's desire?

Only your love, dear Father.

Your words fill me with joy, Beauty, but I must bring you a gift. Name what you would like and it shall be yours.

I would like the most beautiful, fragrant, scarlet flower in the world.

Well chosen, indeed. I promise, with all of my heart, to return with your precious flower.

The audience clapped raucously when Beauty left the stage. Now they were shouting at the Beast. Michail stifled a laugh as he prowled the puppet in front of the curtain. Elvira Maria moved to the edge of the theater to see who was making so much noise. It was a group of street boys. Rowdy and enthused, they laughed and repeated their favorite lines. Toughened by the deprivations that came with winter, their sullen faces brightened as they watched the Beast. Packs of boys usually struck her as devious, even hostile, as they begged for money and cursed those who ignored them, but this morning they appeared innocent as they reclaimed their childhood for a moment. Pavlo, she noticed, had joined them. He was pointing to the stage and strutting back and forth, obstructing their view. An older boy pushed him aside, but he ignored him, and stood in the middle of the group. She scanned each face before she went backstage. The scene changed. She pulled a red cord behind the curtain that brought flowering tulip trees and a mansion with turrets into view.

The Merchant stood beside the large scarlet flower that poked through the stage.

Oh ho! he exclaimed. I have traveled from frosty Siberia to balmy Odessa searching for the perfect flower. At last, I have found it, the most fragrant of them all. Beauty will be overjoyed with her present. He picked the flower and waved it before the audience.

The Beast, jumping out from behind the trees, growled. Halt! You cannot pick my flowers! They're not State property, available to every foolish comrade who wants one.

The Merchant trembled and threw himself at the Beast's feet. I am at your mercy. Please, please spare my life!

Send for your Beauty at once, the Beast demanded, and I shall let you live. But know this, and know it well—she must be a fair maiden and have a brave and loving heart. She will dwell on this grand estate as my prisoner. The Beast sang his lament:

> The witch that cursed me years ago
> Had snarls of hair as white as snow.
> Her eyes were greedy and fiery red,
> A wicked hag—so Satan said.

She came in the night, straight from the East
And changed me, alas, from Prince to Beast.

The performance continued as Beauty discovered the Beast in the garden and horrified, cried out. The Beast, kind and generous, treated her well, and gradually won her love, despite his ugly appearance. Elvira Maria glanced at her sheet of lines, trying to keep up with Michail. Familiar with the story, he improvised his dialog and responded to comments from enthusiastic audience members. She paced Beauty back and forth on stage, hoping the puppet looked worried as the Beast lay dying in the garden, the scarlet flower wilted at his feet. Not sure if the next line was hers or his, she looked at Michail for a cue. He blew her a kiss.

On stage, Beauty knelt next to the Beast. *Oh faithful Beast,* she cried, *you shall not die. I love you. Please live to be my husband.* She kissed the Beast. The witch's curse was broken.

Elvira Maria heard Pavlo's cheers over the rest of the audience. Michail slid the Beast through the trees and exchanged him for the puppet of the Prince, dressed in a Bolshevik uniform. He and Beauty stood together center stage, holding the vibrant scarlet flower. They sang the final song:

Happy ever after comes
When hearts stay true and love has won.
Flowers grow in garden soil
With sun and rain and daily toil.
Take heed, oh Comrades, and blink your eyes
See through the dust, the tears, the lies.
Grief is short, but love is long
Flowers will bloom, if you hold strong.

20

BORIS PARTED THE VELVET DRAPES blocking the dawning light in the antechamber of Heddie's bedroom. "Quite the car," he said under his breath. "They've come in an armored Austin."

For the past two months, Heddie and Boris had expected an official visit from Red Army personnel, but never at seven in the morning. Heddie, dressing hurriedly, fastened her narrow skirt, and brushed the lint from the gray and blue brocade. She smoothed a hand down each leg to straighten the seams of her stockings.

"They're waiting in the alcove in the green salon," Boris said. "I've asked Elena to serve the house vodka and Murads. They're the only cigarettes we've got."

"What have you heard? Is Dudorov part of the Cheka or just a military man?"

"They say he's the General's deputy, but not part of the Bolsheviks' secret police, at least not yet. He's only recently switched over from the Whites' Volunteer Army."

"An opportunist changing sides." She looked in the oval mirror above her dresser and pinned up her hair. "I can't believe it." Her hands trembled as she buttoned her jacket.

Over the years, with each political upheaval in the city, men like these had come to the house. Paper-toting bureaucrats, shameless gangsters, decorated military men—they all demanded special favors and accommodations. Some extorted cash. Others feigning moral outrage, threatened to shut down her business and revoke her yellow-paper license. For as long as Heddie could remember, she'd been a pawn in their political dramas. She played her part as best she could, detesting the need, but knowing her livelihood and personal safety were at stake.

"There's another fellow with the Deputy," Boris said. "Ivan Dashkevich."

"What's his story?"

"Agitator. Used to print Bolshevik propaganda here in Odessa. Could be working for the Cheka, but I don't know."

She rouged her cheeks and traced her lips with a small brush. Boris held out her jewelry box. She sorted through it, found a rhinestone brooch, and fastened it to her suit jacket.

"What do you think?" She turned to Boris. "Too lavish?"

He adjusted the pin, stood back, and nodded.

"Such nonsense!" she said. "I hate playing games. I don't mind being frugal, but looking like a factory frau is not my forte."

She picked up a large silver hairpin lying on her dresser and twirled it between her fingers. "I'll signal you with this if I need you to rescue me." She tilted her head and jabbed the hairpin into the mass of curls on top of her head.

"I'll be in the wings," he said.

In the salon she kissed Vladimir Vladimirovich Dudorov on the cheek, carefully avoiding the thin red scar that wrapped around his right jaw. "Comrade, Deputy Dudorov, it's a pleasure to have you call."

"I assure you, the pleasure is all mine," Dudorov said. Short, fifty-two years old, balding, and sweating, he scanned the room, his eyes resting on a small porcelain figurine, two dancers balanced on a flowered pedestal. His petulant wife, who begged him to buy her Parisian trinkets, would love it. But today was not the day to slip it into his pocket. He was here on state business. He bowed stiffly and added, "I hope you are well."

"As well as can be expected during these extraordinary times. I hear our gracious city has rescued you from Petrograd. Congratulations. General Kotovsky knows a talented deputy when he sees one. Will you be stationed in Odessa?"

"Yes. I'm grateful. My wife and children have never wanted to live anywhere else."

"They certainly have good taste," Heddie said. She turned to her other visitor.

"I've brought Comrade Dashkevich with me," Dudorov said. "He's our new Housing Commissar. I thought you should know each other." He leaned toward her and whispered, as if sharing a military secret. "Residency permits are quite valuable these days. Remember this man, if you need one."

Heddie shook Ivan's hand. She opened a fresh packet

of Murads and offered both men a cigarette, then refilled their glasses. "My dear comrades, how can I be of service?"

Ivan wore a brand new Red Army uniform and freshly polished boots. "Comrade Naryshkina," he said, "my bureau is reviewing the occupancy status of each dwelling and updating the count. Housing in Odessa's at a premium these days. I'm sure you agree that the displaced masses who have struggled during the war deserve a roof over their heads." He handed her a large brown envelope and explained that it was a household report that required the number and names of those living in the house. She accepted the envelope and tucked it under her arm. "Since your girls are public women," he continued, "you must document their yellow ticket status, as well as your own. The second page—"

"One moment, Comrade," Dudorov interrupted. Didn't this upstart understand that *he* was in charge and would dictate the terms? "I need to clarify the Commissar's mission," he explained to Heddie. "You must understand that normally the bureau sends their officers to inspect and evaluate the occupancy of a city dwelling. But in your case, I've encouraged the Commissar to rely on your personal credibility and expertise. We wouldn't want to interrupt your routine."

No stranger to the brothel scene, Dudorov had met General Kotovsky months before the October Revolution in Moscow's red light district. There they drank for five days straight and ran through the girls and boys they fancied. It was a passionate escapade they would never forget. When Kotovsky joined the Bolsheviks' 39th Division, Dudorov remained with the Whites and grabbed a position as a Quartermaster General, an uninspiring post despite the many supplies he peddled for personal profit on the sly. As the Civil War swept through Russia Dudorov nervously watched the Reds claim territory and establish soviets in cities and provincial towns. By the summer of 1919 he knew his days were numbered. Loyal to no one but himself, he changed sides and joined the Reds. Hearing the news, Kotovsky immediately placed him in his camp and toasted their camaraderie. Now as Kotovsky's Deputy, Dudorov ran around Odessa intimidating bureaucrats, restructuring personnel, and poking his nose in the Cheka to see if he could improve their interrogation methods. He was a busy and dangerous man, and like his petulant wife, given to fits of rage and sudden cruelty whenever he felt threatened.

Heddie placed a cigarette between her lips and accepted a light from him. "I'll do my best to assist you with an accurate count," she said. "Commissar Dashkevich, I assume you understand the nature of my business. My clients expect confidentiality, and for that specific reason I have an excellent and very particular staff."

"Would you be willing to expand your staff?" Ivan asked.

"Comrade, my current employees are perfectly capable of attending to the needs of my clients and guests, especially those associated with the city's government and our brave military."

Deputy Dudorov put a firm hand on Ivan's arm. He looked at Heddie. "It may be helpful to increase your staff. I imagine you're quite busy these days with so many new officers arriving and needing a bit of entertainment." He picked up the packet of Murads and helped himself to another.

"What do you have in mind?" she asked.

"Commissar Dashkevich has a friend, a young woman, who needs a place to live and work." Dudorov handed the Murads to Ivan. "Tatiana Kovaleva will arrive tomorrow."

"Should I know anything else about Tatiana before she settles into my house?" Heddie asked.

"Only that she'll be useful to us both," Ivan said. He picked up his glass and offered a toast.

She adjusted her hairpin and twisted a curl around her index finger. Boris, a stack of letters in his hand, entered the salon. He placed a calling card on a side table.

"Comrades," she said, "I look forward to meeting this young lady and will be pleased to add her to my occupancy report." She walked to the table and picked up the card. Holding it to her bosom she shook her head regretfully. "I have a pressing engagement, I hope you'll excuse me."

"But Heddie," Dudorov said, "we expected some entertainment on our first visit."

"Boris," Heddie said, "please direct these gentlemen to the piano." As she took her farewell she smiled at Deputy Dudorov. "You will love Elena's beautiful voice. She sings like an angel."

Alone in the private dayroom adjoining the kitchen, Heddie placed the envelope in her desk drawer and locked it. She tucked the key in her bosom. Her lace camisole was damp. Those people! How had it come to this?

Elena's lilting voice echoed along the hallway as she sang a ballad. Heddie appreciated her support. All the other girls were sleeping, oblivious to the crisis.

A soprano, Elena had studied at the local conservatory

since she was a child, but her hopes of singing with the opera were ended by the pogrom. She was one of the many Jews left destitute, mourning, and sifting through the ashes of home. After years of struggle she knocked at Heddie's kitchen door and asked for employment and shelter. Heddie turned her away, knowing she was not suited for the sexual work her clients expected. But weeks later she returned with the libretto of the Italian opera, *Aida*. In minutes the house filled with Heddie's favorite music. That had been twelve years ago, and ever since, Elena's artistry was one of the things that had always convinced the latest regime that Heddie's house was no rough-and-tumble brothel like the ones on Glukhaya Street in the Moldavanka. These Bolsheviks, though. Who was she fooling? These men didn't care about music.

She drummed her fingers on the windowsill and recalled each word, each insulting innuendo, she'd been forced to swallow. She was annoyed, but also frightened that a stranger, especially a young commissar, could enter her house and behave in such a brash manner. And then, there was the girl—a spy coming to live under her very roof.

Boris entered the kitchen. "They seem to be enjoying Elena," he said. "The Deputy's joined her at the piano and is striking a few keys for amusement."

"I hope she has enough charm to prevent them from sniffing around and counting the rooms. No one goes upstairs without my permission. That's the rule, and I won't bend it, not for a bloody Cossack and not for a damned Bolshevik."

"She can handle these two."

They waited. Boris stirred the coals in the samovar. He poured Heddie a glass of tea. She read three chapters of a spicy French novel she'd recently found in the upstairs lounge. The laughter and music continued. Dudorov, shouting to Elena to pick up the pace, began to sing "La Marseillaise." Heddie tossed the book on her desk.

"Don't they have something better to do?" she asked.

"But Heddie," Boris mocked. "This is an *official* visit."

"I've got to get some air. I'd better take a walk before I do something I'll regret." She reached for her spring coat, white wool with sky blue trim.

"Take the alley if you're going to Deribasov Garden," Boris said. "They might have someone watching the house."

"Heavens, I hadn't thought of that." An anxious look crossed her face. "I won't be gone long."

She picked her way through the furrows in the dirt path and followed the alley behind Ekaterinskaya Street. Now late morning, housewives were checking the fluttering sheets on their clotheslines and shooing beggars and rag pickers from their kitchen doors. The flat, sour smell of boiling potatoes mingled with the musty odor of winter mold still clinging to damp limestone and rotting wood. Although a resident of the neighborhood for over forty years, she rarely walked along the alley, preferring instead the tree-lined front street, which led to the Stock Exchange, Opera House, and Odessa Club. But now they were closed, and like the vacant cafés and abandoned shops on nearby Deribasovskaya Street, had seen better days.

She entered the garden and paused at the lion statues, surprised to see Michail Lukashenko packing up his puppet theater.

"If I'd known you were here I'd have come earlier,"
she called out. She passed a group of excited children
and embraced him. "I'm thrilled to see you!" She pointed to the stage with both hands. "It's a jewel, absolutely
delightful."

"I'm honored, Heddie." He kissed her cheeks. "What
are you doing out here this morning?"

"Darling, don't ask." She waved a hand, as if sweeping
away an unpleasant thought. She noticed the red flower
he held. "What did you perform?"

"*The Scarlet Flower*. Sorry you missed it. People were
enthusiastic."

"I'm sure they were, Michail. You're a talented, energetic Beast."

"Careful now," he laughed, embarrassed. He beckoned
Elvira Maria to join them and introduced the women.
Elvira Maria Andrushko, he said. A performer, his partner. And Heddie Naryshkina. A dear friend. A patron of
the arts.

"It must be amusing," Heddie said, "to work with a
puppet theater."

"I'm enjoying it." Elvira Maria smiled shyly. She noticed Heddie's stylish coat, and felt shabby in the black
dress she'd worn for ages.

"Lovely," Heddie said. "I certainly hope I hear about
your next performance. I don't want to miss it."

"We'll be here next week," Michail said. He bowed,
and with a flourish, presented her with Beauty's scarlet
flower.

Her eyes lit up as she accepted the large blossom. She
turned to Elvira Maria. "He's a charming man, isn't he?"

Elvira Maria blushed. "Excuse me. I need to gather a few things before we leave."

Michail took Heddie's arm and steered her toward the garden's entrance. "She's the woman I told you about months ago. Her children are still missing. Every day she makes inquiries. It's difficult."

"She's prettier than I'd imagined, Michail. I'll have to swallow my jealousy." Heddie pressed the flower to her heart. "I'll be in touch if I have news. Locating missing people is really out of my range, but you never know these days. My clients are changing. It's not the old Odessa crowd anymore."

She waved goodbye. When she reached the street, a lorry driver parked at the corner started his engine. Black exhaust billowed across her path. Annoyed, she retreated to the lion statues and waited for the vehicle to move on. Then fanning the air, Heddie crossed the intersection to walk beneath the trees on Ekaterinskaya Street.

21

TRAILED BY A BOISTEROUS GROUP OF URCHINS, Elvira Maria and Michail headed back to the tenement along Gogolya Street. Vendors, their pushcarts loaded with garden pots and urns, wrought-iron fencing, and decorative sundials, jolted toward a nearby alley where cast-off items and black market goods were sold. They guided the heavy carts along the street and shouted at pedestrians. Elvira Maria stepped aside as the carts swayed precariously past her. Who could afford to buy this merchandise when food prices were soaring and rations smaller each time she stood in line? Behind her, Danya and Pavlo occasionally stopped to panhandle. A couple leaving the Labor News reading room gave them a coin. The boys shoved one other, then dashed across the street with the larger group, dodging into the traffic.

"Danya," Elvira Maria cried out, "watch for the lorries." But he was gone, running behind his brother. She shifted the weight of the bundle in her arms.

"Let me take it." Michail hoisted her sack over his theater panels. "I'm used to carrying everything."

She shook her head. "I want to help. It isn't heavy."

"Not this time. I have my reputation to maintain."

"What do you mean?"

He grinned. "If you think I'm charming I don't want to spoil your opinion of me." She laughed. He stopped and rested the panels on the walkway. "You did agree with Heddie, didn't you? That I was charming?"

She turned away.

"Come now, am I charming or not? You can answer me, can't you?" She refused to look at him and laughed again. "I'm glad to see you're happy," he said, "but you're avoiding my question."

"Yes, I am."

"Elvira Maria Andrushko, what can I do?" He feigned bewilderment. "You are a mystery with your dark moods and contagious laughter. Do you understand I'm in love with you? I think about you every day. God help me, I'm charming enough to do anything to please you."

"Michail, stop." A unit of soldiers walked past them and turned around with interest. "We must move on."

"So, you have no answer?" He settled the panels and sacks on his back and sighed with exaggerated disappointment. He offered Elvira Maria his arm. She took it and they continued down the street.

In the vestibule dust motes floated through a shaft of sunlight that danced in the cool air. Yagna, Tolya's wife, and her younger sister greeted Elvira Maria as she navigated her way through the piles of bedding and dirty clothes on the floor.

"You got a washtub we can use?" Yagna's sister asked.

Overworked and sallow, her back hunched, fingers red and blistered, the thirteen-year-old was worn out as an old woman.

Elvira Maria pointed to the shed. "Ask Michail to give it to you. He's in there now." She stepped over a scatter of rags and hurried up the stairs, avoiding an exchange with Yagna, an ill-tempered drinker. Her high-pitched voice, shrill with complaints, rang through the house each day. At night she and Tolya went to the taverns and begged along the seawall and Odessa Steps. When they returned, stumbling through the door, they sat on the stairs and argued for hours. Yagna would berate Tolya for his poor health or declare that their neighbors in their building were stingy. Sometimes she would cry. Those same neighbors, trying to sleep, shouted for silence, but were ignored or insulted. Danya and Pavlo drifted in and out of the vestibule and managed alone. Irritated with her sons, Yagna claimed the family's misery was Pavlo's fault. He'd stolen the sacred communion chalice from their village church and the priest had cast them out. Elvira Maria was thankful to be tucked away in the small space she had to herself, far from the newcomers.

The water from the pump splashed into the washtub. Nadia, shouting from her bedroom window, demanded to use it next. The little girls were with her, laughing and excited about pigeons flying over the shed. Elvira Maria thought of Ana. If she were here they'd have played together; set up house beneath Nadia's kitchen table, sipped make-believe tea from old saucers, and cradled their dolls to sleep. Now Michail greeted the girls and they called back, their voices singing into the wind. Since they'd seen the puppet show he'd gained their affection.

Elvira Maria sat at her desk and mused about their flirtation. But as she heard his footsteps on the stairs she felt nervous. She held her breath and prayed he would pass her door and continue on to the attic.

The stairs creaked as he climbed higher, heading to his room. He closed his door. Furniture scraped across the floor. She sat still and listened. All was silent. Perhaps he was smoking a cigarette at his workbench. Perhaps he was carving a new puppet for another show. Perhaps he was scheduling a new show, more shows, so they could be together. When she was busy and didn't see him for days, she missed his laughter, the way he gently interacted with street children, and how he embraced life with a certainty and strength she had left behind in Kos. But a romance? She looked at the children's postcard tucked in the niche by her door. What would Ana and Sasha think?

22

THE PUPPY IN TATIANA KOVALEVA'S ARMS was restless. She held him tightly while she pounded on Heddie Naryshkina's front door. The brass knocker was shaped like a mermaid. Above her, flowers were carved into the lintel. Heddie had money. Ivan said she lived like a queen, that her table was always full of food and drink. He promised Tatiana that she and her dog would be fat within a month, and she'd live in a palace with a balcony of her own. Her job would be simple: listen to house gossip and tell him what clients said about the new regime.

Despite the enticement of food and comfort, Tatiana had avoided Ivan for weeks. She knew Heddie and her girls were whores who thought they were high class and could rule the roost because they were rich. She didn't mind the fact that the girls turned tricks for a living—she did that herself—but working for Ivan was a different matter. Her reputation on the street would suffer once the word got out she was a snitch. Boys who were tough and demanded the sexual favors that kept her safe would beat her up. They might even wring her neck. But Ivan, who refused to understand her situation, had insisted she live at Heddie's, and if she did not, he would take away her dog, the only thing she truly loved. She was angry and indignant. He'd have to buy her another new dress and a fancy necklace with rubies if he wanted her to cooperate. She pounded again on the door.

"Yes, yes," Elena called, running down the stairs. She ushered Tatiana inside and gasped at the little dog. "Look at his sweet pink nose." She held out her arms. "Oh please, can I hold him, just for a moment?"

The puppy thrashed in Tatiana's grip and suddenly sneezed. "I better hang onto him," she said. "He won't like you."

"Why not?" Elena's welcoming smile faded.

"He's afraid of strangers—and he's skittish. He was left alone in an abandoned house on Pushkinskaya Street, without food or water. Commissar Ivan found him and gave him to me. Commissar Dashkevich's my friend."

"I promise I'll be gentle."

"No," Tatiana said, petting the dog. She looked furtively at the golden glass chandelier, the forest-green velvet drapes, the damask wallpaper, and the finely carved furniture in the front vestibule where they stood. She pointed to a paperweight shining on a nearby table. "I've seen one of those before. Does it have snow?"

Elena turned the glass globe upside down. A flurry of confetti showered the tiny winter skaters. "Oh, how beautiful!" She held the paperweight toward the morning light streaming in through the lace curtains.

"Elena," Boris called from the back hallway, "bring
her to the kitchen, now." He frowned as he entered the
vestibule and bolted the front door. "You should know
better than to knock at this entrance," he said to Tatiana.
"In the future go around to the alley and use the back
door. What's this animal you've got with you?"

"His name's Dima." Tatiana held the puppy firmly
under her arm and asserted herself. "I got permission from
Commissar Ivan to live here with my dog. Ask him and see
for yourself."

"My dear, I plan to," he said. "Hurry along and remember your place. You're not on the street anymore."

Boris herded both girls to the kitchen. He studied
Tatiana as she walked in front of him. Thin to a fault, yet
graceful. Stringy blonde hair down her back. Not badly
dressed. She wore a short woolen cape buttoned over a
blouse and a skirt that flared with alternating red and
yellow panels. Both garments appeared to be as new as her
shiny leather boots.

"When did you last bathe?" he asked.

"That's my business," Tatiana said. She stopped and
turned around to glare at him.

"Well, I'm making it mine." Boris snapped his suspenders and waited for an answer.

"You'd better tell him," Elena whispered.

"Don't get involved, Elena," Boris said. "If she wants
to stay on the back porch, that's fine. As for the dog, he's
going out there now."

"I'm keeping Dima with me," Tatiana said.

"That's right, and you're sleeping in the kitchen beneath
a counter *next* to the back door. Elena, bring down some

bedding and get her settled." He turned to Tatiana and pointed to the dog. "If you want your sweet little Dima to stay safe, you'd better do as I say and change your smart attitude. Do you understand?"

Now mid-afternoon, Boris stood inside the curtained threshold of Heddie's bedroom. She looked up from her playing cards. "Dudorov has sent a messenger around," he said. "Seems he wants the entire house for a party this evening. Thirty officers around eleven o'clock. All the Deputy's personal friends."

"What did I tell you? He's a manipulator. A little man with a big promotion." Unable to finish her game of patience, she gathered up the cards. "Has he sent any money?"

"Twice the usual amount. Must want special treatment."

"He probably needs to impress his comrades," she said. "It's certainly not generosity. He doesn't have the class or the rubles." She checked the edges of the cards with her index finger and returned the deck to its box. "How annoying. I thought he'd disappear for a few days— distribute proclamations to the masses." She sighed. "Take what you need to buy the drinks and put the rest in the safe. I'll tell the girls to get ready for a long night."

"Commissar Dashkevich's ward has arrived," Boris broke the news. "I put her in the kitchen, with her dog."

"A dog? We now have a dog?"

"Yes. I expect the girls will be excited. Elena is already infatuated. It's small, it looks like a puppy."

Heddie walked to the window and parted the velvet drapes a crack. Two men, wearing black leather jackets, the attire of the Cheka, stood in the doorway of the house across the street.

"My, my," she said, "how amazing. A puppy in Odessa. I haven't seen one in years."

23

Tolya hustled Pavlo out the door of the tenement and saluted Ivan Dashkevich, perched in the driver's seat of the idling lorry.

"Climb in and let's get moving, Comrade," Ivan said. "It's late. Don't sit on the crates, they're empty and fragile." He shifted into first gear and held the brake as Tolya and Pavlo jumped on the running board and crawled under the back canvas flap. Putting his foot on the accelerator, the mud-streaked vehicle jerked forward and barreled down the dark road.

Pavlo scratched a match on the floor and held up the shaking flame. The sulfurous smell engulfed the cold stale air inside the covered lorry. "What's this?" He pointed to the jumble of wooden crates that surrounded them and looked at his father crouched on the floor, both hands wrapped around a metal side bar. "Where are we going?"

"Never mind," Tolya shouted above the roaring engine. "Put out that light." Several crates slid across the floor and hit the tailgate.

"I just want—"

"Shut your ugly trap and keep it that way. The Commissar needs our help. He's got influence. Follow orders and be respectful. No questions, understand? I don't want no trouble from you."

Ivan blasted the horn and swerved to avoid soldiers and refugees on the street as he drove across the city to the Moldavanka. He overtook a droshky, strapped with household goods and people on the move, bumping along behind a weary nag. Recklessly continuing on full throttle, he passed the dimly lit hospital, rumbled through an intersection, and slowed down only to turn into an alley riddled with potholes.

"This gets worse every time," he muttered. He cursed into the windshield and downshifted, bouncing violently until he reached the back door of a shophouse. He turned off the motor. The aging vehicle shuddered to a halt.

"Stack the crates out here," he said to Tolya and Pavlo, pointing to a dilapidated lean-to jutting off the side of the building. He climbed the porch steps and unlocked the back door and entered a long hallway that led to a closed storefront comprising two rooms. As he parted a set of striped portieres that hung in the entrance of the main space his eyes adjusted to the light of a paraffin lamp on a side counter. Ribbons, plates, liquor bottles, combs, and a broadcloth helmet cluttered a long table in the middle of the cold, dingy room. Fifty open crates loaded with munitions lined the floor, their lids slanted to the side waiting to be fastened.

"Sonia," Ivan called into the adjoining space, "bring some straw over here and we'll close these." He knelt beside a crate and counted the guns. An adolescent girl, wearing an oversized day dress, emerged from a dark corner. She dragged a large gunnysack.

"Did you get the food I sent last night?" he asked, looking at her tired face. He reached in his pocket and handed her a tin of biscuits.

She examined the turquoise letters on the tin and set it on the table. Then picking up a comb, she parted her auburn hair, separating the curls that fell to her shoulders.

"We need to finish this now," he said. Sullenly, she put down the comb. They rearranged the guns and layered them with straw.

"Is Tatiana coming tonight?" she asked.

"I don't know. She's busy now. It's not a good time."

"All of us miss her. Dima too. I wish you could—"

"Not now," he said. He put the lids in place and nailed the crates shut. When he finished he put his arm around her waist, knowing he'd been too abrupt. It was his nerves—about the shipment. "Is everyone sleeping?" he asked.

"Yes, they drank too much last night."

"Go rest for a while." He kissed her cheek and gestured for her to join the others in the side room. "My men need to take these out. I don't want them to see how pretty you are."

She picked up the biscuits. As she crossed before the lamp her long shadow lingered on the opposite wall before it disappeared.

Ivan exhaled into the damp air. He checked his watch and went to the alley to get Tolya and Pavlo. Tolya came as far as the portieres. He stopped, a dirty hand to his mouth. Seized by a coughing fit, he doubled over, his body shuddering with convulsions. He spit blood into his sleeve and gasped for air.

"Go outside and stay there," Ivan told him. "Pavlo — you get to work."

Pavlo, struggling with the heavy crates, dropped the end of a large box. Ivan stood over him, shaking his head in disgust. He grabbed the other end and together they carried the munitions to the lorry. Determined to finish the job with just Pavlo, he ignored Tolya's pleas to help. He trotted back and forth, and pushed and stacked the crates. His arms ached, his fingers were sore. Next time he would remember to bring gloves. He brushed the straw from his greatcoat. "Get in the damn lorry," he said to Pavlo and Tolya. "We've leaving."

He paused on the steps. The headlights of a car in the nearby lane flickered along the fence, exposing the dozens of tire tracks that crisscrossed the yard. He looked up and down the alley. The light disappeared as the driver turned onto the main street. Only a faint glow coming from the house remained. Brambles from the vines choking the porch had blown onto the lorry's windshield. He picked them off, one by one, and threw them in the yard.

He climbed into the cab and sat for a moment. Guns were still in demand. Dealers flush with cash came to the shophouse to buy. But his days as a printer were over, his once blackened fingers wiped clean by new obligations. Deputy Dudorov kept him busy with ambitious schemes he claimed would enhance his standing with General Kotovsky. Ivan's appointment as a housing commissar depended on pleasing the Deputy. One moment he was Dudorov's gunrunner and spy; the next his driver and drinking pal. "Expand your vision of the revolution," Dudorov had told him. "I'm bored with your gloomy, self-righteous behavior. Develop a sense of humor. Enjoy the opportunities that come our way." Ivan thought about it. He could expand his vision—the Party was already doing so by empowering the Cheka to rout out political enemies. But taking things lightly had never been his way. An hour late with Dudorov's shipment, and expected to join him for another party, this time at Heddie's, Ivan started the motor. The lorry pitched to and fro as he drove along the alley and passed the loading docks of deserted shops. Reaching Preobrazhenskaya Street, he stepped on the gas and headed to the dockyards.

Startled awake, Elvira Maria pulled her blanket over her shoulders and turned toward the rattling window to look at the cloth scraps she'd stuffed in the frame to diminish the draft. They shifted as the wind shook the glass and dropped to her desk. The calm and starlight of hours past had been replaced by storm clouds chasing each other across the dark sky. The noise from the street grew louder as the gale sent scattered debris hurtling into the late night.

    Unwilling to leave her warm bed and tend to the window, she closed her eyes and returned to the fitful images that had circled through her dreams just moments before. They folded in upon each other twisting her along a wooded path that ended at the stream below the farmhouse in Kos. She and her neighbors bent over the cold water, mud swirling as they rinsed the stringy flax they'd buried in the banks. Was that her mother splitting the stalks with her nimble fingers? Wearing the apron she'd embroidered in red and blue threads? A treasure she'd sewn for the harvest feast, and here she was working in her finest. Overjoyed, Elvira Maria reached to embrace her, to feel her warmth and love. But no, the woman looked up and it was Yagna—Yagna smiling scornfully and pointing at her. Elvira Maria cringed. Instantly, she was running up the slippery bank and through a sunlit meadow, her heart pounding as the thick amber grass opened before her and Ana and Sasha rushed to her side. They tried to keep pace with her strides and catch her flying skirts. She shouted their names into the vast white sky as the wind swept them forward, and she and the children ran with abandon into the burning sun.

She opened her eyes. Wrapping herself in the blanket, she stumbled to the window, streaked with rain. Thoughts of the children, of her mother and neighbors remained with her. Should she return to the village or stay in Odessa? Had Kos been destroyed as everyone said, or was it still there, its golden fields fallow, its dusty roads busy with horses and carts? The cold rain seeped through the frame and pooled water at her feet, but she stayed at the window and stared down at the long, deserted street leading to the port. Overhead, she heard Michail cross the floor in his attic. She quietly mounted the stairs and found him standing in his doorway, waiting. She walked into his arms and felt them fold around her, their shadows cast on the wall by the fire burning in the grate.

In the years to come, when they lay side by side weak with hunger, famine gripping the city, she would remember this night. How he'd taken her to his bed, where their bodies, lit with passion, found a boundless joy over and over again. How the sunrise had colored the drab attic walls an iridescent rose, and they stayed in each other's arms all morning long, their whispers soft, their breath alive.

24

DEPUTY DUDOROV DROPPED HIS PLATE of caviar on a table in Heddie's green salon and staggered to the piano. He leaned over Elena, whispered vulgarities in her ear, and kissed her on the bosom. She brushed him aside and struggled to continue playing the marches he wanted to hear. He held his empty glass aloft and demanded somebody fill it. Officers, entranced by a circle of dancing girls, sang loudly, ignoring him. They whistled as the girls waved silky scarves above their heads and a colorful rainbow arched toward the gleaming chandelier. Dudorov shouted over the uproar, insulted that no one was by his side. It was his party, he'd paid a fortune for the drinks, and the service was lousy. He demanded vodka all around until he said otherwise. "Hell," he grumbled, shaking his glass, "do I have to bring my personal flask to this whorehouse?"

Heddie, wearing a black velvet gown and amber jewelry, pushed her way through the noisy crowd. She took a bottle from the sideboard and hurried to Dudorov. "I hate to see an empty glass," she said. She poured him a drink and stepped back to avoid his advances. "It's a marvelous party Deputy Dudorov. Just what your comrades need to celebrate and lift their spirits. We're all grateful for your generosity."

"Here, here, don't placate me," he said. "I know you're a shrewd businesswoman. You escaped the last pogrom just to pick my pocket—isn't that right?" He threw back his vodka. Coughing as the sharp liquid caught in his throat, he brought his hand to the scar now throbbing along his jaw line. "Damn Turks. Vicious fighters, every one of them."

She raised a questioning eyebrow.

"A duel, my dear Heddie," he said, "Happened in Stamboul years ago. I'm proud to say that I won."

"Thank God."

"God had nothing to do with it." Swaying and flushed, he turned and headed toward an officer waving a bottle of whiskey.

The house was packed with more guests than she'd expected. Already three in the morning, the rooms upstairs were full, leaving the remaining men adrift and drinking heavily. She hoped they would soon tire of the party and take to the streets and port where they could carouse until dawn.

The officers at the piano sang another chorus of a wartime ballad, their bloodshot eyes watering with nostalgia. Heddie, exasperated by their singing, asked Elena to play a farewell song that would move them out the door. "Merci, ma petite chanteuse," she said, kissing Elena's cheek. "You've played your heart out this evening and sung your best." She was peering into the mirror behind the piano, removing the lipstick caked in the corners of her mouth, when Boris approached her.

"Heddie," he whispered. "I think you'd better come to the kitchen."

"Oh dear, have we run out of liquor?"

"Come with me."

A rhythmic jingle of bells floated through the back hallway. He opened the kitchen door, pulled her inside, and shut it, displacing a cluster of drunken officers standing in their way. In the candlelight, clouded with hot breath and cigarette smoke, a flash of sequins twirled in the center of the room. Two boys danced arm in arm. Dressed in red pantaloons and matching embroidered jackets, the ten-year-olds snapped their fingers as they shook the bells and coins sewn to their Turkish costumes. A dozen officers, Dudorov among them, clapped and yelled obscene encouragements as the boys swung their hips seductively and pointed their dirty feet.

"No more trips to Stamboul," Dudorov said. "We've got dhimmi boys right here. My little surprise—a present for you all." Excited and disregarding the strands of greasy hair falling in his eyes, he snatched a hat from one of the boys. He laughed as he held it out to the men. "Put your rubles in here, Comrades. Remember, they have to eat."

"What else do they do?" a young officer asked.

"Find out for yourself!"

The men scuffled to fill the hat, manhandling the boys who stood close together and eyed them with caution.

Ivan Dashkevich, standing in the corner, remained aloof, but watchful. Dudorov was indulging himself, taking advantage of his position to control everyone in the room. Ivan felt the watch in his pocket ticking the hours away. He was wasting his time. Tatiana, wearing a gold Turkish scarf and a new red dress with puffy sleeves, stood next to him. He handed her a large tambourine and leaned against the wall, his arms folded across his chest. She raised it above her head and shook it wildly. As everyone turned toward the sound she pushed two small girls forward. Sweeping around the circle of bawdy men the fair-haired girls, layered in pink chiffon, pranced like fanciful birds and swayed their skinny arms from side to side.

Dudorov, sloshing vodka on the floor as he filled the empty glasses of the men, proposed a toast. "To young blood, Comrades. Fresh from the countryside up north. They've never been touched."

Lewd remarks and more laughter rippled around the steamy room.

Heddie stepped forward. "Deputy Dudorov, your party is over." Her unexpected voice cut through the raucous din. She gestured for the girls to stop. The room was quiet. She fixed Dudorov with a look of icy hostility. "Get these children out of my house at once."

"What's this, a meddlesome whore?" he sneered. "How dare you tell me what to do?" He raised his hand and struck her across the face. She fell against an officer and collapsed on the floor.

Shrieks from the children, curses and shouts from the men, broke out. Boris rushed to Heddie's side and helped her stand. Blood streamed from her nose and mouth. He reached for his handkerchief. Her dress and now his white shirt were streaked with blood.

"Comrades, comrades!" Ivan raised his voice and swung open the back door. "Everybody outside. That's an order. Come on, it's time to go."

The men, leaning on each other for support, shuffled outside. Slurred complaints followed by laughter and singing drifted along the alley as they tromped off into the dark. Ivan listened to their rabble. They'd find a portside brothel soon enough. Irritated with the evening and with Dudorov's demands, he threw his cigarette butt after the men and jerked open the door of the lorry. He ordered Tatiana and the children to jump in. They all had to abandon Heddie's before the Red Army guards patrolling the district arrived. And Tatiana, his well-planned informant, the girl he'd bribed with a puppy and gifts he'd bought with his own rubles, now would have to move back to the shophouse. Boris would surely throw her out of Heddie's house. Dudorov, the self-serving drunk, had made a mess of everything. One foot on the running board, Ivan hollered at the man to get moving. But Dudorov was threatening Heddie and Boris.

"You'll be hearing from me!" he said. Then, lurching through the doorway, he tripped down the back steps and toppled into the muddy yard.

25

TWO DAYS LATER, SUNLIGHT STREAMED through the attic window. It was an encouraging sign. Michail was scheduled to perform at noon in Deribasov Garden, and he hoped a crowd would be there to enjoy the warmer weather and his new production, Ilyá Múromets. He bound together two handfuls of dark brown feathers and attached them to the breast of the large puppet, Solovei, a nightingale with fierce eyes and a crooked orange beak. Slipping the puppet over the wooden stand on his workbench, he stepped back to view it from a distance. He circled it. He ruffled its feathers. Elvira Maria stopped sewing to watch him. She could feel his excitement. He'd carved and stitched for days, crafting the new puppet with materials he'd stripped from ones he no longer used. Pavlo, holding a tree branch at the other end of the attic, waited.

"It's ready," Michail said. He picked it up, spread its enormous wings, and flew it across the attic. It glided smoothly. He pumped his fingers inside the mitt as he tested the strength of his stitches and circled the room again, twisting its beak and talons. He perched it in the straw nest tucked in the branch, then squawked loudly. They all burst out laughing.

He ran to his workbench and turned around to look at it. "Pavlo, hold the branch straight and push those leaves aside," he said. "They'd look better above the nest, away from his head."

Elvira Maria went back to stringing a tiny crossbow with silver thread. Smiling to herself, she remembered Michail's gentle touch of the night before. A surge of warmth rushed through her. She tied a delicate knot at each end of the bow.

"I'll fasten the tree to the stage," Michail said, "but right now I need to be sure Solovei won't be hidden. We can't fix these details once we're in the garden and people arrive."

"They always come backstage," Pavlo said. "They shouldn't do that."

"They're curious. It's all right. Once the show starts they go out front to watch. You have to be generous in this business or you can't survive."

Pavlo put down the branch and brought the puppet and nest to the workbench. He picked at the straw. "My pa says you're foolish to run around with a puppet show." He placed a twig between his teeth and waited for a response.

"Is that what he says? Maybe so, but I'm in better shape than he is these days."

"Yeah," Pavlo said. "You don't moan and holler all the time."

"Your father's not well, Pavlo," Elvira Maria said. "That's why he gets upset." She fastened the arrow to the crossbow and held it out to Michail.

"He'd get better if he went to the hospital instead of helping Commissar Dashkevich," Pavlo said. He snapped the twig in two and cast it on the floor.

Michail retrieved it, threw it in the stove. "What sort of help does he give him?"

"Loading boxes at a shophouse in the Moldavanka for some officer, an important deputy."

"Who's that?"

"I dunno, but he orders everybody around. You should see him. He's got a scar on his face from here to here." He traced a broken fingernail around his jaw. "Somebody cut him real bad."

"Did you meet this fellow?" Michail asked. He took the crossbow from Elvira Maria and attached it to the padded shoulder of another puppet.

"Nah, but I seen him at the dockyards when he counted the crates we packed in the lorry," Pavlo said, proud to know something that Michail did not.

"Put the nest in that sack Pavlo and bring it along with the other props," Michail said.

He placed Elvira Maria's shawl on her shoulders, leaving his hands there until she turned around. As he met her gaze he almost kissed her, but thought better of it with Pavlo nearby. The boy was crafty, and his remarks made Michail want to know more about this deputy and his connections to Ivan and his comrades. The city was full of intrigue. People claimed that gangs and conspiracies were on the rise. With destitute refugees flooding the streets, everyone guarded their food, their backs, and their rubles. Would the Bolsheviks bring a better day? How many more nights would he hear gun shots in the streets, or see a child peddling clips of ammunition they'd gotten from God knows where? His questions and worries were endless. He lifted a sack of puppets and headed off to the one thing he was certain he knew.

Michail hovered the puppet, Solovei, before the scenery of a devastated meadow and faithfully recited lines from the popular story. The small group assembled before the stage admonished the nightingale with shouts and boos as Michail described his evil deeds.

The nightingale screamed. Not an ordinary scream, Comrades, but a maniacal scream that shattered the clear blue sky. All the grasses in the meadows wilted. The purple wildflowers (my favorites, and yours) lost their petals. The deep, dark woods bent down to the earth and trembled. All the people from near and far lay dead. Comrades, it was worse than any war, much, much worse. Alas, nothing, nothing at all, was spared by Solovei, the ruthless and fiendish bird.

Solovei, now perched in the nest, shook his talons at the beloved Ilyá Múromets, the valorous knight destined to save the world. Ilyá drew his crossbow and released a poisonous, lethal dart into the bird's eye. The audience cheered. Backstage, Elvira Maria covered her ears a moment before Pavlo blew the pishchik whistle. He blasted and sputtered its shrill volume while he beat a metal pan, until the bird, writhing in agony, fell over. Michail laughed at his enthusiastic sound effects. He sobered his voice and sang the final stanza of Ilyá's triumphant marching song:

> *Evil is vanquished both here and abroad,*
> *I am the hero who deserves your applause.*

Never a worry
No care should you fear
Ilyá Múromets is finally here.

When the curtain closed Danya rushed to his brother. He grabbed his arm and reached for the whistle, begging to have it.

"Slow down," Pavlo said. He shook Danya loose and waved the pishchik above his head. "Ask Michail, it belongs to him."

Michail, returning with the money he collected, counted a few coins into his purse. "That's fine," he said. "Give it to him." He knelt beside Danya and demonstrated. "Blow through this end, just a little, not too hard. The performance is over."

"If people hear it," Pavlo said, "they'll think another show is starting. Right Michail?" He watched his brother strain to emit the chirping sound from the pishchik.

"Yes," Michail said. "Everybody knows the signal."

"Even me, Comrade," Volodya said. He walked toward them, waving a hand.

Michail looked up. "Oh ho!" He pounded Volodya on the back. "All good things come on a sunny day. How are you, old friend?"

"I could be better. Market's barely open. Ration slips nowadays." Volodya turned an empty pocket inside out. "No food, no customers, no rubles."

"I didn't earn much today, either."

The men shook their heads and commiserated with each other. "Here," Michail said, "have a smoke. It's mahorka. Pretty rough, but it does the job." He lit a match. "How's the family? What's your boy, Yuryi, doing?"

"Ah, that's a fine story," Volodya said. "He's gone. Ran off with a girl, an anarchist. Got hold of a pistol, a Webley no less, and went up north with some other foolhardy souls."

"I'm sorry to hear that."

"He wouldn't stay home, not even when the missus cried and carried-on. She's heartsick, won't leave the house. Yuryi was her last, her darling."

"The war's been hard on everyone. Makes people desperate."

"He was hellbent. More so, after he heard about that riot in Kyiv."

The men smoked in silence, remembering the reports of several weeks past:

Hundreds of starving people, shouting for bread, had marched on a distribution station. They battered down the bolted door and swarmed the meager shelves. Red Army soldiers, firing into the crowd, killed seven people and wounded countless more. Three of the corpses were never claimed. Frozen in pools of blood they'd lain on the street for days. A gusty wind blowing over the bodies loosened the long scarf of one, and tore off the buttons on the skirt of another. The clothes rippled and snapped until they were shredded to pieces, and patches of white flesh glinted in the daylight. Despite efforts by the soviet to censor the news in the press, the story spread quickly by word of mouth, angering people in Kyiv and beyond.

Volodya pulled Michail to the side. He tilted his head toward Pavlo. "Is that boy helping you?"

"He's trying. He needs something to do besides wander the streets."

"He's been a pest at the market, stealing bric-a-brac and peddling it on the side. Watch your wares, he's a professional."

"Thanks for the warning," Michail said. "I'll keep an eye on him."

"I tell you now, he'll come to a bad end."

They watched Pavlo gather up the props and hand Solovei to Elvira Maria, who wrapped the puppet in muslin. Together they dismantled the stage and folded-up the panels.

"See you next time," Volodya said. "Got to get home before the missus starts to worry." His lean body, once heavy and robust, was so stooped the ties of his leather apron touched the ground.

Michail reached to pick up the theater panels, but stopped as Elvira Maria pointed to a small figure running across the garden in their direction. The sun in his eyes, he squinted and saw a boy carrying a large red flower. Breathless, the boy pushed through the group and dropped it at Michail's feet. Cutting between the lion statues, he raced on to the intersection, where he disappeared behind a droshky loaded with wood.

"Should I get him?" Pavlo asked, ready to toss the banners on the ground and run. "I'll catch him, if you want."

"No. No, don't bother." Michail tied the rolls of scenery together. "Take these home. That's more important right now. I'll follow with the rest shortly."

He bundled the scenery onto Pavlo's back and watched him head across the city garden. Cautious of Cheka agents staked out nearby, he briskly ran his fingers across the flower, searching for a message. There was none. He tucked it inside the sack of props. He scanned the intersection, hoping to see a trace of the boy, but he was gone.

"Come here, Danya," he said. He handed him a coil of rope. "You can carry this back to the shed, but stay with Elvira Maria. Don't cause trouble by running ahead." He pointed to the traffic. "You see that lorry over there? And those army trucks coming down the boulevard?" Danya eyed them and shuffled his feet. "The drivers can't stop if you dart in the street. Remember that, if you want to work for me."

Elvira Maria touched the petals of the flower and closed the sack. She nodded to Michail.

Boris directed Michail to Heddie's kitchen. He looked up and down the alley, then locked the door.

Michail glanced at the silver trays of dirty glasses and plates on the counter and followed Boris. As he entered the green salon, now shuttered and draped in late afternoon, he stopped and bent down to remove a small object from beneath his boot. It was an onyx cufflink. He set it on a side table cluttered with bottles.

"Please disregard the mess," Heddie said. Her voice came from the opposite side of the room where she lay on a divan, several pillows supporting her head. Dressed in a gray walking suit, and in her stocking feet, she held out her hand and asked him to sit beside her. As she turned toward the dabbled light filtering into the room from the vestibule transom he saw her bruised face and swollen eyes.

"Should I get a doctor, Heddie?"

"I've a bit of medicine here. I'll be fine in a week or

so, unless they drag me to Siberia." She smiled and winced, the pain spreading through her cheek.

"What's happened?" he asked. She hesitated. "Tell me," he urged. "You must have earned that black eye somehow."

"Deputy Dudorov was here with Ivan Dashkevich, who I think you know. It was a private party for selected officers, a special evening that turned ugly yesterday morning, right before dawn." She slowly shook her head. "My mother warned me years ago that if the worst happens, it happens at that hour. When guests are liquored to the brim, desperate for attention, and won't go home to their foolish wives. Why didn't I remember that and call an end to things earlier?"

She told him what had happened. Dudorov bringing the dhimmi boys to the kitchen and offering to hand them over to the officers. The little girls too, picked up from the streets. Her ordering everyone to leave—and Dudorov's blow that had knocked her off her feet.

"My God!" Michail said. "You took a tremendous risk by crossing him."

"I couldn't control myself. For years I've seen his kind oiling their way through society, thinking I'll support their perversions."

The clinking of glassware came from the stairway as Boris carried trays to the kitchen.

"They've got an operation set up somewhere," she said, "and Tatiana's part of it."

"Tatiana?" He was taken by surprise, hadn't seen her since the day at the market when she'd been so upset about the missing girls.

"Dashkevich had her living here, with her little dog. I expect she knows quite a lot. Elena tells me she's mentioned your name."

"I helped her last winter, but it wasn't much."

"You're too kind, Michail. She's cunning and needy. In my opinion, that's a dangerous combination."

Traffic lumbered past the house. A unit of soldiers, patrolling the nearby intersection at Deribasov Garden, shouted cadence. Heddie listened, a worried look in her eyes.

"You'll close the house?" he asked.

"I'm afraid so." Her voice was bitter with resignation. "It's taken me all day to send discreet letters to my regulars thanking them for their business. I've sent everyone off, except Elena and Boris. If Dudorov wants to arrest me or shoot me, he certainly can. But he may choose to keep things quiet. I suspect he's connected to a lot of nasty business if he's turning up with dhimmi boys and street urchins. Get a hold of Dashkevich, he'll tell you more." She looked around the room at the cigarette ashes smeared across a marble table, the stained carpet, the smoky mirrors, and the cut glass chandelier, now missing a row of crystal beads. "I've gotten old, Michail. I've had enough. I don't have the energy to fight this regime and I don't have the stomach to go along with it." She ran her hand over a tear in the velvet upholstery of the divan. They were silent. Finally, she looked at him and smiled. "I wish I could go on holiday."

"On holiday?" he laughed. "Where the hell to, Martinique?"

"Wouldn't that be nice?" She retucked the combs in her hair. "I should have left Odessa years ago, when I was young and still turned a head or two."

He could see that beautiful young woman for a moment in the way she smiled, the way her face, despite the bruises, softened. Then quickly that girl disappeared, and her eyes widened with fear. "I haven't told you why I sent for you," she said, clutching his arm. "I've heard something. Nothing definite, mind you. This terrible war has led us all down twisted lanes. But I do have news. It's about those children from Kos."

26

THE CATHEDRAL BELLS TOLLED SIX O'CLOCK, eventide. Elvira Maria went to the landing window a second time, hoping to see Michail among the men in the street whose voices carried up to her room. He was not there. Her empty stomach tightened, leaving her feeling more anxious than she'd been before. Already the sun was casting a band of purple and orange in the west. She thought about Heddie Naryshkina. Why had she summoned Michail in such a mysterious manner? What was the glamorous woman up to? Why was Michail so quick to respond?

She returned to her room and examined the black woolen bodice lying on her bed. Except for a few narrow pleats, it was plain, similar to the one she was wearing. At least the pleats had impressed Monsieur Oury and helped her gain employment, but now the well-worn garment needed a new set of sleeves and another collar. She sat on her bed and picked apart the seams. But the light was poor; it was impossible to sew.

Twilight lasted longer in Kos, filtered through the birch trees setting everything aglow. The children had played with their shadows or chased each other around the yard, avoiding their bedtime. She scolded them, but it had been useless. Only Lev could make them obey. Thinking of it now, she was glad they'd had so much fun.

These playful evenings had disappeared when the soldiers charged down the road in a rage and swarmed the house taking Lev. The drawing she'd made of the guardian spirit of her home and hearth sat on its shelf, dead as the paper itself. Her offerings of porridge, salt, and bread had been food for the rats. How could she have believed a domovoj would protect her household? The Bolsheviks knew better; placating spirits was superstitious nonsense.

Restless, she folded the bodice and left it on the bed and took Michail's keys from her pocket. In the attic, cold without a fire, she inhaled the smell of paint, oil, cinders, and cigarette smoke. His workbench, readied for a new project was cleared of everything other than his delicate brushes in jars and a ceramic pot of glue. He was neat and organized and loved his work. If she'd met him in Kos, she would have run away in fear, mistaken him for a Ruska Roma come to rob the village.

She touched each of the puppets hanging beneath the eaves, the last rays of sun spreading across the row of fairytale figures, their varnished faces shining and animating the wall. She stopped before Father Frost and put her hand inside his furry robes, imagined the warmth of Michail's right palm, where it had rested and turned the puppet to and fro, creating the magic that spectators loved. Comforted by her gesture she proceeded down the row slipping her right hand, and then her left, inside several others. She was proud to work with him and marveled

at his ability to bring the puppets to life, to sing their
songs and make people laugh during such an uncertain
and difficult time.

She reached Solovei, the nightingale, roosting above
the puppets. Crafted from feathers, its yellow glass eyes
glowing on either side of its crooked orange beak—it was
so impressive. She took it down and placed her hand deep
inside its wings. As she moved her fingers a large fan of
feathers arched toward her shoulder. She felt the grooves
in each wing caressing her fingers, grooves where Michail's
hand had held the puppet, his strong fingers extending
and stretching as the nightingale flew over a meadow or
perched in a twisted branch. The bird was enchanting, but
also frightening as it came alive. She withdrew her hand
and returned it to its peg. Stepping back, she heard something drop and jingle on the floor before her feet.

She lifted her skirt to the side and picked up a small,
blue satin purse. A violet ribbon, laced through the
top, was tied in a bow. "Did this come from you?" she
asked the nightingale. "Is this your special bell to ring
for attention?" She ran a finger along the bird's smooth
breast. Turning back to the purse she untied it and shook
out the contents. A gold wedding ring and a tiny silver
locket in the shape of a heart slipped into her palm. She
stared at the items. Then quickly returned them and tied
the ribbon. She took down the nightingale and slid the
purse inside its wing. Struggling to settle the puppet back
on its perch, she hoisted it over several others, causing
them to tumble to the floor. Close to panic, she picked up
each one and hung them in place. She hurried to Michail's
workbench and sat down to calm herself.

She lit a candle. The faint light cast jagged shadows on the rafters. The nightingale was slanted precariously on its perch. She got up from her stool, stood before it, and straightened it. She felt the tip of its wing, and was relieved that the purse was still there.

Shivering, she hurried to the grate to build a fire and knelt to select scraps of wood. She thought about the ring and locket. She knew nothing at all about his private life. Nothing. They'd always talked about her past, rarely his. But as she stuffed a handful of straw in the stove, she remembered that last week, while they shared a bowl of soup, he'd mentioned his family in Minsk and something about an epidemic that occurred years ago. A neighbor, begging him to repair a broken lock on the shed before nightfall, interrupted them, and Michail had left with the fellow without finishing the story. What had he wanted to tell her? She rubbed a streak of soot off her wrist and looked at her bare fingers. Lev could not afford a wedding ring. Could Michail? How had it not occurred to her, a man like Michail, such a good man—why would such a man be alone? So many men had fought in the war and never returned. And here he was, available—or was he? "I must be strong enough to stand on my own, if need be," she whispered. She looked around the room, searching for clues that would tell her more about what she'd found in the purse.

Michail opened the door.

She rose, hadn't heard him on the stairs. "You're back," she blurted out. For a moment she wished she'd stayed in her room, where the cracked walls and slanted ceiling were familiar and offered solace. "I thought I'd make a fire. I hope you don't mind."

"No, not at all. Perhaps you should light it?"

She reached for the flint and fumbled, dropping it on the floor.

"Here, give that to me." He took the flint from her cold hands and looked at her tense face. "Are you all right?"

"I'll be fine once I'm warm."

"We're lucky tonight," he said. "I've got two onions we can cook. They're from Heddie, who sends you her regards."

"That's generous." She took his satchel and put it on the workbench. "Is she all right?"

"More or less." He lit the fire and pulled the mattress closer to the grate. Kicking off his boots he sat and tucked his feet beneath him. "Come here," he said, "come sit next to me."

She remained standing.

"I have news of the children." Before she could react, he corrected himself. "Not as to where they might be. But information that might help us find out."

She quickly took his hand and joined him. "Does Heddie know something?"

"Yes." This time he chose his words more carefully. "She has reason to believe that street children are being abducted." He stopped, seeing the horror in her eyes. She was too naïve. She'd been to all the official places that handled missing persons and had searched the streets until she knew each one. Poverty, crime, and hunger were all around her, and yet, she hadn't let herself reach the next and obvious conclusion. "We can't dismiss Heddie's news. Sasha and Ana might be impossible to find because they've been hidden away or because something more sinister is going on."

She felt colder, as if she would never be warm.

He watched her twist a loose button on the cuff of her sleeve. He searched her anguished face. "Do you remember the shophouse with the little dog?" he asked. "The one where you saw Tatiana?"

"Yes."

"We must find it."

"Could Sasha and Ana be there?"

"I don't know. But Heddie claims Tatiana is working for a gang in the Moldavanka and hustling street children." Though he wasn't certain, he suspected the shophouse Pavlo had mentioned was a drop-off point for trafficking guns and vulnerable children. He feared Ivan was involved with both.

Elvira Maria paused, taking in the news. She'd heard rumors of gangs selling street children, but she'd somehow believed she would find Ana and Sasha one day on the street or in an orphanage. Other children, not hers, were victims of this kind of abuse. "Heddie knows about this?" she asked.

"She's lived here a long time and has connections in places beyond our reach."

"What kind of connections?"

Now Michail paused. It was foolish not to tell her. Heddie and her business were well known in the city, and the house, one of the grandest in the central district, was right across the street from Deribasov Garden where they performed. "She runs a brothel," he finally said. "Her clients are wealthy and influential and she's a smart woman who keeps her ears open."

"I see." Elvira Maria got up from the mattress and walked to the other side of the room. Heddie. This assertive, well-spoken, and beautifully dressed woman, this patron of the arts Michail had introduced her to, was more than she appeared to be. If she was a prostitute, she certainly wasn't the tawdry-looking kind like the ones who loitered in front of the tenement, desperate and drunk. Heddie had valuable information and if she was right—Elvira Maria returned to Michail and placed her hands between his to warm them. They would go to the shophouse tomorrow.

27

ELVIRA MARIA WATCHED THE STEAM evaporate from the iron pot sitting on the workbench and fidgeted with the fringe on her shawl. Michail handed her a cup of broth.

"Eat mine," she said. She went to the window to watch the street below. "I'm not hungry."

"Did you say you're not hungry? Everyone in this city is hungry. Come, we must eat when we can. It's good. You liked it last night." He placed the warm cup in her hands and urged her to join him at the workbench.

Sitting, she stirred the broth, bringing to the surface a piece of onion. She slipped it into her mouth and chewed slowly, relishing the sweet flavor that in better times had been a daily staple. "Have you always cooked for yourself?" she asked, watching him ladle the broth into his cup.

"Not always. My mother was a great cook. It tortures me to think of the tasty dishes she put on our table, especially on feast days. Sometimes I dream about draniki and

borscht." He sat and wiped his wooden spoon on his sleeve
and began to eat.

"Was there anyone else?"

"What's that?"

"Did a woman, a woman other than your mother,
ever cook for you?"

He set down his cup. "Elvira Maria, what do you want
to know?"

She looked across the room at the nightingale. "I want
to know if you've ever been married or if you're married
now."

"Ah," he said. He tried to draw her eyes to his, but it
was impossible. "Yes to your first question and no to your
last. And just to satisfy your curiosity, she was not a bad
cook."

"Can you tell me what happened?"

He pushed his stool away from the workbench. "It was
a hard time."

"Please tell me. I'm ready to listen."

"My wife died of scarlet fever—ten years ago."
Hesitating, he thought of his loss, and then told her about
that summer, how the fever had swept through Mińsk
when the harvest workers came. "Some were sick," he said,
"and it spread quickly." He'd been performing with Ivan in
the old town of Vilnius when he heard that his wife wasn't
feeling well. He had a show scheduled that evening for a
wealthy patron he didn't want to disappoint. The season
had been poor and he needed the money. Rather than
rushing home, he kept the engagement. When he returned
his mother-in-law hurried him to the sickroom. His wife
was delirious. "Soon after," he said, "Kalina was gone."

"Michail, I'm sorry."

"I should have come home at once, tended to my family."

"But how could you have known?"

"The fever took my daughter as well. She was three." He swallowed, his voice full of sadness. "I tied a wedding ring around her neck to break her rising temperature, as friends insisted, but even as I was doing it, I knew it wouldn't work. I lost them both."

Elvira Maria walked to the other side of the workbench. She stood behind him and wrapped her arms around him. "I never imagined your life was so hard," she whispered. "I had to ask."

"It's all right," he said. "I've wanted to tell you."

"The last time my mother was sick she told me that life has no meaning without pain."

"That sounds familiar." He rearranged the paint brushes on his workbench. "Many people believe that, but I'm not so sure. I'd just as soon do without the misery. It makes you bitter."

"Were you bitter?"

"Yes, for a few years," he said, "but I'm not anymore."

"What made you change?" She leaned her cheek against his.

"I couldn't live that way. I couldn't perform my shows for children. And my love—" He turned around and kissed her, "—if I'd stayed bitter I wouldn't have noticed you at all."

The walkways, so crowded earlier in the day, thinned as people headed home, tired from hours of standing in line to collect their rations. A Red Army convoy sped toward Nikolaevskaya Boulevard and the port beyond, whirling past the monument of Catherine the Great, recently enshrouded by a large tarp tied in place by the Bolsheviks. Undaunted by the soldiers blasting their horns, a droshky loaded with withered corpses plodded steadily along, the driver making his weekly rounds to collect the dead from houses and apartments, lanes, courtyards, tunnels, and bridges. Starvation and disease were devastating Russia, claiming thousands of lives each day. Years of war had ravaged fields and displaced farmers. Those who remained on the land with limited livestock struggled and complied with Bolshevik mandates to feed the Red Army. As officers confiscated grain, fodder, and animals, seasoned farmers predicted ruin. Cities like Odessa waited for food, residents tightening their belts.

And yet, people attended to their lives. Elvira Maria and Michail, swept along by a stiff wind at their backs, crossed the noisy street and passed the massive Preobrazhensky Cathedral. They followed the tramline to the hospital. Hours later, they entered the neighborhood of the shophouse. Elvira Maria remembered the curtains in the windows and hoped they were still there.

"Does the shop face east?" Michail asked.

"Yes, with the sun over there." She turned to check the horizon. "But by the time I left the hospital it was hidden by storm clouds."

Michail worried. As they walked on he wondered if they'd taken a wrong turn. "I've never been here before," he said. "The district must have been prosperous once." He scanned the boarded windows, padlocked doors, and colorful and gilded signs of pastries, poppy seeds, chocolate, and bread. Soon these gave way to faded posters of stylish fashions, luxury fabrics, and sewing notions. "Does this look familiar?" he asked.

"There it is!" Across the street, a pair of green curtains hung loosely in the display windows of a building. "There's the metal latch I tried."

"Let's walk to the end of the block and find the alley. I want to see if there's a rear entrance." He beckoned her.

Uneasy, he took note of the people on the street. Most were refugees hauling their belongings on their backs as they trudged along seeking shelter before nightfall. Forced to walk into the grit now blowing through the air, their faces were covered against the brittle assault, their identities uncertain and haunting. "Don't stop," he said. Elvira Maria held her mantle in place as they passed the anonymous figures, her skirts billowing.

In the alley, cluttered with broken fences and ransacked garbage, two men bent over a smudge fire.

"Comrades," Michail said. "Hard to keep a fire going, isn't it?"

"Depends who's asking," the older of the two said. He spit to the side. He placed wood chips on the dwindling flames and sat down on the edge of a loading dock, his felt coat belted with a rope, his boots without heels. He smoothed his black mustache against his upper lip.

"I work with the Housing Commissar," said Michail. "I have a rendezvous at a shophouse nearby." He nodded toward his destination. "You live here?"

The man, surprised, gestured to the other, a skinny fellow in a dirty sweater, still crouching by the fire. "We was just passing through. Taking a break from the devil's wind. Gotta eat sometime."

Michail looked at the smoking fire. Blighted potato peelings roasted in the ashes. "I'll leave you to it," he said. "Put out your fire when you're done. You don't want trouble." He saluted the men and steered Elvira Maria in front of him.

They passed deserted loading docks surrounded by overgrown weeds and thistle, the backs of the narrow shophouses poking several stories into a gray sky. A stinking outhouse, clinging to a patch of chalky dirt, shook with each gust of wind. Farther on, a battered and stranded lorry stripped of its wheels, waited for a final heist. Soon they heard someone laughing in the yard of the house in question.

"Wait here," Michail said.

She stood behind the lorry. As she caught her fluttering mantle and held it tightly to her chest she gripped her pendant. She heard the laughing again, then a girl's voice. "You've learned how to catch your toy," the girl said. "Go get it, Dima!"

Seconds later a knotted rag ball, followed by an eager puppy, bounced across the alley toward Michail. Scooping up the ball in one hand and the small dog in the other, he approached the startled girl.

"He's a smart dog, isn't he?" Michail said. He smiled, guessing the girl was five, perhaps six. Her dress was rumpled, her left cheek bruised. He put the ball in her hand and stroked the excited puppy until he stopped squirming.

"Oh yes," she said. "Yes, he is." She clutched the ball with both hands.

"I had a dog like this years ago. He followed me everywhere. Loved to ride in my father's droshky on the front bench, nestled in my coat."

"Dima can't do that. He has to stay here." She put the ball in her torn pocket. "I need to go inside now." She held out her arms for the dog and looked anxiously over her shoulder through the open door.

"I'm glad Tatiana shares her puppy with you," Michail said, handing her the dog. He climbed the porch steps with her and followed her into the dark corridor. "Is she here?"

The girl called out in a hushed voice, "Tatiana, someone wants to see you."

Tatiana's voice came from a side room. "Get in here!" she yelled. "Start obeying me or you'll get a whipping. Don't go out there. I told you that before. Can't you stay upstairs with the other girls?"

Tatiana, emerging from the set of portieres, grabbed the girl and pulled her inside. She scowled into the daylight beyond. She looked haggard, her thin face smeared with rouge, her hair matted from sleep. Her big blue eyes, rimmed in kohl, were ghostly. When she recognized Michail standing in the hallway she stopped shouting. She put her hands on her hips and stood stubbornly in front of the curtains.

"It's been a long time, Tatiana," he said. "How are you?"

"What are you doing here?"

"I'd like to ask you the same question."

"Go away." She pointed to the door. "I don't need nothing from you, Michail." Cold from standing in the windy corridor, she wrapped her arms around herself, her blue silk robe shimmering across her bare legs and feet.

"What's the operation here?" he asked. "You should know better than to get mixed up with Ivan's illegal weapons."

"Mind your own business!"

"I wish I could."

"Wait til I tell Ivan you're meddling in his affairs."

"Tatiana, don't make me laugh. Ivan's an old friend of mine. I know his affairs."

She cursed and told him again to leave. Instead, he stepped toward her. As he did, Ivan Dashkevich parted the curtains.

"Go upstairs," he ordered Tatiana. She stamped her foot and fled. Ivan, cigarette in hand, and dressed in a faded linen tunic and dark trousers, walked halfway down the corridor. Michail noted the new lines etching his forehead. His fair hair, once glossy and well combed, was flecked with gray, unruly strands shoved behind his ears. "I'm glad to hear we're still friends, Comrade," Ivan said. "I've missed you."

"I'm sure your life has been far too exciting for that to be true," Michail answered. "All the intrigue. All the deals. All the exploitation of children. Far too busy for me or even for . . . what was it?" He squinted reproachfully. "Bread, peace, and land?"

"You remember the slogan. We did a good job." Ivan laughed. "Michail, I've always admired your persistence and your never-ending interest in whatever I do. I should

have known you'd turn up and make a nuisance of yourself." He sighed and took a box of Murads from his pocket.
"Want one?"

Michail shook his head at Ivan's guile. Disgusted,
he wanted to abandon his search, but thought of Elvira
Maria, waiting behind the lorry. He snatched the Murads.

Overhead, the dog barked. Slaps and cries echoed
through the house. A door slammed.

"I saw her from the window upstairs," Ivan said. "That
lorry's not much camouflage. Tell her to come here."

"She wants her children, Ivan." He stepped forward.
"If you don't tell me what you know, I'll make damn sure
you regret it."

Ivan crushed his cigarette on the floor. "Tell her to
come here before I change my mind."

Silent and wary, Michail and Elvira Maria waited on the
porch for Ivan to return. She had not seen Ivan since he'd
been shot in the alley and taken refuge with Michail.
Though she knew he was Odessa's new housing commissar,
Michail never spoke of him and their broken relationship.
She assumed political differences kept them apart, but
now, realizing Ivan was at the shophouse with Tatiana,
she was certain he was trafficking children. Michail had
walked away from Ivan, but had failed to tell her exactly
why.

Out on the street, the lone cry of a peddler selling
rags pierced through the rumble of evening traffic until a
screeching lorry drowned him out. Elvira Maria clenched
her fists in her pockets and focused on the door latch.
Finally it stirred, and Ivan joined them.

"No one recognizes the girl," he said. He handed Michail the photograph of Sasha and Ana. "But the older girls know the boy. He stole a vendor's purse in Privoz Market a while back and was arrested. Deputy Dudorov got involved and got him released. They say he's still with Dudorov, who keeps him right by his side." Ivan looked at Elvira Maria, his eyes sharp and unflinching. "They haven't seen him lately."

Elvira Maria steadied herself against the porch railing. She felt sick to her stomach.

"What about you?" Michail asked. "You work for Dudorov. Have *you* seen him lately?"

"Listen, I'm trying to help you," Ivan said. "I'm trying to steer you in the right direction." He pulled out his watch, checked the time, and snapped the lid shut. "You'd better come in. I have dealers coming."

Michail went inside, but Elvira Maria remained in the yard. She needed to think, to pace. The children would never forgive her. She was responsible for the abuse they faced every day. She walked in circles, the wind casting dust across her wet cheeks and rattling through the lorry, shards of window glass flashing in the twilight.

She thought about the way Ivan had looked at her when he said Sasha was with Deputy Dudorov—the meaning behind that glance—and she couldn't help picturing an officer's groping hands claiming her son.

But it was more than that. She'd been searching for her children in parks, the railyard, among gangs of urchins, never admitting to herself that there were worse places they might be, far worse people they might be with. Her refusal to see war-torn Odessa — the world — as it really was had cost her time and had cost the children so much more. Even Michail, the man she loved, hadn't told her everything he should have. She had somehow believed her children were more protected, more loved by God, than Luka, than Tatiana, than any other mother's child. She wiped the grit from her face. No, her children were like all the others displaced by the war — lonely, frightened, exploited, and helpless.

She returned to the house and strained to see Michail and Ivan through the open door. Ivan was pointing upstairs. Seconds later, and what seemed without warning, he gripped Michail's shoulders and pinned him against the wall. They struggled in each other arms, until Michail freed himself. He turned to leave, but Ivan pulled him back and held onto his sleeve, his face worried and forlorn. Elvira Maria waited, the time swirling beyond her into the gale. At long last, the two men shook hands.

She headed for the alley, Michail close behind. But before she reached the lorry she stopped and turned around to look at the shophouse. She imagined the girls upstairs, trapped and frightened, hungry, drugged on alcohol or marafet. She walked toward the porch, ashamed that she'd stayed in the yard to cry, hadn't climbed the stairs and barged into the room to help them.

"No!" Michail grabbed her arm. "It's too dangerous." As he pulled her to his side he felt her resist. When they reached the alley she shook her arm from his and hurried on. He stood for a moment and watched her, her back straight, her body a stream of black fabric, her step determined. It was then that he heard the racket: a pounding on the front door of the shophouse and the harsh voices of men calling for Ivan. He glanced over his shoulder.

Tatiana stood in the upstairs window, Dima tucked in her arms. She raised her hand and slowly waved, her heart-shaped face exhausted.

SPRING
1920

We reached Odessa just after a fire had completely
destroyed the main telegraph and electric stations,
putting the city in total darkness. As it would require
considerable time to make repairs, the situation
increased the nervousness in the city, for darkness
favored counterrevolutionary plots.

—Emma Goldman

28

Odessa

IN THE YARD, ELVIRA MARIA SCRUBBED her petticoat
against the side of the washtub. The murky water
floated across the patches she'd sewn along the bottom
months ago. It hardly matched the delicate organdy camisole she'd pinched from Monsieur Oury, but hadn't had
the courage to wear. She hoped the petticoat, her only
one, would last through the summer. Lifting it out of the
gray swirl, she plunged it into the water once more, and
worried about Sasha.

Aleksander Lyova Andrushko was her first born. As
his mother she demanded his fierce loyalty, and like all
honorable sons she expected that he would care for her as
she grew older. This was his duty. Who else would uphold
the family name? Who else would pray for her soul when
the hour of death assumed its power? Ana would marry
and leave her, but Sasha would sow and tend the fields,
barter for salt, tools, and cloth, and guard their household
from thieves and vagrants, the plague of the countryside.

She had been blessed. Her son was no simpleton. He was curious and skillful. Despite his station in life, he'd taught himself to read.

Only eleven years old, it appeared he'd been preyed on by Dudorov. There was a time she would have believed he'd been ensnared by Satan and needed to change his ways, to beg God for forgiveness. Now she knew he was blameless. To survive he had fallen into the hands of a powerful and manipulative man. Despite the danger, she would find him. God's grace would protect them both.

Verging on tears, she removed the petticoat from the washtub and flung the wastewater toward the acacia trees. The red tassels attached to the corded waistband shed drops of water. Ana had sewn them on just before they'd left Kos. Each time Elvira Maria tied the cords in place she thought of happier times. Ana had taken to sewing at an early age. After learning never to waste a length of thread or yarn, she spent hours unraveling worn-out clothes, saving the stronger threads for new projects. Elvira Maria draped the petticoat over her arm and took it to her room to dry, away from devious neighbors she knew would steal it.

Yagna and Tolya were sleeping. Since installing themselves in the vestibule months ago they spent most of their days coughing and lying fitfully on a bundle of rags that served as their bed. Elvira Maria avoided them, fearing a confrontation with the sick and quarrelsome couple. But now she stared at their unkempt and heaving bodies and listened to their gasping, snivels, and groans. She was startled by a profound pity the human sounds and exposed intimacy made her feel. She quickly mounted the stairs.

She hung the petticoat on the nail next to her desk. "They have no shame, no shame at all," she said under her breath. She looked at herself in the chipped hand mirror she'd recently found in the trash. She removed her scarf, smoothed back her uncombed hair, and ran her hands down the front of her wrinkled bodice, checking the five tiny clasps that kept it closed. Since she'd arrived in Odessa she'd been so absorbed in her search for Ana and Sasha that she too had neglected herself; hadn't always repaired her worn-out clothes or minded her appearance as she'd once done in Kos. She, like many of the refugees she saw on the streets, had carried on as best she could, made compromises she told herself were temporary, and hoped that she retained a semblance of dignity. "At least I haven't started to drink," she whispered and set down the mirror.

Two weeks had passed since they'd seen Ivan at the shophouse. Each day they expected to hear news of Ana and Sasha, but Ivan hadn't sent a word. Elvira Maria now hated him and wondered how Michail had ever known such a man. Ivan claimed his revolution would free the masses. How could he justify holding children hostage? Perhaps he was following the Deputy's orders and was also trapped, as Michail suggested, but she didn't care. She would never excuse or forgive him. She understood, after a tearful confrontation with Michail, that Ivan had trafficked the girls from the shed for guns, and that Michail had been too afraid to tell her. Begging her to forgive him, he'd promised to stalk Ivan until her children were found. But that was dangerous and reckless. While they waited for news, Michail had asked her to be patient, but she knew he too was anxious for an update. She kept busy, trying not to panic. During the day she sewed cuffs and collars and buttonholes, practiced her lines, cleaned the wood stove, and wrote lists of words she wanted to remember. But at night she lay awake and imagined the children locked in a shophouse or hidden in the cellar of the Red Army barracks. Perhaps Ivan was silent because they were sick with typhus or were dead. If so, would he have the courage to tell them?

To distract themselves, she and Michail walked to the hills above Coal Harbor just to have something different to look at. They sat on an outcropping of sandstone surrounded by violets and spring grass. The morning fog was lifting. A dizzy flock of gulls trailed in the wake of a steamer headed for Constanţa. Its turbines groaned as it slowly propelled forward, gushing smoke from its double stacks. She tucked a strand of hair beneath her scarf and pressed down her wind-blown skirts. "If Sasha's with Deputy Dudorov, we need to find his office at headquarters," she said. "Can't you ask around?"

"Ivan will contact us when he has a plan." The dark circles under her eyes, the new lines furrowing her brow worried him. She seemed never to sleep. Sometimes he woke at dawn and found her sitting at the grate looking at her photo, as if she could will the children to her side. "If we don't hear anything in the next few days," he said, "I'll track him down."

Broad-backed and muscular, the dockers at Voenni Pier sorted huge bales, lumber, and crates. They worked steadily, as rhythmic as the waves rolling in. The sails of the dories anchored nearby rippled in the cool breeze. The water was vast, shimmering in the first sunlight. Like the wheat fields, Elvira Maria thought. "I realize it's useless to think about Kos," she said, "but sometimes I fantasize that we'll return. It's springtime now. If I were there I'd be planting the fields, tending the lambs, or preparing for Easter."

He took her hand. "I often have trouble accepting the past is gone forever, too. But Kos was burned to the ground months ago."

"Yes, I know, but sometimes I don't. I think I'll never believe it unless I go back and see for myself."

"Believe me," he said, "there's nothing there."

The proof of his words was all around them. Homeless families camped and begged along the dockyards and Odessa Steps. They'd come in droves. Their villages had also been destroyed.

"I've always hoped . . ." she said, then gave up on the thought. As destitute strangers wandered up and down the grand steps, she focused instead on another cargo ship leaving the harbor, beginning its crossing of the open sea.

29

"THE RED ARMY HAS TAKEN CHARGE of the trains," Boris announced. He sat on the sofa across from Heddie in the reception room. "They're transporting new recruits and the able-bodied wounded along the old Kyiv-Odessa line. The station is terribly chaotic. I saw Roza this morning and she told me the latest news. Securing train passage now is out of the question."

"Ah, Roza's still there," Heddie said. She remembered her former employee fondly. She put down the outdated newspaper she was reading for the third time. "Even with her beloved Louis gone. How is she?"

"Getting by," he said. "They relocated her tea stall near the main entrance so she's serving more customers. But I don't envy her. The soldiers are brazen and she's struggling day and night to keep the samovars lit. She's got to buy fuel from some black marketeer who's unreliable and wants a fortune."

"Poor girl. I wish I'd been able to keep her. She was the best cook we ever had."

"I doubt if she'd be able to work her magic now," Boris

said. Thoughts of a savory roast beef with dumplings and horseradish crossed his mind. "The kitchen shelves are empty."

"Please dear, don't remind me." She approached the large potted fern set before the curtained window and removed a handful of dry brown fronds. "Let's move this to the kitchen. It's going to die without any light or fresh air. Perhaps we could put it out on the porch."

"Heddie—"

"Boris, securing train passage has always been difficult, but if we don't try we're going to rot here like this plant." She threw the crumpled fronds on the table and glanced at him, gloomily slumped on the sofa. "I'm sorry. I should take twenty lashes for getting you into this mess. And now, I'm the rudest person I know. Not that I see anyone, mind you."

"It's a wretched time and Dudorov made it worse," he said. Although they were fearful of Dudorov's next move, Boris was proud she'd faced him head on. At least she'd fought for her principles and hadn't been intimidated by the tyrant. Her loyal clients would remember her as not merely elegant, but heroic. Since his arrival Dudorov had been embroiled in Odessa's underworld, and Boris, who followed the rumors on the streets, had known he was nothing but trouble. Speculators and criminals despised the man, and though they did his bidding, they took a hefty cut, laughed behind his back, and cursed him to the devil. "I should have shot the scoundrel when he first came to town," Boris said.

"We'd both be dead if you had." She sighed heavily. "So many people owe me favors and now when I need their help and influence, no one's to be found. It makes me furious. I'm glad the house is closed. I'm sick of spending my precious time with selfish, lecherous hypocrites." She walked to a gilded mirror and examined her face. "At least my bruises are disappearing. Thank heavens I didn't lose my eyesight."

"You look much better."

"I'm going upstairs. Keep track of those awful spies across the street. I need to count our treasure and see what's left for the days ahead."

30

THE BABUSHKAS FROM THE COUNTRYSIDE wore shawls, layered skirts, and flowered kerchiefs on their heads. Their drawstring leather pouches, tied to their aprons, rustled with coins. Late April, they sat beneath the trees in Deribasov Garden with mounds of dandelion greens, acorns, thyme, and sunflower seeds spread out before them on checkered towels. The wild onions and thick yellow tubers, included in several displays, created a stir among the customers who bargained aggressively for the rare produce. The old women pointed their thick fingers at each item and shouted their final price, their round faces and steely blue eyes unyielding. They had combed the hillsides since dawn, collecting spring flowers and greens, groundnuts, and herbs to sell.

Long familiar with foraging, they'd finally won the respect of city folks who had dismissed them as illiterate bumpkins when they'd first arrived with iron sickles or a hay knife slung across their backs, cloth bundles in each arm. Now customers were not only buying, but also asking for cooking instructions and herbal remedies to banish dysentery, worms, and fatigue.

Elvira Maria, with Danya in tow, greeted them as she headed to the center of the garden where Michail and Pavlo had set up the stage for the morning's performance. She'd sat with the women on occasion, sewing and exchanging news and family stories. They were tougher than their customers imagined. They snapped their fingers when they got the price they wanted, and waited for the next transaction, serious and watchful, ordering pushy customers to stand back, shouting at anyone who dared try to touch the produce. Widowed, they had suffered through years of war, losing their homes and loved ones. She admired them and wondered if someday she would be a version of them, using her country knowledge to earn a meager living. Some days it seemed the best she could hope for.

She checked the props and puppets for the show and took her place beside Michail. As he blew the pishchik whistle she smiled. He handed Pavlo a string of bells and a drum, then ran out front to welcome the audience.

Spirited Comrades, brave revolutionaries, mighty masses of Odessa, friends and foes. Come gather around for your favorite story — the delicious and unforgettable 'Khinkali.' This story will touch your hearts, feed your soul, and fill your belly. Children of all ages, welcome!

The crowd moved closer to the bright little theater. Pavlo beat the drum while Michail went backstage and slipped the puppet, Dedushka, over his hand. The puppet, stout, bearded, and costumed in a tunic and breeches, hobbled on stage and stood before a kitchen backdrop. He opened an empty cupboard and moaned. Elvira Maria

placed Grandma Babushka, his wife, beside him. Her
button nose and cheeks poked out from a blue kerchief
that matched her apron. She waved a wooden spoon while
Dedushka rubbed his jiggling belly and complained
loudly.

Comrades, I'm hungry. Come to think of it, I'm hungry
morning, noon, and night. Such a terrible, unbearable, dilemma.
We have nothing to eat. Dear Grandma Babushka, come here.
Listen to my poor, empty belly grumble, tumble, and rumble.

Babushka put her ear to his belly and jumped back.
Aghast, she threw her hands in the air and turned from
side to side. She leaned toward the audience and cried out.
It's groaning and moaning!

It echoes across this land, Dedushka exclaimed. Without
a helping hand! Where are the farmers, so valiant and brave?
he asked, spreading out his arms. They must be at a meeting.
Greeting a fleeting—delegation—sent to save our nation.

Out front, people murmured and exchanged furtive
glances. They shifted on their feet and hid their smiles.
There were rumors that Cheka agents were planted in the
audience. Pavlo beat the drum, imitating a military march.
Elvira Maria looked at Michail, her face tense. He'd wandered from the script, as usual, and now was taking Pavlo
with him. He seemed determined to speak his mind and
risk arrest. As she bobbed Babushka's head and wondered
how she could intervene, Danya tugged on her skirt. Eager
to see the show, he pointed to the crowd, and dashed off.

Michail continued. My belly deserves to be fed, Dedushka
cried.

Yes, Yes, Grandma Babushka agreed. She stuck out her
belly. Mine too!

Dear Grandma, Dedushka said, make me the most delicious, the richest, the tastiest round dumpling in the world. Bake
me a soft, warm khinkali.

Babushka shook her spoon and wiped her brow with
her apron as Dedushka sang:

> Scrape the cupboard to look for flour
> Sweep the floor and gather more.
> Don't be afraid to sift and stir
> Crumbs in the corner and near the door.
> A stuffed khinkali I want to eat
> With cheese or meat that's more than sweet.
> Beef or pork, it's on your fork
> Every glorious day.

Babushka, he said, taking her arm, we must let this
steaming khinkali cool on our platter. Let's take a stroll and visit
our old friends at the grand Odessa dockyards. We'll eat when
we return.

Elvira Maria and Michail trotted their puppets off
stage. She slid them over the spindles and handed him the
round, embroidered Khinkali, a puppet she'd made. He
nodded to Pavlo. Accompanied by a jingle and drumbeat
he bounced the dumpling from the platter to the floor.
She exchanged the kitchen backdrop with a colorful one
depicting trees, flowers, and birds. Khinkali hummed
merrily as he bounced through the forest. But when he
came upon hungry Sister Fox he stopped, then shimmied
to the drumbeat. Michail glided through the story as
Khinkali ran away from Sister Fox into the woolly arms of
Brother Bear. Each time he met a hungry animal he sang
his favorite song:

I'm a khinkali dumpling, plump and sweet.
The very best meal you will ever eat.
But if troops arrive, they'll have a surprise.
I'll be gone in a flash, to the forest at last.
So clever and smart, and with a good start
I'll run, run, run — far away, far away.

While Elvira Maria stood beside Pavlo and listened for her next cue, a girl, about eight years old, dressed in a tunic smeared with charcoal, ducked in front of her. She whispered to Pavlo and took hold of his wrist, distracting him from keeping pace with Michail.

Elvira Maria pulled her aside. "Talk to him when the show is over," she said. But Pavlo, alert, thrust the bells and drum into her hands, and without a word, ran after the girl.

Michail frowned. He called out the closing lines of Brother Wolf, a mangy-looking puppet with a red star, the symbol of the new regime, sewn to his forehead. *Sing the song again sweet Khinkali. Hop onto my tongue so I can hear you better. I've always loved your song.*

Khinkali, puffed up with pride, jumped onto the Wolf's tongue. But before he could sing, Brother Wolf opened his enormous mouth and swallowed the tasty dumpling with a loud *chomp!*

Elvira Maria shook the bells and beat the drum vigorously as Michail strutted the cunning Wolf before the audience. The curtain closed. She put down the instruments and made her way through the dispersing crowd. Before long, she saw the girl with Pavlo and Danya at the distant edge of the garden. They were pointing and shouting at another boy who stood in the street beside an idling lorry.

Unruffled, the well-groomed, flaxen-haired boy lifted the
visor of his docker's cap and placed a cigarette behind his
ear. Pavlo and the girl continued to shout, but he ignored
them and kicked his leather boots in the dust while he
looked into the park, as if searching for someone.

Breathless and irritated, Elvira Maria approached
him. "What's going on here?" she asked. She pulled Danya
away from the grinding vehicle and stood in front of
Pavlo. Instinctively, she shook the arm of the boy in the
cap, and looking into his surprised face and widening
gray eyes recognized her son.

"Sasha, get in the lorry—now," the driver said, his
voice angry.

"No, no!" Elvira Maria grabbed her son by the shoulders
and held him before her. "I'm here Sasha," she said. "My
dearest boy. I'm here. It's Mama. It's me."

"Get in this lorry," the driver yelled again. "Don't play
me for a fool." He cursed and revved the engine, spewing
black exhaust into the air. He leaned out of the window
and pointed at Sasha. "If you run off on me," he threatened, "I'll hunt down your sister and slit her throat!"

Sasha broke loose and jumped up into the cab. He
slammed the door shut. Elvira Maria reached for the steel
handle and gripped it tightly, refusing to let her son go.
The vehicle careened around the corner and she swung
against the door, a sharp pain jolting through her body.
Seconds later, she felt Sasha's hands savagely beating
her own. She screamed his name as he pried her bloody
fingers, one by one, from the handle, and she fell headlong
into the gravelly street.

31

Pᴉɴᴋ sᴛʀᴇᴀᴋs ᴏꜰ ʟɪɢʜᴛ ᴡᴀsʜɪɴɢ ᴏᴠᴇʀ the rafters above her head. Gulls streaming past the window, their shadows lingering briefly in the room before disappearing into the breaking dawn. Alone on Michail's mattress and still wearing her clothes from the day before, Elvira Maria drifted in and out of consciousness, not certain she wanted to wake. She bent her bruised and bandaged fingers. They tingled beneath the soft cloth wound around her knuckles and palms, her exposed nails caked with dried blood. She remembered Sasha standing before her, his aloof expression changing to astonishment as he'd recognized her face, her voice, her reprimand.

"I finally found you," she whispered, not daring to utter the words aloud. She sat up, a dull ache throbbing in her chest, and searched for her pendant. The Blessed Mother had answered her prayers. She kissed it, knowing she would seek her mercy again and again. She thought about the lorry driver's menacing words. Ana was alive! Why else would the horrid man have made such a threat?

He had terrified Sasha, forcing him to abandon his own mother and his chance to be free.

She thought too about the lorries that parked on the edge of the garden, idling loudly and choking their audience with toxic fumes. Michail had warned Pavlo and Danya to be careful as they ran into the street, dodging the vehicles. She'd always assumed the drivers parked there to see the puppet shows. Perhaps this lorry had been among the others every time. Perhaps Sasha had been watching their performances for weeks. Alarmed, she struggled to her feet and went to the window to consider the possibility.

Michail came in with Pavlo and Danya. He put his arms around her, then went to the bed to get her shawl, as she requested.

Pavlo pushed Danya aside and dropped a pile of banners on the workbench. "That boy was in the audience," he said, "offering hungry kids cigarettes and bread if they'd get in the lorry." He turned to Elvira Maria. "He was trying to kidnap Danya!"

"What?" she said. She stumbled on a crate as she stepped back.

"I've seen that photograph you've got. It was him. Your son! Danya was lucky I got there before that muzhik carried him off."

"He wasn't going to get me," Danya said. "I wasn't climbing into that lorry."

"Deputy Dudorov was there too," Pavlo said. He ran his finger across his jaw. "The girl told me. He was sitting on a bench next to the old women who sell sunflower seeds and grass."

"You're talking about the officer you've seen with Commissar Dashkevich?" Michail asked.

"Yeah. Those two are criminals. You can count on it."

"But why kidnap Danya?" Elvira Maria asked. She put her hands on Danya's shoulders.

"He's an easy mark," Pavlo said. "Doesn't run with a gang like I do." He pulled Danya away from her and shook a finger at his brother. "You better keep your eyes open."

"Everyone settle down," Michail said. He took a seat at the workbench. He needed to think carefully about what had happened in the garden, and how he would confront Ivan, force him to secure Ana and Sasha before Dudorov bartered them off in a lucrative transaction.

He cut pieces of bread from his ration. The green-colored loaf, made from ground pea shells, bore little resemblance to the hearty dark ones of years past. He took a small chunk and handed another to Elvira Maria, before passing the rest to Pavlo and Danya. They fell silent as they ate their meal of the day. The rhythmic cries of newspaper boys and washerwomen drifted through the open window. But the comforting sound of the district vendors soon disappeared as the shouts and thunder of a mounted battalion tore down the alley, flinging dust into the air. Sporadic gunshots echoed in a nearby street. The riveting of a machine gun answered at once. Elvira Maria closed the window.

She wondered if the girl was lying—wanted to impress Pavlo with a wild story. Cautious of his reaction, she asked him how the girl knew about Sasha.

"She lives in Deribasov Garden," Pavlo said, "watches out for trouble. She reports to *me*." He raised his voice. "I tell you, your son's not a petty thief like most of us working the street. Ha! He's a lousy decoy in a criminal racket."

"Pavlo, that's enough!" Michail said. "Take your brother downstairs."

"He'll be sorry when we get him," Pavlo said, pushing Danya out the door. "I'll make him pay, one way or another."

Michail collected the banners and stacked them against the wall. He sat across from Elvira Maria and wiped the surface of his workbench. He searched his leather pouch for threads of tobacco. It was empty. Reaching in his pocket for a clove, he found only lint and his pishchik.

"Michail." She hesitated before she sought his support. "I knew finding Sasha would be difficult, but I never expected—" She stopped, unwilling to give voice to Pavlo's verdict. "I have to find him. I need to help him."

"He's caught up in a dangerous business," Michail said. "I doubt if he's had much choice if he's been working for Dudorov."

Deep in thought they sat together as the afternoon faded and a fiery glow filled the windowpane. Downstairs, Tolya and Yagna began their nightly quarrel. Unable to sit still, Elvira Maria finally rose. She rearranged the cloth set aside for costumes and counted the spools of thread she'd gotten from Monsieur Oury. Sasha had been too afraid to leave Dudorov. And Ana, where was she? Were the children together? Despite the turn of events, she feared she could lose them forever in the shadows of the city.

32

Early the next morning, the occupants of the tenement scurried in and out of their apartments. They called wayward children, shook dusty blankets, emptied slop pails, and slammed doors.

Commissar Ivan Dashkevich, uniformed smartly and carrying a thick file of official papers, knocked on Michail's door. "Housing inspection, open up, Comrade," he said. He turned around to address the people huddled below on the landing, their anxious eyes following his every step. "Go back to your apartments. I'll be coming down shortly. Have your papers in order."

"Good day, Commissar," Michail said. He was glad Elvira Maria was in her room and not in his bed.

"Close the door," Ivan said. He walked to the other side of the attic. Grabbing a crate, he sat down and gestured for Michail to do the same. He lowered his voice and scoffed, "Too many ears. Next thing you know, they'll be hovering on the other side of that door. It's pitiful."

Michail sat next to him and waited.

"I've got the girl."

"My God," Michail said. "You're certain it's Ana?"

Ivan nodded.

"Where is she?"

"I can only tell you this much. She's been with Sasha. He wants to unite her with Elvira Maria. Wants her to be safe, off the streets."

"Did you talk to him?"

"Not for long. He's clever—found out I knew you." He looked intensely at Michail. "I'll pay a price for this one. Remember that the next time you think I'm a heartless bastard."

"What do we do next?"

"Come to the shophouse at ten tonight. Take a droshky and have the driver wait out front. Bring Elvira Maria. The girl won't go with just you. She's got to come."

"Does Ana know what's happening?"

Ivan shrugged. "All I know is she'll be at the shophouse after dark." He looked at his watch and wound the tiny crown. The minute hand advanced, ticking softly. "I've got to go. Here, sign this." He took out a housing document. "If anyone asks, this was official business." Standing, he put a hand on Michail's shoulder. "We've got to do this quickly and quietly. No fuss. When you return to the droshky with Ana you've got to look like an ordinary family on an evening's outing."

While he hustled down the stairs, Ivan wondered if he'd redeemed himself a little, regained Michail's respect, something he'd lost when he'd partnered with defiant comrades who rewrote the rules to gain power. Transforming the old world into a new one was difficult. Inspired ideology, unspeakable anguish, and hope had driven them all to seek answers in dark, violent places. Over time, Ivan had come to believe Michail preferred to work with puppets instead of people, to improvise a fairy tale that rejected the contradictions and complications that belonged to a revolution.

Michail had no idea what Ivan's days were like with Dudorov. How vigilant he had to be, constantly looking for opportunities to nudge the Deputy this way and that, to distract him from abusing some hapless merchant, some struggling family, some abandoned child. A bully who helped himself to whatever he wanted, Dudorov reminded Ivan of the boys in Mińsk who lived in the squalid tenements abutting the Vulica Tannery that spit acid, blood, and misery into the Svislach River. The boys had trailed Michail and Ivan, taunted them, and shoved them into dead-end streets, where they pocketed their coins or snatched a bag of theater props. Laughing, their footfalls hammering the cobblestones, they ran off, leaving Ivan and Michail with bloodied noses and knuckles and the urge to seek revenge. Ivan felt the same urge now. He paused on the landing to reshuffle his papers, the hint of a smile on his lips. Placing Ana in her mother's arms was a way to frustrate Dudorov's sordid game. And even if Dudorov didn't care, it would make Ivan feel better. He had come to accept his own failings, his own despicable actions. It would be a relief to remember what it felt like to do something honorable and to live up to his old ideals.

Pavlo and Danya pulled their blankets off the stairway railing. "If these lousy blankets are a fire hazard why didn't Commissar Dashkevich tell us that when we first moved in?" Pavlo asked. He threw his stained quilt into the corner of the vestibule. "He could have warned us, saved us lots of trouble." He held the blue citation Ivan had given him to the light. Unable to read it, he placed it on his father's pile of bedding and went back to stacking the jumble of pots and pans shoved beneath the stairs. "Tolya's gonna beat us when he comes in."

"Hide it in your pocket," Danya said. He kicked a pebble across the floor.

"You don't understand how things work."

Elvira Maria took advantage of the cleared staircase to sweep the steps, brushing the dust and dirt toward the vestibule and out the door. The spicy scent of acacia flowers greeted her as she whisked the debris into the street. Vendors pushed carts laden with housewares toward a black market tucked behind the commercial school. Tea kettles, pots, and pans swung and clattered as the wheels bumped over cracks along the route. As more and more families struggled to survive, they sold the last of their personal belongings. She greeted the stubble-faced men as they passed her and admired the assorted items she could not afford to buy. When she saw Ivan leave, she stomped the grime from her broom and ran up to the attic.

Michail, his voice steady, told her what had transpired with Ivan. She found herself standing perfectly still, perfectly silent, as if movement of any kind would wake her from what was surely a dream.

"After all this time, I'll finally be able to hold her again!" She clutched his arm, her face beaming. "How am I going to survive until ten o'clock tonight?" She thought for a moment, then asked, "Will Sasha be with her?"

"Ivan only mentioned Ana." Her joy disappeared. "At least we've found him and he knows you're here. We must follow Ivan's plan. He's risked a lot to get Ana. We have to take her while we can and hope for everyone's sake it goes well."

She shuddered a breath and regained her composure. "Michail, I'm prepared to do whatever I must."

He sorted through the lace and colorful cloth on his workbench and selected a piece of green satin. "Let's finish this puppet today," he said. "The Frog Princess is a popular show. We could stage it this summer."

She found her sewing needle and broke off a length of thread. Did he know that in Kos she and Ana often sat beneath the dusty leaves of an oak tree, a basket of mending between them? A quiet child, Ana rarely asked for attention, though she brightened whenever Lev rewarded her work with sweets from the Easter market. When he was taken away by the soldiers, Ana's quiet disposition seemed less a sign of contentment and more a refusal to engage with the world. More than her mother, she turned to Sasha for love and companionship. She followed him everywhere.

While Elvira Maria sewed, Michail tapped his mallet against a chisel as he carved a scenery frame for the theater. Each of his strikes cut through the silence between them. She finished the puppet's tiny slippers and set them on the workbench.

"Ah, your stitches are better than mine," he said, examining her handiwork.

For his sake she tried to smile, before she selected another piece of cloth.

33

THE BLACK MARE WAS AFRAID of the tram tracks. The driver, hunched and bundled against the cool spring evening, cracked his whip against her haunches until the pain conquered her fear and the droshky continued on, past silhouetted trees and grand apartments, past the Opera House with its gigantic cupola looming through the shadows of Cathedral Square.

As the cart entered the Moldavanka Suburb and turned into a narrow street, the budded trees and elegant structures disappeared. Relying on the paraffin lamps glowing in the darkness, Elvira Maria strained to identify the two-story shophouse amidst the rows of neglected buildings cropping up from the broken boardwalks and gravel. Before long, it came into view, the top row of windows lit between sagging shutters.

"Have a smoke while you wait, Comrade," Michail said, offering the aging driver a cigarette he'd begged from Ivan.

Peals of laughter and rowdy shouts drifted down from the upper rooms. The driver arched a bushy eyebrow and pointed to the windows. "If you're going up there for the night I'll lose all my business. I'll only wait a half hour, no more."

"Don't worry, we'll be back in a moment," Michail said. "We're fetching our little girl from a friend."

"I'll be damned." The driver shook his head, dismissing him. "Mind the clock. I ain't got all night."

Elvira Maria and Michail entered the dark alley. They followed the line of broken fences until they found the battered lorry, still stranded in place, and hurried to the shophouse. But they stopped at once when they saw a black Puzyrev passenger car parked near the back porch, polished and gleaming and menacing.

"It's a party," Elvira Maria whispered. Shrieks from the girls now punctuated the laughter. She gripped the knife she kept in her pocket though it hurt her fingers, still not fully healed. Her heart raced.

"Michail, is that you?" Ivan stepped out from behind the Puzyrev. He looked around, his eyes unadjusted to the darkness.

"Over here," Michail called out in a low voice. "What's happening?"

Ivan came closer, following the sound of Michail's voice. "Dudorov arrived a few minutes ago." He turned up the collar of his greatcoat and threw a glance at the car. "He was supposed to be at Pratique Harbor tonight. I was there when his secretary scheduled the meeting. I never expected him, but here he is. Drunk and nastier than usual. Always needing—"

He stopped short as a lorry, its metal flanks rattling, swung into the yard. They scattered to a thicket of small trees at the edge of the property, and huddling together, watched the vehicle back up and stop at the edge of the alley. The driver turned his headlights off and on. Tatiana, a lamp in her hand, appeared in the upper window. She scanned the yard, then set the lamp on the ledge and retied the sash of her robe. The excited voices of girls and men rippled down the shophouse stairs and continued across the yard as the group headed for the lorry and piled in. The driver turned into the alley and drove off.

Deputy Dudorov, brawling for Tatiana to serve him a drink, pulled her away from the window. Seconds later, the dog barked, followed by a sharp yip and whimpering. Dudorov cursed.

Elvira Maria stood before Ivan. "Is my daughter here?"

"She's upstairs."

She could not believe what she was hearing. Ana was with Dudorov and his friends. She wanted to shake Ivan, to rage against him with all the pain she'd endured for months. But Ivan, sensing her wrath, stepped back and held up his hands to stop her from doing anything rash.

"I'm not leaving without Ana," she said, her voice shaking.

"If we wait, he'll get what he came for and move on. He wants Tatiana. It shouldn't take long."

Scuffles on the stairs drew their attention. They remained in the thicket, as far from the light as possible without losing their view of the porch. The back door of the shophouse flew open, the latch clanging against the metal railing. Deputy Dudorov, pushing Tatiana in front of him, stopped on the porch. He struck her with his leather gloves.

"How dare you ignore me in favor of that mutt," he said. Overhead, the lamp threw a shaft of yellow light down the splintered clapboards that illuminated his face, bloated and sweating. Their shadows spilled across the back porch and down the stairs. "You're an ungrateful little bitch, with another bitch under your arm."

Tatiana held Dima inside her robe and leaned against the railing, bracing for another blow.

"Throw that dog into the alley!" Dudorov yelled. "I don't want him in the house. I told you that last week and I'm telling you again."

"I'll put him in the side room," she said. "Please sir, he's no trouble."

He cracked his gloves across her face. "You think I'm going to listen to you?" Dudorov jeered, spittle flying from his lips. He shook the gloves at Tatiana and she flinched. "Every time I'm here he's a nuisance. I don't come here to play with a damn dog." He struck her face again, this time cutting her cheek. Blood spattered to her robe. Tatiana sobbed, but she continued to cling to the dog.

It was a young boy's voice, calm, yet insistent, that broke through the uproar.

"Leave her alone," and Sasha walked through the doorway, tossing his cigarette to the side. He put his hand on the Deputy's arm.

Elvira Maria stifled a cry, but could not keep from taking a step forward. Michail held her back. He looked at Ivan, who seemed frozen with fear.

"Get your filthy hands off me," Dudorov said.

"Sir," Sasha said, "that dog never bothers you."

Deputy Dudorov spat at Sasha and threw off his hand. Stumbling, he reached for his revolver and pointed it at Tatiana. "I'm ordering you to let go of that mongrel."

"No!" she cried. Her wide eyes were filled with tears. Elvira Maria pulled against Michail's grip, but he held onto her.

Dudorov cocked the hammer. He swayed back and forth, squinted his bloodshot eyes, and took aim. Sasha grabbed the gun and struggled to wrench it free. He twisted the barrel away from Tatiana and struck it against Dudorov's chest. The bullet discharged. Deputy Dudorov slumped to the ground, blood gushing from his mouth, the smell of smoke and sulfur filling the air.

"Mother of God," Elvira Maria exclaimed. Now all three of them ran to the porch, Michail and Ivan bending over Dudorov, Elvira Maria taking her son into her arms. As tightly as she held him, she couldn't stop his trembling or keep him upright when he collapsed against the door-frame, trapped and horrified.

Michail placed his hands on Dudorov's chest. He knew the man was dead, and yet he wanted to detect a heartbeat, only for Sasha's sake.

"Leave him be," Ivan said, pulling Michail away. He pointed to the hallway. "Get Ana. She's upstairs. Hurry!" He wrapped an arm around Tatiana and wiped the blood off her face. "Stay downstairs," he whispered. "Hide in the shop." She clasped Dima to her chest and ran down the dark corridor.

Elvira Maria helped her son to his feet. "It's an accident, a terrible accident. We all saw it, all of us. You saved Tatiana's life."

"Ma, what, what will—"

"You're coming with me," she said. She dragged him away from the porch and Dudorov's crumpled body. "You and Ana are coming with me tonight."

"Don't you understand?" he pleaded. "That's impossible. I've got to run—"

"No Sasha, no. We'll protect you." She turned to Ivan. "He's innocent, isn't he?"

"What does that mean anymore, innocent?" Ivan muttered. He shook his head as he looked at the bloody sight in front of him. He picked up the revolver, rubbed it against his sleeve, and tucked it into his coat. Then running to the Puzyrev, he opened the trunk. "Sasha, give me a hand." He pointed to the alley. "Elvira Maria, there's a bucket of water in the outhouse. Wash this down before the stains dry."

She looked at the pool of blood seeping through the porch boards, then at her son, not wanting to leave him. "Ma," he said, "go," but she couldn't. She remained and watched her child help Ivan lift Dudorov's heavy body. More blood guttered from his wound and trailed down the stairs, pooling in front of the car. She ran for the bucket.

The cold water splashed her skirts as she rushed back to the shophouse. There Michail stood on the porch with Ana in his arms. She set down the bucket.

"Annushka," she said. "It's Mama." The little girl, wrapped in a shawl, stared at her blankly. Then touching her mother's cheek, she smiled and recognized her. "Yes, I'm here," Elvira Maria said. "You're mine. You're my sweet girl." She kissed her dirty face and smoothed her greasy, matted hair.

"Elvira Maria, we must go," Michail said. Worried a dealer might arrive any moment, he glanced toward the alley. He thought too of the droshky out front.

"Sasha, come with us," she said. "We've got to stay together."

"No Ma, I ain't leaving the Commissar alone with this."

"But please, I beg you." She stood before him, helpless, desperate.

Sasha shook his head. He steered her to Michail. "You've got to leave, now. I'll find you, I promise." He took a ruble from his pocket and folded it into his sister's outstretched hand. "Do it for Ana."

Michail pulled her into the alley and they hurried to the street. The droshky was gone. He wasn't surprised or even angry. Anyone would have left at the sound of a gunshot at this particular address. They began walking as swiftly as they could without breaking into a run that might arouse suspicion. The lights of the hospital shone in the distance. They would find transportation there.

Sasha watched them until they left the alley and merged with the darkness. He slammed the trunk of the Puzyrev shut. Dudorov was dead but still manipulating everyone, sneering with satisfaction as he went to hell. The bullet had settled the score Sasha had been keeping for months as he suffered through Dudorov's advances and the threats that gave him no choice but to pull urchins off the street. But though those ordeals were over, Dudorov had still won. Now Sasha would be on the run. At least Ana was safe. He'd been afraid that Dudorov, or his cronies, would abuse her or sell her to a pimp. But he'd kept one step ahead of them all, hiding her in the old barns and sheds on the edge of the Vodyanaya Ravine, paying trustworthy boys to keep watch when he couldn't be with her.

Ivan thrust a broom into his hands. Sasha reached for the bucket and threw the water across the porch. The red and brown stains spread, coloring the entire surface of the porch. He got on his knees and began to scrub.

34

THE LILACS WERE BLOOMING ALONG the alley. Heddie sat on the back porch and counted the bushes she and Elena had planted, shortly after the girl arrived. The deep purple blossoms, pungent and intoxicating, made her nostalgic for the past; when the house had been full of laughter, wealthy clients, sparkling champagne, music, and sex. This time of year she would bring armfuls of lilacs into the kitchen and fill every urn and vase she had, then direct the girls to carry them to the salons and the exclusive bedroom suites. Now that her house was shuttered, with the Cheka out front, she hadn't had the energy for flowers. The one time she looked out the kitchen window, the bushes had been clipped severely, and the blossoms were sparse, thanks to the work of market sellers who had raided her beautiful thick clumps to make a few kopeks. Why hadn't she thought of that? She could have had Elena cut them. Boris could have sold them at a black market.

Heddie felt trapped and fearful. Like everyone in the city, she never knew what the next day would bring. Her savings were dwindling, and she'd been reduced to selling her silver cutlery on the sly. Her only hope was that she and Boris could book passage on a train or steamer.

She kicked off her slippers and put on her garden clogs. The few lilacs that remained on the old bushes were better than nothing. She found a pair of pruning shears and went out to cut what was left.

"I managed to get the last copy of Izvestia," Boris called out. He walked up the alley and handed her the newspaper, waiting for her reaction to the bold headline splayed across the extra edition.

"Oh!" she said. "I have to sit down. Here, take these flowers. I can't believe this has happened. They say it was the night before last." Hurrying to the kitchen she set the newspaper on the counter and ran her index finger along the printed lines. "Good Lord, he was assassinated." She turned to Boris. "Well, I'm not surprised. He was such a dreadful man—must have made enemies all over the city. Listen to this. 'Special measures must be taken to fight counterrevolution and sabotage.' I suppose they'll make him a war hero now. A martyr to the People's cause."

Boris leaned over her shoulder and laughed with scorn at the photo of Dudorov in military dress. "The Deputy was an important officer in the Red Army. Can't deny him that, even if he was a bastard."

"Hush! It's dangerous to talk like that."

"They'll scour the city looking for his killer. Does it say they've rounded up anyone?"

"They found his car at Quarantine Harbor. They've brought in five dockers as suspects." She scanned a few more lines. "They've arrested people in the Moldavanka as well."

"Of course they did," Boris said. He put the flowers in the sink. "It's a good opportunity to execute every thug in Odessa."

She tapped her finger on the newsprint. "It will be Fanya Kaplan all over again. She alone guns down Lenin, but somehow over five hundred are executed and thousands more vanished to labor camps."

"Let's keep things in perspective. Dudorov was a significant local player, but he wasn't Lenin. He can be easily replaced."

"Do you think they'll call me in for questioning?" She looked up at Boris, panic in her eyes.

"Depends on what they learn. I imagine someone in the ranks shot him — a revenge killing, that sort of thing."

"Just when I thought our lives couldn't get any worse!"

"If they knock on the door, I'll go with you," he said.

"No, no." She was grateful for his offer, but she knew how it worked. The agents would play them against each other, and they'd both be lost. The cunning and violent Cheka had destroyed the lives of thousands. She set aside the newspaper and wiped the ink from her fingers. "Boris, I'm terrified."

She realized she was shaking. She put her hands on the sink to brace herself. After a moment, she poured water into a blue porcelain vase and filled it with the lilacs. "Lovely, isn't it?" she said. She closed her eyes and took in the fragrance. "So many small and intimate things keep me going these days." She held out her arms to the room. "The sunlight in here is marvelous. I never saw it until now, with all the night-time hours we kept." She picked up the lilacs and headed to the green salon. "Would you please ask Elena if she'd be willing to come downstairs? I'd love to hear some Lysenko. A polonaise is perfect for spring. I need a diversion or I'll go mad."

Michail lit another cigarette and blew the smoke out his attic window. The new shag was rough but at least filled his tobacco pouch. The starlight of early morning still glittered in the dark. He scanned the sky and steadied his gaze on the North Star. He thought again about the Deputy's killing, three nights before. Unable to sleep ever since, he had taken to sitting at the window and worrying about the days ahead. The street below was quiet, except for the faint and intermittent voices of dockers heading to the port for the first shift of the day.

From the corner of his eye he unexpectedly saw the glow of a cigarette shaking in the yard. Drawn to the curious signal, he stubbed out his own cigarette and watched it. It went out, but then, moments later, it reappeared. The small round light traveled up and down, drawing a thin red line that penetrated the darkness.

He glanced at Elvira Maria and Ana, asleep beneath the quilt, their breath intertwined. He crept down the stairs and cautiously entered the yard. Ivan, standing in the cluster of acacia trees, waved him over.

"I knew you'd come sooner or later," Michail said. He embraced him, felt the fear in Ivan's body. He stepped back to take a good look and held him close once more.

"I'm leaving for Stamboul in an hour," Ivan said. His voice was hoarse and urgent. "I don't have any other choice."

"Did the Cheka come to the shophouse?"

"I thought they would, but no sign yet. We covered the tire tracks when we moved the car to Quarantine Harbor. Dudorov had been drinking there all day. We hoped the agents would assume he'd never left."

"Maybe you're in the clear then," Michail said.

"Oh, they'll find the house. It's just a matter of time. The girls are gone, but the guns are there with everything else. Too dangerous to move."

"Where's Sasha?"

"Underground." They had parted after they ditched the car. He'd watched Sasha run between the half-lit shelters and jetties that dotted the shoreline, as he headed north to Peresuip. "He'll have to stay out of sight until he finds a way to escape Odessa. The Cheka know he was Dudorov's pet. He must be their top suspect."

"What a nightmare. Tatiana?"

"She's run off. Disappeared into the streets."

The union bell clanged at the dockyards. The first shift had started.

"You'll take the cargo ship?" Michail asked.

"I know it well. It's easy to slip through when they're loading."

"It's not like we thought it would be," Michail said. "Remember all those dreams we had in Mińsk?" For two years they'd planned their trip to Odessa, saved every coin to make it happen, and like delirious fools, talked of gaining fame and fortune.

"I prefer the dreams we had here," Ivan said. "Those days at the Palmyra." Where they'd sat at the beach-side café and watched the elegant women pass by with their radiant smiles and shapely figures. "Nothing like that back home."

"We should have stayed with my old man—and my uncle, your favorite printer. You know, he loved you more than me."

"Stop that." Ivan shook Michail's shoulder. "Both of them wanted us to go. Make a better life."

"You think we did?"

"Don't ask me that now." He pulled a bundle of rubles from his tunic and handed them to Michail, who pushed them away. "No, take it," Ivan said. "You'll need it. I've got plenty to get me to America and set up some kind of business."

"I'll miss you," Michail said. They kissed and stood clinging to each other. "Go with God, my friend."

"Michail, you know I'm not a believer."

"Hedge your bets anyway."

Ivan laughed as he disappeared into the darkness.

Such bravado, Michail thought. The Bolshevik Revolution, Ivan's passion, had imprisoned him at every turn with its inevitable violence, corruption, and deception. He'd played a dangerous game with Dudorov and the Cheka. And now he was going to America, the citadel of capitalism, armed with a wallet full of worthless rubles. It was ironic, tragic. Michail wondered if Ivan would ever be at peace with himself. Knowing the man like he did, he was sure Ivan would wrestle with his conscience forever, trying to understand what went wrong.

Michail stayed in the yard to watch the sunrise. A breeze from the Black Sea blew through the yard, rustling the leaves of the acacia trees.

Days later, he sat at his workbench, Elvira Maria and Ana nearby. He smoothed the scallops on the dress of the Frog

Princess and offered it to Ana. "You can carry her to the performance," he said. "She's yours now."

Ana looked to Elvira Maria, and seeing her mother nod, eagerly took the puppet. She sat on the floor and ran her finger across the green sequins sewn to its headdress.

"Look," she said. "They sparkle."

"Yes," Elvira Maria said. "Like the fireflies in our old garden." She kissed the top of Ana's head and buttoned her sweater, a hand-me-down from Nadia.

Now that Ana was safely in her keep, Elvira Maria was an attentive mother, assessing her needs and moods as never before. At night she woke to caress her, to make certain she was within her reach. What had she suffered? How had she lived on the streets with all those wild and dangerous children, all those predatory men? Ana said that Sasha brought her food several times a week when she stayed in the ravine above the Moldavanka. Sausages, she said, and cheese. His boss never finished his meals. Sasha said he preferred to drink than to eat. Her belly had been full on those days. But there had been plenty of other days, when he hadn't been able to come, and her stomach had ached. She waited, sat in the doorway of the barn, and sucked her fingers until they were wrinkled and white like the worms she had. Hungry, she went to town with other children who lived in the hills.

"We ate from trash bins on the back steps of taverns," she said. She tugged on a strand of her hair as she spoke to Elvira Maria. "Sometimes we shared a good morsel, but mostly we fought over scraps and burnt mush."

Since her rescue she gobbled everything Elvira Maria and Michail fed her. She discarded her spoon and shoved bread, and even soup, in her mouth with her hands, mewing like a starved animal. Elvira Maria found bread-crumbs and clumps of dirt in her pockets that she saved and ate secretly. At bedtime she curled into a little ball beneath the quilt. It was then that she remembered the stampede at the train tracks, being pushed into a freight car with Sasha, who had held onto her arm. A man with a rifle and sour breath had lifted them onto a stack of lug-gage and told them not to move. She'd screamed time and again for her mother, not realizing Elvira Maria wasn't on board. When she and Sasha arrived in Odessa, they spent hours at the station house and yard, looking in vain for Elvira Maria. Finally, they joined other lost children and roamed the back streets in search of food.

Ana lifted the scallops on the dress of the Frog Princess to examine its long legs and striped stockings. "I found a doll in the tunnels once," she said.

Elvira Maria knew she was referring to the catacombs in the Moldavanka where children lived when the weather was bad. "Did you and Sasha stay there?" she asked.

"No, the boys were too rough. They wanted to cut my hair and sell it."

Elvira Maria stared at her long braids, dry and dull, but worth a fortune to needy children. Each time Ana told her a story like this she was ashamed of what had happened. She felt like an imposter, pretending to be a good mother.

She placed a hand on the banners for their morning show and looked at Michail. "I'm ready," she said, forcing an uneasy smile. "You're sure it's wise to go out today?"

"We'll be safer in Deribasov Garden where we usually perform," he said. They'd been hostage to the attic for almost a week, and he knew Odessans expected to see a performance when the weather was sunny and mild. It would be suspicious if they didn't show. "Just pretend everything's fine," he said. "We're doing what we always do." He grabbed the sacks of props and puppets.

Outside, a noisy flock of gulls rose from the gutter. They arched above the tenement and flew out over the harbor. Gogolya Street was busy as usual. Beggars and street urchins besieged them for handouts as they walked along. Students, gathered before the windows of the reading room, peered at the volumes of Gorky and Lenin displayed in a dusty window. Nearby, another student was summoning a crowd with Alexander Blok's recent prophetic poem, "The Scythians." The broadside quivering in his hand, he implored brothers to sheath their swords and share a feast. Elvira Maria and Michail, impressed with the young man's passionate recitation, paused to hear his final stanza. Before they continued on, she looked across the street at Monsieur Oury's shop. A new sign was posted on his door. The small letters read: BY APPOINTMENT ONLY.

They passed the lion statues and entered the garden, sheltered by the age-old chestnut trees. Elvira Maria felt soothed by the familiar, tranquil place. She watched Ana chase two pigeons on the cobblestone walkway. Greeting the babushkas who sold herbs, she took comfort in the genuine friendships she'd established with them over time. They knew of her loss, had passed her photograph around while she had commiserated with their similar stories of family members who had disappeared, were killed in battle, or succumbed to sickness. Everyone she met in Odessa was touched by the circumstances of an era fraught with war, hunger, and political upheaval. Few could recall a day without worry.

Now introducing her daughter to the women she was happy, an emotion that felt foreign after months of heartache. As astonished, tearful friends came forward to embrace her and dote on Ana, she accepted their joy and their kindness. The shy little girl standing before them was a miracle most could only pray for.

While they assembled the puppet stage Elvira Maria kept Ana next to her. She helped her open and close the curtains and showed her how the scenery panels moved up and down. Vigilant, she steered clear of the strangers who came backstage before the show and let Michail answer their questions. Ana's hand in hers, she scanned the surrounding streets and looked for the lorry that brought Sasha to the garden weeks ago, knowing it was most likely long gone. Still reluctant to accept the fact that he'd been part of a criminal gang that had kidnapped children from Odessa's streets, she held him in her heart and prayed for his imperiled soul. He had protected Ana against the worst and paid a terrible price.

Suddenly, a lorry skidded through the intersection at Deribasovskaya Street. The driver shouted at an old man wheeling a barrow piled high with baling wire. Her body went rigid, but the lorry moved on, passing the edge of the garden in a fury as it headed south.

35

MICHAIL SECURED HIS STAGE AND SCENERY in the shed. The morning's performance had been quiet despite his efforts to rouse the audience with jokes and songs. Although he could never be sure, he suspected Cheka agents had been in the crowd, taking note of his performance and dampening the spirits of an audience that had dwindled sharply by the time he had finished. He checked his purse and was relieved he had enough money to buy rye bread from Volodya, who sold the loaves secretly to a handful of customers he trusted. He didn't relish the long trip to Peresuip, where Volodya sold the precious bread, but the quality and price made it worth it.

That was what he was thinking about—rye bread—when Pavlo ran up to the tenement gate and seized his arm.

"Two men broke into your place," he said. "They just left, headed for the dockyards."

Michail rushed into the vestibule, Pavlo at his back. "Did you recognize them?"

"No. Might be Cheka," he said, excited about the intrigue under his own roof. "They wore leather jackets."

Michail climbed the stairs two at a time, leaving Pavlo at the front door. He joined Elvira Maria and Ana on the landing.

"The door was open," Elvira Maria said. She gripped the railing for support. "They've ransacked the attic, destroyed everything." She followed him up the last set of stairs.

The room was strewn with crushed glass, upturned furniture, torn fabric, and broken pots of paint and glue. Leather dolls and costumed puppets that once lined the walls lay in mangled heaps, their limbs torn apart and desecrated with ashes from the firebox.

He picked his way through the debris, straw from the slit mattress clinging to his boots. At the far corner of the attic he bent down and retrieved the broken wing of his brown-feathered Solovei, the puppet smashed against the wall pegs where it once had perched majestically. He felt for the hidden purse and pulled it out. Kissing it, he tucked it inside his tunic. As he looked at the shattered puppets the memory of his grandfather came to his mind, the bearded old man trotting the Golden Reindeer through the tundra, urging the children out front to paddle their knees, as if they were running along. Michail turned away.

Elvira Maria and Ana stepped around the overturned workbench. Unwinding a strip of soiled cloth from a crate, Elvira Maria set the box at the window and gestured for Ana to sit.

"What's happened?" Ana asked, a worried expression darkening her face. "Why are the puppets broken?" She picked up a small headdress and shook out shards of glass.

"Troublemakers came here while we were gone, Annushka." Elvira Maria put her arm around her. "It will take some time to fix everything."

"We'll need to wash the floor," Ana said. Footprints in the trail of ashes crisscrossed the room.

Elvira Maria went to Michail, still standing with Solovei's wing in his hand. "Come, let's sit down." She lifted the remains of the battered puppet from the wall and guided Michail to the mattress, where she held him gently.

"Such senseless destruction," he said, his voice breaking. He took the puppet and brushed the long feathers still attached.

"It's cruel," she whispered.

"Yes, it is. Part of this endless war." He looked at his carving tools scattered across the floor.

She called Ana and settled her on her lap. Together they clung to each other as shouts and a volley of gunfire rose from a distant building.

Pavlo stood at the top of the stairs and stuck his head through the open door. "I was down the street when they came," he said defensively. "Nobody was here." He folded his arms across his chest and nodded to the string of bells dangling from a leg of the workbench. "They sure didn't spare you nothing."

"They must have been here quite a while," Michail said.

Pavlo entered the room and closed the door. He stopped and stared at a large black and white photograph nailed to the inside panel. "Michail!" he cried. He stepped back, a hand clasped over his mouth.

Michail scrambled up from the mattress and hurried across the room. He looked at the photo and then, shut his eyes and steadied himself against the wall. Moments later, he ripped it from the door and took it to the stove. While red flames twined around the image, he quietly said a prayer in a dialect Elvira Maria didn't know. Unable to tend to the room or his puppets, he sat before the grate.

She'd caught a glimpse of the photo before Michail burned it, the depiction of Ivan's tortured body laid out in a courtyard of garbage, ENEMY OF THE PEOPLE scrawled across it in red letters. Trembling, she began to clean the attic hoping her fears would subside if she kept busy. But instead, memories of Ivan and the shophouse plagued her. After she'd learned he was trafficking children, she had stayed awake each night and prayed that Fate would intervene on her behalf, and ruin Ivan in ways that she could not. Now that it had happened she was not gratified, as she'd imagined she would be, but was stunned and more distraught than ever. She placed the damaged puppets on a clean cloth beneath the eaves in the attic. Each one was once so meticulously crafted and real, she could hardly bear to look at them. Their torn, disfigured bodies made her think of Ivan, painful enough, but then made her think of what the regime would do to Dudorov's killer, if they ever discovered it was not Ivan.

Dusting off Beauty, a puppet that had survived the raid with only a few scratches, she tried to save what could be saved of these wise old grandfathers and babushkas, swooping birds, magical reindeer, and foolish dumplings — the folk history of the region. She and Ana sorted through broken objects most of the afternoon, looking for bits and pieces of puppets, setting aside what could be salvaged.

Later, she took up the broom and swept the room again. She filled a bucket with ashes and straw. The photograph lingered in her mind—Ivan's open eyes, the startled expression on his face. His execution and the violent break-in made her feel helpless. She worried about Michail. His life had been calmer, had been his own, before he met her and had gotten involved in her problems.

The cathedral bells chimed seven, signaling the work-day's end. She took the bucket down to the street. As she emptied it into the sewer she noticed the sparkling tiny crossbow she'd made weeks ago. The bow was cracked and the arrow missing. She picked it out of the ashes and put it in her pocket. Ilyá Múromets, the fearless knight, would need it again. She would give it to Ana and ask her to repair it for Michail. She was fascinated with the puppets.

"Want some help?" Pavlo asked. He stood on the other side of the gutter, leaning against a lamppost.

"I can manage," she said.

"I'm not afraid to help you." He took a step toward her. "Nobody in the house wants to go to the attic or be seen with Michail. They think it's dangerous, think they'll be next."

"That's a shame," she said. "He's been kind to every-one, helping whenever they've asked. He'd appreciate their support."

"They're scared," he said. "Just a pack of hungry wolves afraid of the forest. They'll come around begging in a couple of weeks when they need something."

It broke her heart, the things this war and these times had taught children about life. "Good night Pavlo. I'll let Michail know you're available."

She returned to the attic to find Michail standing in the darkening room before his workbench. He opened their labor books and checked the dates. Setting them aside, he unfolded another document, counted the pages, and placed it on top of a set bearing his photograph.

"Do you have your papers from Kos?" he asked.

She reached into her bodice and pulled out her internal passport, a ration card, and two baptismal certificates, one for each child.

He studied them. "Everything looks fine," he said, handing them back to her. "Carry these on your person. Don't leave them in the attic or give them to anyone. They're difficult to get. We can't move without them."

"Do you think we should leave Odessa?" Still waiting to hear from Sasha, she was alarmed by the sudden prospect.

"If things get worse we'll have to."

She kept her thoughts to herself. It was not the time to discuss Sasha.

He tucked his papers in his tunic and turned to his carving tools. "I can repair these," he said. He examined a curved blade attached to a smooth white handle made of antler. "At least the steel isn't damaged. They don't forge metal like this anymore. Look." He showed the knife to Elvira Maria. "This one has a red agate decorating the shaft."

"Let me see," Ana said. She ran to join them.

Michail bent down and pointed to the stone. "My grandfather had the tools made when he was in Budapest performing for a wealthy Turkish merchant. The Ottomans still lived in the city when he was young."

"Can I have this one?"

"Ana," Elvira Maria said, "don't be so forward."

"It's all right." He smiled. "I'm happy she's impressed."

He placed the knife on the workbench and inspected the rest while Elvira Maria sang Ana to sleep. After he cleaned the glue and ashes from each tool, he wrapped them in cloth and put them in a box. He went downstairs and out to the yard. Thankful no one was there to disturb him, he sat beneath the trees, his head in his hands.

36

HEDDIE READ THE EVICTION NOTICE a second time. She flung the papers on the sofa. In a week, on the seventeenth of May, the Bolsheviks were appropriating her house. It was an outrage. Her mother had opened the brothel on that very day, more than thirty years ago. It was an anniversary Heddie celebrated at the casino ever since Tsilia had passed. Playing the number seventeen at the roulette wheel, she'd always beaten the odds and gone home with a fortune. Now her luck had changed.

Boris examined the notice. The date was stamped on every page. He smoked his last Murad, inhaling the sweet-tasting tobacco deeply. He feared it would be a long time until he smoked another.

"How dare they bother me at six in the morning," she said, remembering the embarrassment of being caught off-guard.

Unable to accept being evicted from her home, she'd listened to the new Housing Commissar read the order, and had hinted that the issue could be settled with a few resources. That was the protocol with city officials and military brass. They *always* accepted a bribe. But this Bolshevik commissar had been too young and too high-minded to understand and follow her lead. Guarding her rubles, for fear of losing them, she'd finally pleaded with him and offered to live discreetly in the upper rooms. But she had been dismissed; informed that her house, the best the district could offer, soon would become the central office for Red Army personnel.

"They're requisitioning it all," she cried. "The entire house and furnishings. They say everything belongs to the People. Whatever will the People do with an oval mirror above a double brass bed?"

"You'd be surprised," Boris said. "They'll sell it or ship it to Moscow." He looked around at the crystal, jeweled lamps, and figurines she'd collected, a small fraction of her valuables. He had counted them all at the end of each and every lavish party. "Should we call in a few speculators and make our own arrangements?"

"I wish we could," she said, "but they're watching. It's too risky. Heaven knows they'd shoot us in an instant. And who's to stop them?" She caressed the mahogany trim on an ornate loveseat. "I knew when I survived the last pogrom they'd make my life hell."

"I never thought we'd last this long."

"Boris, we've done our best — coddled, bribed, entertained, and seduced every man of consequence living in Odessa. I've spent a fortune and calculated every move. I should have lied on that horrible occupancy report and tripled the numbers."

"It's a pity Dashkevich didn't serve the notice," he

said. "We might have worked a deal with him, given his shady connections to Dudorov and his dhimmi boys."

"Why do they keep changing officers?"

"To keep control, *Comrade*."

She laughed at his sarcasm. Approaching the piano, she ran her fingers across the ivory keys. "I can't believe they're taking my Erard. I'll never forgive them. Remember when it came on the train that hot summer evening?"

"If I think about our past I won't survive the future," he said.

She headed to the stairs. "Bring your coat up to my bedroom before you go out," she said. "I need to sew some gemstones into the lining when I'm finished with mine."

"I'll get it from the closet right now."

The lime-colored parrots and emerald vines twisting through the lounge were vibrant in the daylight that entered through the partially opened curtains. After Michail had finished the mural, she'd always seen it at night when the chandelier was lit and an amber glow colored everything in the room. She pushed the curtains aside until they were fully open. Placing her hand on the wall she examined the parrots, the glossy leaves and palm trees. Michail had painted them five different shades of green. They truly resembled the ones in her picture book of Martinique. She stepped back and admired the fleshy girls posed alongside the blue and turquoise waterfall. The ripples sparkled with flecks of shiny white paint. The mural had been the highlight of the house, the amusement that had lifted her spirits when she felt defeated. It would soon be destroyed. Tears filled her eyes, the vines became blurry. She wiped her wet cheeks, annoyed with the smudges of mascara on her handkerchief. "They'll probably paint the walls beige," she muttered to herself. Heddie closed the curtains.

Reaching the third floor, she stood beside Elena's open door. "Bonjour, mon petit chou," she called softly. "It's me."

Elena, dressed in her navy and white walking suit, placed a frilly nightgown in the suitcase on her bed. "I can't decide what to pack," she said. "I have so many clothes and precious gifts from old friends."

"Try to be practical," Heddie said. Within a week Elena would be working in Roza's tea stall at the train station. Heddie advised her to pack a large apron and a comfortable pair of shoes. "Don't be glamorous or you'll have trouble with the customers." She sat on the bed and looked at the contents of the suitcase.

"May I take some sheet music?" Elena asked. She sat beside her.

"Take whatever you like." Heddie refolded a blouse and tucked it in place. "I wish I could give you the piano."

"I'll find another. Perhaps the conservatory will reopen in the fall."

"I hope your new lodging at Fanconi's isn't a wreck," Heddie said. "Since they've closed the café and changed owners the rooms upstairs haven't been renovated. I'd hate to see you sleeping with spiders and mice."

"I'll get by. I won't be alone. The rooms are filled with the other girls. We all need to start anew."

Heddie looked at her left index finger and loosened her amethyst set in gold. She slipped off the ring and gave it to Elena. "I had this made years ago and I want you to have it."

"Heddie!" Elena burst into tears and embraced her. "Are you sure?"

"Yes, it's yours. But don't be foolish and wear it in public. No. Not these days. Keep it hidden next to your heart."

"It's beautiful. Oh, it's exquisite!" Elena placed the ring on her finger and held out her hand.

"If you truly must sell it make sure you get a good price," Heddie said. "When times are harrowing the dealers are ruthless."

"I'll never sell it, Heddie. I promise, I'll keep it forever."

"My dear, I wish I shared your conviction."

37

NADIA, WEARING HER BLUE DRESS and apron, her wild brown hair now streaked with gray, sliced a piece of potato and tossed it in the pot. It joined the shreds of a carrot and turnip she'd saved for at least two weeks. She'd been reluctant to cook all the vegetables at once and deplete her supplies. Usually she measured and divided their food, or stretched it out until it was watery gruel, and, at the end of each week, she refused to eat and fed the children her portion. But her husband had threatened to kill a rat and roast it in the yard if things didn't improve and today was Lydia's sixteenth birthday and Nadia was sick of being frugal. She'd take the chance that rations would be better in the days ahead, now that it was spring. Meanwhile, her skinny daughter deserved a good meal.

The steam from the pot rose and circled the portrait of Lenin that hung in the kitchen. There was a knock on the door: Elvira Maria and Ana. She pulled them into the room and kissed their cheeks. "I can't believe I'm out of bread," she said. "How can we eat a soup without it?"

Elvira Maria handed her a bunch of sorrel she'd picked earlier in the day. "Perhaps this will help."

"Thank you, ten times over."

Ana, carrying her Frog Princess, joined Nadia's younger daughters in the bedroom. Elvira Maria set the embroidered headband she'd made for Lydia on the table and removed her shawl. She was wearing a dress Heddie had sent her. Loose-fitting, and cut from jacquard crepe, it was pale yellow and printed with blue and green ferns.

"Look at you," Nadia said. "You've walked out of a fashion magazine." She rotated her hand above her head and Elvira Maria spun around to model the dress. She laughed, felt self-conscious. It had been difficult to pack up the black dress she'd been wearing for so long and put aside her mourning, but she knew her life had changed. The old one, threadbare and faded, the skirts drooping, belonged to Kos. Michail loved the new one, and the organdy camisole she now wore with it. Nadia examined the fabric and asked how she'd gotten the dress. "Most people wouldn't give a treasure like that away," Nadia said. "They'd sell it." She pointed to her sleeve, ripped at the elbow. "Look at this," she laughed. "You're more fortunate than me."

"In some things I am," Elvira Maria said. "In others, not at all." She was thinking of Sasha, but Nadia inquired about Michail.

"He hasn't slept for two weeks," Elvira Maria said. "Just sits by the window all night."

Rumors had circulated quickly after the break-in, and were fueled by government reports that charged Ivan with Dudorov's murder. Some occupants in the house claimed

Ivan worked for the Cheka and got what he deserved. Others whispered that Dudorov was the first of many on his hit list. Elvira Maria was thankful no one had mentioned Sasha. But people had seen Michail with Ivan, and several asked her about that. She reminded them that they too had old friends who changed during the war. Besides, she added, Michail had incurred the wrath of the Cheka by criticizing the regime when he performed. Everyone knew that.

"I'm sorry his puppets are ruined," Nadia said. "But Ivan's to blame. If he killed Deputy Dudorov, like they say, he put Michail at risk." She added the sorrel to the pot and stirred. "He must have had accomplices, don't you think?"

Elvira Maria quickly opened the window and shook out the tablecloth. Then turning to Nadia's dishes, she selected a blue plate and matching bowl for Lydia. As she picked up the silverware she noticed Ana had returned to the kitchen. She was stacking the other girls' dolls, blocks, and clothes in a corner behind the laundry basket. The girls complained, but she continued to trot back and forth. Finally, standing in front of the pile, she waved a hairbrush and told them to leave her alone.

Elvira Maria dragged her to a chair. "Sit down," she said. "If you want to play you must share." Ana burst out crying. To stop her tears, she chewed the paw of her Frog Princess. "I don't know what to do," Elvira Maria said. "She was never like this before."

"What can you expect?" Nadia asked. "She's been on the street. Give it time."

Michail arrived with Lydia and Nadia's husband. They sat around the table and rolled thin cigarettes while they waited for the soup. He asked Lydia about her boyfriend, a writer who'd posted a free speech manifesto on the street and now was standing trial.

"He'll win in the end," she said. "Truth will prevail. That's my birthday wish."

Michail took out his flask of vodka and lined up five glasses. "It's the last," he said, holding it up while everyone cheered. They toasted Lydia and drank. The vodka he'd stretched since New Year's warmed their throats and kindled Lydia's wish.

The next day, Elvira Maria washed the floor in her room. As she opened the window a warm breeze, smelling of fish, salt, and seaweed, greeted her. When she first arrived the strange odor had made her nauseous. She kept the window closed. Nadia told her that sailors read the weather by putting their noses to the wind and recommended she should do the same. Instead, she watched the clouds, as she had in Kos, and based her predictions on how they moved across the sky, changing from silver to black in minutes when a storm rolled in. Now she was accustomed to the smell and welcomed the moist air that came with it.

She sat at her desk and remembered how insecure she'd felt clumsily holding a pencil to write her first letters. Not wanting to waste paper, she'd traced them in the dust on the windowsill and glass, always fearing someone might come to her room and discover how foolish she was, sitting there with dirt on her lap. When she heard Michail move about in his attic she felt guilty she now cared for a man other than Lev. How many hours had she turned in her narrow bed, longing for the children, listening to the night? The room had been her refuge, but it was full of worry. Thankfully, she no longer needed it.

Michail and Boris climbed the last round of stairs. She jumped up and got out of their way. They were carrying Heddie's steamer trunk, their muscles straining, sweat lining their brows. The trunk was massive. They struggled to pass it through the doorway. Once inside, it took up most of the room. They pushed it beside the desk, as out of the way as possible, and collapsed on the bed.

Heddie stood in the hallway catching her breath from the steep climb, a heavy winter shuba in her arms. "I'm sorry," she said. "I couldn't leave with just a suitcase."

Elvira Maria took the last of her things, a small tin box containing three hair pins and a sliver of soap. "I hope you'll be comfortable," she said, handing Heddie the key.

"Thank you for giving me the room." Heddie tucked the key in her bosom.

Boris stood, still panting a little, and tipped his cap. "I'll stop by this evening to see if you need anything," he said. He had moved to Fanconi's Café and would sleep in the linen closet, a stuffy alcove full of napkins, curtains, cushions, and flittering moths.

When he and Michail reached the street they spoke in hushed voices. "It's been a terrible shock," Boris said. "I hope she'll adapt."

"We'll do what we can to make her comfortable, but it's rough over here." Michail nodded toward a woman slouched against the hood of a parked car, a dark green bottle in her hand.

"She's convinced it's temporary," Boris said. "She wants to book passage on a steamer. One day we're going to Hamburg, the next to London, then suddenly she's talking about Paris. If she comes across a Zionist tract, we'll be headed for Palestine."

"Do you have travel papers?" Michail asked.

"I've been working on that for some time," Boris said. Forged documents and counterfeit papers had always been available in the city, but since the war business was thriving. The urgency of the moment and the thousands of people wanting to leave Russia kept underground printers busy. "Why?" he asked. "Do you need a set?"

"I'm fine, for now," Michail said. Though he had a contact, a friend of Ivan's who'd lost faith in the Bolsheviks, he knew that Boris and Heddie were connected to more reliable and discriminating sources.

Boris kept his eyes on the soldiers loitering nearby. "I'm terribly sorry to hear about your theater. The destruction is one thing but the personal violation is quite another. We must be on our guard with these hooligans in charge."

"They made their point," Michail said. "I hope that's the end of it."

"I didn't realize Dashkevich was an old friend of yours."

"We grew up together, toured with the show. We had our differences, but still stayed in touch."

"I pity anyone who had to deal with Dudorov. I can't say I liked Dashkevich, but he deserved a trial. The execution was barbaric. And I don't mean to be presumptuous, but I don't trust the reporting or the gossip. I think Dashkevich was a true believer — couldn't have been a gunrunner for the Imperial Army. I'm not even sure he pulled the trigger, seems too far fetched. My guess is the manhunt is continuing."

"Who really knows?" Michail said.

"I hope you'll get back on your feet soon." Boris clapped Michail on the shoulder and shook his hand. "The Cheka must miss your delightful puppets. I imagine their agents have enjoyed every show."

He proceeded down the dingy street, his thick silver hair shining beneath his cap, his face clean-shaven, head held high. At the intersection he joined a klatch of intimidated pedestrians held hostage to the edge of the street by the lorries swerving between horse-drawn carts and armored cars. Impatient, he stepped forward and raised his hand, stopping the traffic. Screeches of tires and brakes and curses of drivers ensued, but the traffic stopped. He took the heavy basket of a sullen-faced babushka and guided her and a trail of shop girls safely through the mayhem.

Michail headed back to the tenement, crossing Gogolya Street to avoid the Red Army soldiers patrolling the district. Children, armed with balls and sticks, headed home from Deribasov Garden. They called to each other as they ran along the walkway and skipped over cracks. A scrawny boy, crouched beside the tenement door, held out his hand as Michail passed. He slipped him a few coins, and, heavy-footed climbed the stairs to the attic.

38

The month of May ended as the street lights surrounding the tenement flickered and then blinked
out. The neighborhood was plunged into darkness. The
power outage, the second in a month, had come just as
Elvira Maria had started reading the Izvestia she'd gotten
from Heddie. She wondered which insurgent faction had
sabotaged the station this time, and if all the lines in the
city were damaged.

With the help of the moonlight, she trimmed the
wick of the tallow lamp and lit it. The flame sputtered and
caught hold. A spiral of smoke rose to the rafters.

As she waited for Michail to return from Volodya's
with the bread he'd been determined to buy she agonized
about his safety. Robberies were common, and with the
bulky loaves under his tunic he'd be an easy target. If the
tramlines were down she prayed he would hire a droshky
to bring him home. Peresuip, with its factories, twisted
lanes, and overcrowded tenements, was heavily policed,
but dangerous despite the surveillance.

She could hear Pavlo shouting to the vagrants gathered in front of the shed. She looked out the window, but could not see him. He spent his time with a gang of homeless boys who stole from passersby and prowled the dockyards looking for contraband. She'd seen him several times in the yard, polishing a knife or holding hands with a young girl who propositioned soldiers in the alley. He looked rough in his dirty clothes, his boots without laces, his face tired and bruised. Since the break-in he'd avoided Michail, despite his initial promises of support. Only Danya climbed the stairs to the attic now, to cadge a piece of bread or see if Ana wanted to play. He said that Pavlo had argued with Tolya and wasn't allowed to sleep in the vestibule anymore.

When she thought about Pavlo, she thought about Sasha, the two boys of similar age. Was Sasha in Odessa still or had he run to the countryside where life was perilous in a different way, famine closing in? Perhaps he had gone to Kos, though that would have been hard. It was so far away and arranging transportation would be difficult if he had to remain undercover. Besides, Kos wouldn't offer safety. The Cheka would be sure to search there if they suspected he was involved in Dudorov's murder.

Ana, sitting on the bed in the dim light, chattered to her Frog Princess and fed it imaginary food. Her arms and legs were like sticks; her face still as colorless as the night she'd arrived, but she was calmer, at least when she played by herself. It would take time for her to recover. Nadia was right when she'd said children were resilient if they were loved and protected, had shelter and food. Elvira Maria could give Ana those vital necessities, but not Sasha—if he remained a fugitive. She wondered if it would always be so, and if she would struggle with that grief for the rest of her days.

She heard Michail greet a neighbor on the landing and ran to open the door. She threw her arms around him. "Are you glad to see me or the bread?" he asked. He returned her embrace and kissed her cheeks, then pried her arms away so he could hand her the small round loaf. "Volodya couldn't spare any more."

"It's wonderful," she said. She closed her eyes and inhaled the sweet fragrance of rye. It reminded her of Kos, when she'd seasoned her loaves with caraway seeds. "What's happening out there?"

"It's dark everywhere," he said. "Plenty of activity. Soldiers and Cheka on the streets protecting us from counterrevolutionaries and thieves."

"Of course."

"Rumor has it they'll repair the station as soon as they can get the parts."

"Just like the last time."

"Isn't it good to know some things are predictable these days?" he asked.

"Let's eat." She placed three bowls on the workbench. She'd scraped together some beet greens and garlic, even had found a patch of chicory on the hillside. "I've been quite resourceful while you've been gone."

"Me too," he said. He went to the stairs and returned with one of the old gunnysacks he'd used for stage props.

"What have you got in there?"

"Our supper." He handed her several puppets from the sack. Then smiling triumphantly, he pulled out a plump, dead pigeon.

"Oh, Michail!" She touched it, considered its size. "Were you in Deribasov Garden?"

"Shhh."

"You could have been arrested."

"I want a feather," Ana said. "Please Mama?" She jumped up and ran to look closely at the bird.

"Here's a long one," Michail said. He plucked a gray plume from the bird's wing. "See how the color changes when you hold it to the light?"

"Such a surprise!" Elvira Maria said. "Thank goodness we still have a pot to cook it in." She handed Michail her knife. As he plucked the bird she set aside the feathers, knowing he would use them for his puppets. "Ana," she said, "knock on Heddie's door and tell her to join us. We'll have a feast tonight."

As Ana rushed down the stairs Elvira Maria watched Michail, his face aglow in the lamplight. She stood close to him and whispered. "Remember that day in the city garden when I met Heddie?"

"Yes," he said slowly, indulging her while he focused on the bird.

"She was right," Elvira Maria said. "You really are a charming man."

SUMMER
1920

With white eyes gleaming and through slits in her mask, history is watching us.

—Yuri Oleysha

39

Odessa

The majestic oak trees along the central lane in Alexandrovsky Park honored Emperor Alexander II, who had planted the first of them in 1875 during the park's opening ceremony. A monumental column commemorating his visit rose above the trees and could be seen from far and wide. The park was the largest green expanse in Odessa. Located in the southwest quarter, it stretched between Maraziliyevskaya and Uspenskaya Boulevards, and extended to Lanzheron Beach, a popular bathing spot.

In the early nineteenth century, when infectious diseases such as the plague and cholera had threatened the ports of the Black Sea, the area had been a quarantine site, known as Serf's Garden. But by the 1840s, a time of philanthropic investment, it was transformed into a luxurious public garden, designed by Francesco C. Boffo, a Swiss-Italian architect. Known for his neo-classical style, Boffo had also created the city's marine façade, which included the gigantic Odessa Steps, crowned by a statue of Armand duc de Richelieu, one of the city's earliest builders and governors.

The park's central lane took visitors past lush gardens, bowling greens, a shooting gallery, a gilded carousel, the Green Theatre, and d'Alexandre Café. Elvira Maria walked beside Michail, taking in the sights she'd heard so much about, but had never seen. She was equally delighted to watch Ana and Danya, freed from the hot attic and enjoying the sea breeze, chase each other across the grass.

She and Michail paused to read the colorful posters plastered to a kiosk. One advertised the forthcoming performance of Leonid Utyosov, an estada singer and comic actor from Odessa's Jewish community. Michail had seen him several years ago at the Rishelyavsky Theatre, and had loved his charisma and wit. A new agitprop poster featured a cheerful peasant girl standing in a wheat field, a wooden rake at her side. She pointed to an insert that curved across the paper and depicted huge tractors and combines. Headlined, POWER TO COMRADES WHO WORK THE LAND, the poster promised a safer and more efficient harvest. Elvira Maria wondered how much the complicated machines cost. The girl was costumed in an embroidered skirt and matching vest, a luxury outfit no woman in Kos would ever have worn in the fields. The soviet had replaced the sweat and endless work she'd known with an image that looked modern, effortless, and romantic.

They followed the signs to the carousel, but when they reached it, it was cordoned off with a barbwire fence, leaving the fierce tigers, exotic elephants, and prancing horses inaccessible, like animals in the zoo.

A group of street urchins stood nearby grumbling. "If it's busted they should fix it," a boy said. Stocky and well built, his clean face surrounded by curly brown hair, he was eleven or twelve years old, and carried a rucksack over his shoulder. He was taller than the other boys, who threw stones at the painted animals. He squinted at Elvira Maria and walked up to her. "I know you," he said, a broad smile on his face.

She recognized him too. He was one of the boys who'd been at the train station in Kos, the night she'd lost Ana and Sasha. "I can't believe it," she said. "Have you been here all winter?" She remembered he wanted to ride the rails with his idol, a boy called the Wind Shark.

"Yeah," he said. "Not many trains running. It's boring here, nothing to do."

Elvira Maria introduced him to Michail. The other boys, pocketing their stones, gathered around and listened. Ana eyed them cautiously and took Elvira Maria's hand.

"That's your girl, ain't it?" the boy said. "That one your son?" He pointed to Danya.

"No," she said, "he's a friend. My son is Sasha. He's still out there."

The boy nodded. He bummed a cigarette from Michail. "I never caught up with the Wind Shark," he said, a bit of regret in his husky voice. The Wind Shark, he explained, had joined the circus in Odessa, and had gone on tour. Now an acrobatic star, his name was in lights. "Some of us get lucky," he said.

They went to the beach. The tide was out and the waves rolled in gently. She and Michail stood arm in arm at the water's edge, their bare feet wet with foam. They watched the sun inch its way toward the horizon. Ana and Danya splashed each other and ran along the shore. Other children, with their young mothers and nannies, built sand castles ringed by moats with drawbridges. Soldiers sat on the rocks and watched them, some whistling through blades of grass trying to get their attention. It was hard to imagine that a bomb, rumored to be planted by local insurgents, had exploded in Quarantine Harbor just the week before, destroying the bow and rigging of a freighter from Crimea.

Michail picked up a piece of driftwood caught in a swirl of seaweed. He examined the twisted branch and shook off the sand embedded in a large knot.

"Does it look like Baba Yaga?" he asked, holding it out. He was referring to the witch in an old Russian folk tale.

She took the branch. It was heavier than she'd first thought. "It *feels* like Baba Yaga," she said. Since the break-in he'd been reluctant to repair the puppets and return to performing. He sat night after night in the attic, sadness and worry in his eyes. She hadn't wanted to pressure him to get back to work. Hoping he'd come around given time, she'd taken in more piecework from Monsieur Oury to cover their expenses, but she'd been uninspired, felt a dull ache in her body as she hunched over her needle. It was one thing to sew for yourself, but quite another to work for a shop that needed everything completed right away. But, also, she felt something missing from their lives. The puppets, the performing, expanded their world and their relationship. "You want to perform again?" she asked.

"Take my hand, dear one," he said. "Baba Yaga is willing and waiting."

The next day, while Elvira Maria was out delivering an order to Monsieur Oury, Ana sat beside Michail and watched the wood chips fall from his knife. They were full of sand, smelled like the sea. Though it was hot in the attic, and she could have taken her Frog Princess to the yard or downstairs to Nadia's, where it was cooler, she was eager to help him make Baba Yaga. Earlier that morning he'd moved the workbench near the open window and lined-up his carving tools, paints, and glue. She'd seen a few of his knives before, but had never realized he had so many. One was big, like a butcher knife, but the others were smaller, with sharp curved blades and pointy hooks that looked like they'd be dangerous if you weren't careful. He nodded to the one at the end of the row, and she handed him a tool that resembled a dart.

"This is an awl," he said. "It makes holes in wood, even leather." He examined the small head he'd been carving. It had sagging cheeks and an open mouth that followed the curve of the driftwood. But the crooked nose with the knot on top, its main feature, was what made it look like a witch. He set it in the vice fastened to the workbench and tightened the grips. "The awl is very useful when you need to be exact," he said. "See?" She leaned closer and watched him slowly twirl the point into the nose to carve a nostril. He blew away the flecks of wood and made another. "I'll drill smaller holes for her eyes," he explained, "but I'll need you to blow so I can see what I'm doing."

When he finished carving the head, and they agreed

it looked like Baba Yaga, he gave her a piece of sand-paper and she rubbed off the splinters until the wood was smooth. She wiped the surface with a cloth and ran her fingers along the grooves to be sure they were clean. Michail said she was more meticulous than he'd ever been.

Then they selected the colors for Baba Yaga's face. While she stirred the jars of brown, red, and blue paint, he told her how his grandfather had purchased colored stones from an apothecary, the only source for paints in Mińsk. Michail, the same age as Ana, sat at the bench with his grandfather and ground the stones into powder. "They came from the Far East," he said, "from India, China, and Persia. They smelled old and musty like the mountains and caravans." These days he bought his paints from Saul Feodorovet, who sold them in the back of his stationery shop. Most of the colors were ready-made, but some like cadmium yellow and jet-black, came in tubes he mixed with linseed oil and turpentine that made his eyes smart.

By afternoon the paint was dry enough to give Baba Yaga hair. They put oil on a piece of wool to make it stringy and gray, then glued it to the crown of her head. A foul smell filled the attic, and they coughed and laughed. "She's a vengeful old hag," Michail said. He placed the head closer to the window.

"Does she deserve a heart?" Ana asked. She knew the other puppets had hearts beneath their costumes or hidden under their wings or hoofs.

"Of course," he said. "She might be mean, but she's got to have one. That's the rule."

Puppets with hearts came alive on stage, he told her. He'd learned this from his grandfather, who learned it from his teacher, a Turkish puppet master. The djinn empowered puppets with hearts to touch the audience in a special way. Did she know what a djinn was? It was a magical spirit, mischievous but mostly kind. When the curtain opened and the pishchik blew, the puppets with hearts reached out and made the audience — especially children — happy and generous. It made them openhearted.

"Could you make Baba Yaga's heart, please?" Michail asked.

Ana found a piece of red fabric and started to sew. Michail tacked Baba Yaga's head to a large woolen mitt and dressed her with a kerchief, skirt, and shawl. He sorted through a sack of props and found an old broom she could fly on. Placing the puppet on his left hand, he worked his fingers back and forth. He wanted the mitt to be flexible so he could hold the broom and have the witch wave her arm at the same time.

He placed the puppet on the workbench and Ana stood over it to sew the heart beneath Baba Yaga's shawl. They'd decided that was the best place. When she tied the last knot he encouraged her to put her hand inside the puppet. It was too big, but she poked her fingers in place and held it upright. Michail put his hand to his ear, and tilted his head to listen. She cackled three times and felt Baba Yaga come alive.

40

NOW MIDSUMMER. Dark gray skies and thick clouds hung over Odessa and threatened rain. Michail and Elvira Maria, assembling the theater in Deribasov Garden, hoped the storm would wait until the show was over. Michail fastened a banner to the top of the stage and stood back to look at the two castles on either side.

"Move it a little to the right," he said to Elvira Maria. He tightened a guideline attached to a stake and tied another knot in the rope as she made the final adjustment.

She slid the curtains in place and went backstage where Ana was tying the broom to Baba Yaga's mitt. She had informed Danya, who waited nearby, that the morning's show was named after the witch. Elvira Maria checked the new props and hung the tambourine and bells on their hooks. She was excited to perform again and knew Michail, who couldn't stop fussing with the stage, was eager as well. They'd spent weeks repairing broken puppets and torn costumes, a tedious and expensive task. But today, with luck, they might earn the rubles they needed to recoup their losses.

Michail shouted with enthusiasm to the curious crowd gathered before the stage.

Welcome Comrades, boys and girls, dockers and sailors, soldiers and tailors. You've come to the right place. We offer you excitement, mystery, and grand entertainment:

> *The flowers are blooming in this garden today*
> *The wind is gentle, the sea is at play.*
> *My puppets are waiting and ready for you*
> *Come gather before me,*
> *My story is true.*
>
> *No need to ask questions, no need to be sad*
> *You have every reason, my friends, to be glad.*
> *The morning is lovely, the sky ever blue*
> *My curtain is opening now,*
> *Just for you.*

He blew his pishchik, then dashed backstage. Elvira Maria opened the curtains to reveal the first scenery panel, depicting grand houses, boulevards, and the golden bell tower of Preobrazhensky Cathedral. It was Odessa.

Ha, ha, we meet again, dear Comrades, said Dedushka, the old Grandfather. He stood center stage and waved to the audience. *Today I present the thrilling story, 'Baba Yaga and Vasili, The Brave.' Ah, this is an old tale, a terrifying tale, a tale of witches, cauldrons, and ghastly deeds.*

Dedushka shook his hand at a docker in the audience who was leaving. *You in the sailcloth,* he called out, *don't be scared. Don't abandon us. Stay, the children will protect you!*

The docker, stopped by a laughing crowd, turned around and pointed at Dedushka. "I'm counting on Baba

Yaga to knock you one with her pestle," he shouted.

Yes, yes, Dedushka cried over the catcalls. *Baba Yaga is always ready to trouble an old man like me. Comrades, hear me well, the evil witch has stood on my doorstep three times: the first time to ruin my reputation, the second time to steal my wealth, and the third time to shatter the wisdom in my heart. Beware!*

Dedushka moved to a row of bent tulips pasted before a grand house. Elvira Maria brought out Vasili, costumed in a short tunic and ragged breeches. She walked him to Dedushka, swinging his long arms and tall body to and fro.

Davnym-davno, Dedushka said. *Long ago, in this beautiful city, I adopted Vasili, a wild and careless lad.* He pointed at him. *Vasili, you were raised by bears in the great forest before I found you. We've lived together for many years, but alas, it has been a terrible struggle. You still are wild despite my attempts to tame you. You are clumsy and rough. The neighbors complain (as they always do)! You break their tools, trample their flowers, and frighten their children.* Dedushka leaned toward the boys and girls standing close to the stage. *Vasili cannot ride the tram because he's too tall*, he said. *Think about that!*

The children exchanged glances and murmurs.

Dear Uncle, Vasili said, *I've grown too fast. My arms and legs strike everything that gets in my way.*

You cannot live in Odessa, Dedushka declared. *Return to the forest, my boy, where you belong. I cannot protect you from our bourgeois neighbors, or from the proletariat dockers who sneak away from our performance.*

The audience whistled, giving Michail time to place a large club in Dedushka's hands. He gave it to Vasili, singing:

> Go Vasili into the woods
> Bears and wolves are waiting.
> Now is the time for us to part
> Stop your silly shaking.
>
> Take this club. Protect yourself
> Bind my courage to you.
> Travel the road until it ends
> Darkness might pursue you.

Dear Grandfather, Vasili cried, I wish to return someday. Take pity on me!

Forever a troublesome boy, Dedushka said, shaking his head. All right. You may return. But ONLY if you bring me a treasure that will make me famous, make me rich, and make me wise.

I promise to search far and wide until I find it, Vasili shouted.

The puppets left the stage. Elvira Maria and Ana dropped a new scenery panel in place. It was Baba Yaga's home of dark mossy trees, low flying birds, and green and purple skies. A fence constructed of twigs carved and painted to resemble human bones stood beside her upside-down hut. Ana reached for the crank Michail had fastened beneath the hut and spun it around and around.

Tramp, tramp, tramp! Vasili complained, marching across the stage. I've been walking forever. But oh, aw, oh! He wailed and sniffed the air. This place smells rotten. He swung his club at the fence and scattered the bones across the stage.

Ha, ha, ha. Ha! Ha, ha, ha. Ha! Baba Yaga's screams echoed from backstage.

Michail held the witch aloft and sailed her before the audience, her gray hair sweeping behind her twisted

face and fierce red eyes. Small children cringed, while
street urchins jeered. Michail landed the witch before the
shaking Vasili.

Ha, ha, ha. Ha! Baba Yaga cackled loudly. I smell the
blood of a Wayward Boy!

Have mercy great witch of the North Woods, Vasili said.
I'm an outcast, an urchin, a poor besprizorniki.

A besprizorniki? Baba Yaga repeated. She turned to the
laughing crowd. They're everywhere these days! She glared
at Vasili. How dare you invade my forest and destroy my fence.
Stand still, you shaking fool, so I can kill you.

The puppets lunged at each other until Vasili scurried
up a tree and hid. Baba Yaga hissed. Vasili peered down
at the witch, shook his arms and legs, and vaulted to the
stage. He struck her with his mighty club. She staggered
and fell to the ground. Cheers rang out as Baba Yaga lay
dead. Backstage, Ana felt sad for the old witch, but rattled
her tambourine anyway. Danya, his face lit by a devilish
smile, shook the string of bells. He was proud to partici-
pate in the show as Pavlo once had.

Vasili jumped up and down, distracting the audience as Elvira Maria reached through an opening in the
stage floor and clamped a lantern to the end of his club.
Instantly, sparkling glass and sequins flashed in the sunlight that now streamed through the heavy clouds.

Look, oh look! Vasili shouted. He held the lantern for
all to see. It's a burning light in the dark forest. I've found the
treasure!

Ana rolled the scenery of Odessa in place as Michail
stood Dedushka beside Vasili.

Dear Grandfather, Vasili said, I've brought you a treasure like none other. This is a magical lantern, my gift to you.

Vasili, this is a worthy treasure, Dedushka exclaimed. It will make me famous, make me rich, and make me wise. This lantern will shine forever and dispel darkness in our troubled world.

Dedushka held the glowing lantern while Vasili, The Brave, opened his arms to the joyful crowd. They sang the final song:

> The old Dedushki, wise and true
> Have sung their story alive for you.
> A witch destroyed and treasures found
> Our hearts are happy, goodwill abounds.
>
> But oh my friends beware of Fate
> It comes and goes at every gate.
> Despite all efforts great and few
> Trouble and woe may follow you.
>
> So hold a lantern in the night
> To signal hope, to shine pure light.
> We take our leave, our song is clear,
> Vasili, The Brave, is ever near.

41

HEDDIE FOLDED THE LAST OF HER LAUNDRY and placed the clothes in her steamer trunk. She looked with dismay at her chapped hands and torn cuticles. Overwhelmed by the heat of a steamy July, she opened first the window and then the door of her cramped little room, trying to create a breeze. The pallid movement of air stirred the dust from the brittle plaster walls.

"This is a far cry from my usual routine," she said to herself. "I used to spend hot afternoons in a cool bath thumbing through fashion magazines." She sat on the bed. Leaning toward the window, she looked down at the yard. The outhouse door was open again, exposing the large hole on the rough wooden bench. A catalog, torn to shreds, was lying on the dirt floor.

Sobered by her dire situation, evicted from the lavish house and lifestyle she'd enjoyed for so many years, Heddie was ready to leave Odessa. The heartbreak of saying goodbye was diminished by knowing that Paris, her destination, would offer her safety and a cosmopolitan atmosphere. There would be no hooligans on the streets, no scavengers picking through trash bins, no agents of the Cheka on her doorstep. She would find a quiet apartment near the Luxembourg Gardens and open a chic café or elegant tearoom with reasonable hours, a reliable income, and patrons who had no idea about her past. She'd spend time with other Jews, members of the avant-garde, luminaries she'd read about for years.

She fanned herself with a newspaper. Sweat dribbled down her temples. Of course she'd never get there so long as the trains continued to be canceled or sabotaged, like the one derailed outside of Kyiv just days ago. Since she'd purchased train tickets and illicit travel permits at an exorbitant price, she clung to the hope that she and Boris would leave within the month.

Elvira Maria and Ana stopped at her door. "We're going to the city garden," Elvira Maria said. "Would you like to join us?"

"That's a lovely idea," Heddie said, "but I'll stay here this afternoon and have a rest."

"I'm sorry you're not comfortable going out," Elvira Maria said. "Perhaps the house will be cooler tonight."

"We can only hope so." Heddie forced a smile. "Enjoy yourselves. The garden's beautiful." She handed Ana her parasol. "Protect yourselves from the sun, my darlings."

"Oh, it's gorgeous!" Ana cried. She twirled the blue parasol, trimmed with yellow ribbons.

"Careful, Annushka," Elvira Maria said, "Heddie will use it in Paris." Ana pulled her down the stairs.

"Summer's finally arrived," Michail said to Heddie. He stood in the hall, on his way to the yard. "Can you handle the heat?"

"I'm trying my best." She pointed to the attic. "It must be sizzling up there."

"The wind will pick up later. This is the worst time of day, when the sun's beating on these walls."

"Michail," she said in a hushed voice, "why don't you leave here? You could pack up your show, bring the girls, and travel with Boris and me. There's still time. I'll bribe someone, get you the tickets and papers."

"That's a tempting offer. It's the best I've had in ages." He sat next to her and handed her a cigarette. "But Elvira Maria won't leave until she has word from Sasha."

Heddie accepted his match and blew the rank-smelling smoke toward the window. "Doesn't she realize he's gone?" she asked. "I'm glad I'm not a mother. I'd never be able to cope."

"She's done well," he said. "I'm not going to dash her hopes after all that's happened." He looked earnestly at Heddie. "We wouldn't have found the children without you. She's grateful — so am I."

"You had some help from Dashkevich as well."

He nodded.

"Why were you friends, Michail? He was so disagreeable."

"Not always." He finished his cigarette and put the dregs in his pocket. "After my wife and daughter died I couldn't have lived a day without his support. He believed in the Bolsheviks' cause, even when they used him and betrayed him."

"Look where that got him." She shook her head, then tossed her cigarette stub in the yard and gazed out the window, as if to reconsider the animosity she felt for Ivan. "Did he have any dreams?" she asked.

"To spend a night with one of your girls."

She burst out laughing. "Oh Michail, you're terrible! Just incorrigible." She swatted him with her newspaper. He jumped up for the door.

"I've got to check my scenery panels," he said, grinning. "I hope everything's still there."

Pavlo and his gang crouched in the afternoon shade of the acacias. Scruffy and raw-boned, the boys tossed a pair of wooden dice in the dirt, cursing and whooping until a winner snatched the rubles. Michail wet his kerchief at the pump and passed the cold dripping cloth over his face. He got out his key. As he swung the shed door open and entered, a blanket of hot air closed around him. He coughed, adjusted to the musty smell of old straw that lingered in the vacant horse stalls. Walking to the back, he pulled out the top scenery panel and counted the stack leaning against the wall. The five panels were still in place, glowing faintly in the shaft of light that streamed in. A pine forest with wild birds, a woodcutter's thatched hut, a golden palace and rose garden—they were all in good condition, ready to use with the painted rolls he kept in the attic.

"Better rest now, we'll be busy soon," he whispered to the stack. He dusted off each panel with his hand and straightened them.

Bending down to retrieve a gunnysack of old banners lying on the dirt floor behind the panels, his foot tapped the bottom board of the wall. It fell back, exposing a narrow opening to the outside. He knelt beside the unexpected opening and examined the nails at the edge of the board. They were still in place but slightly bent. A thief looking for something to steal or a vagrant looking for someplace to sleep, he thought. He set about replacing the board right away.

When he was done, he looked around to see if anything was missing. Everything looked the way it always did. Shovels and scythes belonging to the neighbors, the washtub, his own theater panels and backdrops were where he expected them to be. The horse stalls were empty. He examined the collection of leather harnesses that hung from the metal hooks attached to the stalls. Each set, draping to the ground, was complete and looked sturdy, despite a few cracks in the tangled reins. He often wondered how it was no one had sold them yet.

He checked the perimeter of the shed, nudging each board with the toe of his boot and looking for footprints. As he moved a rake away from the wall a rat scuttled across his feet and ran out the door. He cringed and hurried to leave. Remembering his banners then, he abruptly turned back and saw that the harnesses in the first stall were swaying, as if someone had pushed them from behind. Stepping into the stall, he could now discern a pair of leather boots dug into the dirt opposite his own.

He pulled aside the harnesses. The boy hiding behind them winced.

"Sasha!" he said. "How long have you been here?"

The confident boy in Deribasov Garden was gone. It was a child standing before Michail, haggard, biting his lip, tears welling in his tired eyes. His shabby clothes, streaked with dirt and stains, hung on his thin frame.

"How long have you been living here?" Michail asked.

"Not long," Sasha said. "I came last night."

Michail drew him close and held him. He expected the boy to resist, but instead, exhausted, Sasha sobbed quietly into Michail's shoulder. Outside the gambling boys shouted and swore like seasoned gangsters. In the alley, children called to each other as they played a game of stick ball.

A large shadow moved on the wall of the shed and caught their attention. Startled, they turned and stared into the light. Pavlo stood, feet planted apart, blocking the entire doorway.

"I never took you for a cry baby," he said. He smirked. Keeping his eyes on Sasha, he bent down slowly and pulled a knife from his boot. He wiped it back and forth on his sleeve.

"Pavlo, put that down, right now," Michail said. He stepped forward.

Pavlo laughed. He swiped the air with the knife. The handle was swallowed by the darkness, but the blade, backlit by the sun, glinted. "I can't hear you, Michail. That muzhik tried to kidnap Danya. Get out of the way. He's mine."

Sasha grabbed the rake. He dashed to the door and heaved the tool, tines forward, at Pavlo. Pushing past him, he stumbled into the yard, ran along the fence, and slipped through an opening in the broken boards. He headed for the street.

Pavlo dodged the sharp prongs. The rake struck the door and clattered to the ground. He let out a shrill whistle. "Get him," he shouted to the boys in the yard. "He's the one we want."

The boys scrambled for their coins first. Only then did they jump to their feet, abandoning the dice in a scatter of leaves. They ran after Sasha, howling like a pack of wild dogs. Michail followed them, struggling to keep up as they charged through the tenement gate and around to the alley. The younger children snatched their sticks and balls out of the way and watched them streak past. When he reached Gogolya Street, Michail could see Sasha zigzag between the droshkies, lorries, and cars. Drivers, cigarettes clamped in their teeth, their red faces drenched with sweat, yelled and cursed. They cracked their whips and blasted their horns as they swerved to avoid him. Outmaneuvering each other, they drove down the street in haphazard lanes.

Sasha, now at the busy intersection, pushed through the shoppers waiting to cross, upsetting a bag of oranges in someone's arm. The oranges, a high-priced luxury, rolled in front of a grinding lorry and were smashed at once. A fragrant smell filled the air. It was swallowed by fumes and dust.

He continued on to Nikolaevskaya Boulevard and raced along the tram tracks. The gang, with Pavlo in the lead, picked up their pace. They dodged an armored car and crossed the street. Intent on their target, they ran next to the sea wall and avoided the traffic while they closed in. Wheezing, Michail stopped at the intersection and held his aching side. A siren blared up the street. People stopped to stare at the armored car parked at the curb, the doors and hatch flung open. He grabbed a lamppost and bent over to catch his breath. As he raised his head, he saw three Red Army officers drag Sasha from the tracks.

Pavlo, yelling and waving, caught up to them, the other boys at his heels. He pulled aside an officer, and pointed at Sasha. Michail could see he was angry, out of control, his mouth twisted as he shouted, the siren still raging. Sasha, breathing heavily, wrestled against the officer holding his arms. He leaned forward and spat at Pavlo. The officer struck him across the face, cuffed his hands behind his back, and forced him into the armored car.

Nearly full, the moon cast a silvery light on the dirt floor. Sasha, curled up in his wet tunic and trousers, rolled onto his side. The earth beneath him was cold and damp and smelled of urine and dirty straw. He ran his tongue across his teeth. Two on the bottom, next to his cheek, were loose. He pushed them into his gum with a finger and fished out a piece of seaweed. He rubbed his aching jaw, moved it back and forth a little. His mouth was caked with blood and salt.

He opened his eyes and squinted at the small window. The thick steel bars were vertical. Not like the ones at the Cheka station where he'd been interrogated earlier. Those had been horizontal and were covered with a metal grille. It was a curious detail to remember, but his head was floating, still in the bucket of water.

Someone coughed and grunted in the corner. Other men were in the cell with him. He couldn't tell how many. Four, he thought. Maybe five. Their breathing was heavy. They moaned now and then, muttered to themselves. But no one snored. Perhaps they were young, hadn't yet developed the annoying habit. Dudorov claimed he never snored, had prided himself on his good health. But Sasha had heard him sputter and snort, and also knew he had nasty sores on his feet.

He was glad he'd confessed, glad he shouted at the Cheka agents that the bastard had deserved more than one bullet. They'd accused Dashkevich, but had gotten the wrong man. They were stupid, and he had told them so — in between the blows they dealt him with a rubber hose. A muscle-bound agent, toting a file of papers, had shown him a photo of himself sitting in Dudorov's office chair naked. Dudorov had taken it. Had he given it to the agents or had they discovered it? Didn't matter. They knew what was going on, but had supported Dudorov anyway, taken a little bribe here and there, hustled a promotion. Spitting blood on the floor, Sasha told the agent to give the photo to his daughter. Enraged, the man tore it up and crammed the pieces into his mouth. Before he could spit them out they'd grabbed him by the neck, ripped him off his stool, and plunged his head in a pail of icy seawater. They dunked him over and over again. The pieces of the photograph eddied around in the water, scratching his face, his ears. He shut his eyes, squeezed them tight, and saw his father, dusty from the fields, standing before him with open arms. He held that vision, lost count of the times he gasped for air, had been shaken and slapped. Finally, he had passed out.

Finding his feet, he stumbled to the window. He grabbed hold of the bars, not sure how long he could stand on his own. The waves crashed on the other side of a huge quarried wall that extended as far as he could see. The breakers rolled in, thundered. Flecks of foam danced above the wall. They looked like falling stars. He thought of his mother, and of Ana. They'd loved watching the night skies in Kos, believed every star was an angel.

Someone coughed again in the corner. "Did they break any bones?" a man asked. His voice was rough. He sounded old.

Sasha felt his arms and legs. "I don't think so."

"Good," the man said. "Take my coat if you're cold. You need to sleep."

He hesitated. He was wary of older men. The offer of warmth, the pretense of care. But now at a loss and near collapse, he limped to the corner and accepted the coat.

42

BORIS PUT HIS ARMS AROUND HEDDIE and tried to console her. It was no use. She continued to cry. He felt claustrophobic in her sweltering room as they stood near a candle wavering on the desk, mosquitoes flitting past his shoulder. She had to collect herself. He needed air, needed to clear his head, now that she'd told him what had happened that afternoon.

"I've never trusted Pavlo," Heddie said. "He's always made me nervous, running up and down the stairs and lurking about in the yard." She wiped her tears. "How could he be so cruel? Elvira Maria will never recover."

"He runs with a vicious gang," Boris said. He took her crumpled, wet handkerchief and offered his own.

"I sat with her for an hour before you came," she said. "I've never seen anyone so distraught."

"Pavlo got his revenge."

"She wants to go to the garrison."

"Michail won't let her. Definitely out of the question."

"But she's his mother. She'll follow him to his grave."

"She's Ana's mother too," Boris said. "She won't leave her daughter."

"Or Michail. I hope she won't think of leaving him. He adores her, Boris. I've never seen anyone so smitten." Heddie sat on the bed, her energy spent.

"They have a life together and a little family. We must trust they'll work it out."

"Oh," she said, "I can't wait to get out of here." She looked around the dreary room. "I never imagined anything like this—living cooped-up and hungry, fearing for our safety, watching friends deal with violence day after day."

"Please." He raised his hand. "Autumn of 1905 was worse. Don't you remember the pogrom—the murders, the destruction? The community still hasn't recovered. Look at Deribasovskaya Street."

"I can't," she said. "I try not to think about it."

"You paced the floors until the carpets wore out."

"But then I had allies in high places. I had money, influence, and the house."

"Now you have a different set of allies, and Michail and Elvira Maria are more trustworthy than the wolves that prowled through your house and threatened us with violence."

"Yes, yes," she said. "I've never had real friends before. I've never shared anyone's pain. Not like this. To be honest, respectable people have always shunned me, despite the money I've thrown at their cultural events." She twisted the wilted handkerchief as she remembered the haughty women at the Opera House who refused to say hello when she greeted them. Who did they think had paid for the beautifully embossed programs they held in their gloved hands? "I'm devastated just thinking about what's happened to Sasha," she said, "and I've never even met the boy."

Exhausted, Boris opened the door. Elvira Maria's soft voice trailed down the stairs, the words of an old country lullaby. He put on his cap and nodded goodnight. "It's late. I need to move on."

Pavlo's whistle pierced through the yard, followed by the stomping feet of boys running down the dark alley.

"Boris," she called, "be careful."

"Don't worry, Heddie. I'll be fine."

The cicadas droned in the midday heat, tucking themselves beneath wild roses and ragweed growing in the back alleys of the city. Residents, drained from the long hot summer, lingered beneath the leafy trees on the spacious boulevards. Mothers, sun hats protecting their drawn faces, pushed prams and exchanged gossip, their toddlers running ahead or falling behind.

Michail and Boris enjoyed none of this. Two days after Sasha's arrest, they were headed to the garrison to visit the boy and make inquiries about his release. They walked to the tram stop, a block from the tenement, and joined the dockers and stevedores who shifted on their feet, smoking, coughing, and waiting. Michail, on guard for the secret police, looked around cautiously. He noticed Boris was doing the same. It had become routine.

"I appreciate your coming with me," Michail said.

"I wouldn't let you go without me," Boris said. "I'm happy to lend my support."

Aboard the tram, they shared an overhead strap. The car lurched from side to side, screeching along. The men were quiet. A breeze from the open windows blew the smell of grease, sweat, and stale tobacco from one body to the next. They passed blocks of grand apartments, their walkways shaded by awnings. Jews, prayer books in hand, entered the Brody Synagogue through its double doors. Sonorous chords from the pipe organ, the first in Odessa, flooded the tram as it trundled past and turned into Zhukovskago Street. Boris caught a glimpse of the Polyakov Brothers Confectionery. Heddie and the girls had shopped there every Thursday, for as long as he could remember. Now it was closed. The colorful displays of caramels and cocoa that had enticed customers of all ages were gone.

As the tram veered away from the coastline, the garrison, perched on the jagged cliffs to the south of Quarantine Harbor, came into view. Rumbling through a desolate plain of thick grass and purple thistle, the tram sprayed dirt and pebbles to the side until it came to a stop at an open-air depot, the end of the line. A rocky hillside covered with blooming yellow gorse jutted to the west and dropped sharply to the sea. Built centuries ago, the quarried fortress with its high walls and watchtowers dominated the windswept landscape.

Michail and Boris hailed a droshky and headed down the long road to the military headquarters of the Red Army. They approached the open gates on foot and stopped before the guardhouse. The soldier, stepping down to examine their papers, beckoned them to stand back as a mounted battalion nearing the gate returned to the garrison. The horses, lathered and snorting, trotted past, kicking up dirt. Michail waved aside the dust and sought directions to the prison.

"Enormous facility," Boris said, scanning the ramparts. "The Ottomans built it to last."

"It must be that alcove." Michail pointed to a large opening in the far wall flanked by Red Army flags and Red Brigade banners. Guards, armed with rifles and bayonets, stood at attention.

They walked across the parade ground, the scorching sun overhead. At the alcove, they placed their identity cards on the reception desk as their eyes adjusted to the dim light of the vaulted space. A breeze from the west fluttered a stack of papers held in place with a stone.

A young Commissar entered their names in a ledger. "Your business, Comrades?"

"I'm here to see a prisoner," Michail said, "Aleksander Lyova Andrushko. The boy was arrested Monday afternoon on Nikolaevskaya Boulevard."

The Commissar turned to a thick roster behind him and looked through several pages of names. Moments later, he left his desk and called for a prison guard to open the iron gate framing a dark corridor. He handed the guard a ring of keys. The two men entered the corridor and disappeared.

Michail and Boris stood alone in the alcove and waited.

"I escaped the military," Boris said. He stepped closer to Michail and lowered his voice. "Dodged about for years. I hid with Heddie's mother until she paid a fortune so I could put my head out the door. What about you, ever served?"

"No. I had counterfeit papers made in Mińsk. My father's younger brother was a printer."

"Imagine, spending your life with a rifle, mucking through trenches and land mines."

"Thousands have," Michail said.

"Yes," Boris continued, "and look at them, poor souls." He threw a glance at the guards gathered in front of the stables. "Hung over from a rough night, arrogant, headstrong, without a pension to count on."

"Your words are harsh," Michail said. He thought of the heated conversations he'd had with Ivan. "Some of these fellows think they're changing the world order for the better. I have to respect them for that, even if I don't agree that waging war or sending the Cheka to my attic will solve the problems of class struggle."

"Think what you like, but I recognize trouble when I see it." Boris frowned as he studied Michail. How could he be so generous after suffering such a violent break-in?

In the distance, churned-up waves battered the wall. Seagulls circling the ramparts pumped their white wings against the gusting wind, the cloudless sky bright blue. The soldiers brought out a stack of bayonets and cleaned them with greasy rags. The smell of kerosene hung in the air.

A jingle of keys, followed by the clang of iron doors, drew their attention. The glow of a torch lit the cavern. The Commissar returned, herding three babushkas before him. The women, carrying canteens, wept and clung to each other. They shuffled past Michail and Boris and headed across the barren parade grounds.

"Why are you interested in this boy?" the Commissar asked, resuming his place behind the desk.

"I'm here on behalf of his mother," Michail said.

"Comrade, he's marked for transport. No visitors allowed for this one."

"Transport to where?" Michail asked.

"He's headed for Solovki." The Commissar paused, reading the stunned expression on Michail face. "Given the charge the sentence is merciful."

"What is the charge?"

"Murder."

Michail flinched. He was overcome with a fear he had not anticipated.

"And this transport you speak of, Comrade," Boris said, stepping forward. "When will he go to Solovki?"

"He'll take the next train to Kyiv and transit to Moscow."

"And then?"

"On foot to Belomorsk, the crossing for Solovetsky Island."

"My God," Boris muttered under his breath.

"He's lucky to be alive," the Commissar said. He returned their identity cards and stood at attention and saluted. The inquiry was over. But as the worried men took their leave, he added a word of encouragement. "A boy like that? He'll survive."

"How can you tell?" Michail asked.

"He's young—and stubborn."

Too dispirited to converse, they waited for the evening's last droshky, the sun sinking slowly beyond the dark blue horizon. In the distance, the Vorontsov Lighthouse, perched on the tip of an outlying peninsula, cast its shining orb out to sea.

43

SINCE EARLY MORNING, Red Army soldiers had stopped people in the alley and checked their papers, looking for suspects linked to a recent warehouse fire at the dockyards. The blaze had blackened the August skies for days and sent the gulls that perched on the tenement ledges and chimneys down the coast. At least they could escape, Elvira Maria thought—unlike Sasha. Alarmed by Michail's report from the garrison, she prayed the judicial commander in charge would reconsider sending a child to Solovki, but as she sat at the attic window and watched the soldiers harass and arrest a friendly peddler she knew, she had her doubts.

She returned to the sewing in her lap and took comfort that Heddie was there to distract her from thinking about Sasha. She pointed to the letters she'd embroidered onto Ana's jumper. "Are the stitches large enough?" she asked Heddie, wanting to know if they could be read easily.

Heddie looked at the jumper, then at the paper in her hand with Ana's name written across the top. "Yes dear," she said. "You've copied the letters exactly."

Elvira Maria studied the next letter and continued stitching Ana's long name inside a back muslin panel. "I should have done this ages ago," she said.

"It's a good idea," Heddie said. "I wouldn't have thought of it."

Elvira Maria concentrated on her sewing. She remembered her painful trips to the detdom, where the orphanage staff had reprimanded her for failing to provide Ana and Sasha with identification. "Are you packed for your trip?" she asked, wanting to change the subject. "I'd like to give you a hand."

"I've crammed everything into my trunk." Heddie thought about the clothes, shoes, journals, and keepsakes she couldn't leave behind. "I wish it wasn't so heavy."

"It's easier carrying it down the stairs than up." Elvira Maria smiled at her. She tucked the paper in her pocket, knowing she would use it again when Ana outgrew her jumper and needed a new one embroidered with her name.

"Would you mind helping me with these?" Heddie asked. She reached into her bosom and brought out a little velvet purse. "I need to stitch the stones into my suit jacket, but they're so small I can't manage."

She stood at the workbench, selected a square of fabric, and poured out five sapphire crystals. The stones glittered against the black cloth.

"Oh!" Elvira Maria said. She got up at once and rushed to the workbench. "Oh, I've never seen anything so beautiful."

"They're lovely, aren't they? This one's deep blue." Heddie pointed to a stone that was darker than the others. "Look."

Astonished, Elvira Maria bent over the sapphires to examine them closely.

"Where did you get them?"

"An admirer gave them to my mother. He got them in Sutara, in the Far East. I've had them for a long time."

"I wish Ana were here. She'd love to see these."

"I used to have seven, but I had to pay a steep debt after the pogrom." Heddie looked wistfully at the small stones.

"Perhaps you should keep them—where you had them." Elvira Maria looked at Heddie's bosom, embarrassed to speak of it.

"No. If I'm stopped or searched I'd lose them right away. Besides, I have to carry rubles in my brassiere." She picked up her white suit jacket with black collar and cuffs and turned it inside out, smoothing the wrinkled lining. "It's better to hide something this precious in a secret place."

"Have you been keeping these in your room downstairs?" Elvira Maria asked, excited by the prospect.

"Heavens no. They've been with me," Heddie said, patting her ample breasts. She confided in a whisper, "There are a few more in my shuba. Not sapphires like these, but garnets and such."

"Really?" Elvira Maria was amazed. She thought about the coat, now more intriguing than ever. When moving into her old room Heddie had carried it up the stairs and refused to hang it from the rusted hook on the back of the door. Red wool felt, trimmed in black sable, the fur-lined shuba was handsome and warm, an exceptional garment Elvira Maria could never afford, no matter how hard she worked. Heddie had often brought it with her to the attic where Ana had stroked the fur and traced the scrolling gold embroidery with her small fingers.

"You have to be smart and on your guard when thieves are all around you," Heddie said.

"I'm glad you'll be traveling with Boris."

"Yes, thank goodness." Heddie looked at Elvira Maria and hesitated. "I hope I can start all over in Paris."

"Of course you can." Elvira Maria reached for her hand and held it tightly. "You're a strong woman—and you're wealthy." She pointed to the sapphires. "This is a fortune, isn't it?"

"It's enough." Heddie laughed, realizing Elvira Maria had no idea what the stones were really worth.

Elvira Maria examined the jacket. "Do you want them sewn together or in different places?"

"Whatever will be the most secure."

"I'll make a little pouch and attach it inside the lining," Elvira Maria said. "That way they'll be together and won't get lost." She felt the edge of the jacket.

"Wait a moment," Heddie said, "I almost forgot." She turned to a large gray-colored winter tunic she'd set at her feet and handed it to Elvira Maria. "I want Boris to take one. Give him the deep blue stone."

Elvira Maria ran her fingers along the seams of Boris's tunic. "What about here?" She opened the front placket, near the top button.

"Perfect." Heddie pulled her stool closer to Elvira Maria. She studied her serious face, then leaned forward and kissed her on the cheek. "I can't bear to leave you! I so wish you and Ana were coming with us."

Elvira Maria blushed, struggling with her emotions. The spool of thread, escaping her lap, dropped and rolled across the floor. She got up and retrieved it, laughing nervously. "That's impossible, Heddie. You know that." She tried not to speak of Sasha's sentence and her hopes of a reprieve, at least not with Heddie. Her strong opinions were too intimidating.

The sunlight moved across the slanted walls as the morning disappeared. The calls of children playing in the alley came and went. Elvira Maria finished her work on the jacket and turned to the tunic, her meticulous stitches hiding the valuable stone.

"You're a talented seamstress," Heddie said. She lifted Elvira Maria's chin and looked into her eyes. "It's probably none of my business, but if you change your mind and come with us, I know Paris would welcome you *and* your sewing skills."

When Heddie left, the garments draped across her arms, Elvira Maria wondered if Heddie's words were true or simply flattery. She listened to her descend the stairs, her walking shoes clacking loudly on the wooden steps. The shoes were beautiful, made of leather, and an unusual shade of maroon. Elvira Maria adored them and envied Heddie's sense of style. Her fashionable attire was the kind only the affluent could afford. Even when she tried to dress simply, she couldn't help looking elegant. She might wear a used garment purchased from a peddler, trying to blend in with her neighbors, but her red lipstick, the sweet scent from her soaps, and her dignified carriage set her apart.

As she folded Ana's jumper and heard the door to her old room open and close, Elvira Maria knew she had never met anyone like Heddie. Heddie spoke with authority, lit up the room when she entered, was educated, and generous—in surprising ways. Elvira Maria was dumbstruck by her forthright emotions, and by her ability to command the attention of men with just the lilt of her voice. Women in Kos deferred to men and kept their feelings hidden beneath a veil of resentment, prayers, and gossip. Older babushkas might speak their minds, but those who were married walked around with thin tight lips. Quiet and unassuming, they worked hard in the fields and struggled to keep their families fed, believing Fate was ultimately in charge. They rarely voiced their true desires, and certainly not their dreams.

The other tenants had frowned and raised their eyebrows when Heddie moved into the house. Some whispered that she'd owned a brothel. Yagna told anyone who would listen that Heddie was a parasite living in their midst, who'd made her money peddling immorality. Elvira Maria told her to keep her foul mouth shut. Nadia, who knew the Bolsheviks had converted Heddie's house into a new commissariat, claimed Lenin had shut down every brothel in Moscow and was purging thousands of prostitutes from other cities. After hearing that Elvira Maria worried about Heddie's safety. She felt forever beholden to Heddie and dismissed her questionable background as best as she could. Heddie had been instrumental in finding Ana, and her knowledge of Dudorov's criminal activities had led her to Sasha, as well. Once or twice Elvira Maria considered asking Heddie how her life had taken such a turn. But she was a woman from the countryside and would reserve that question for another day. Until then, she watched and listened as Heddie revealed moments of her colorful past, trying to reconcile her new life. Impressed with her passion Elvira Maria held her in her heart. She did not feel the need to press for more.

44

THE FOLLOWING MORNING, the neighborhood women trooped into the vestibule. It was nine o'clock and time for the monthly meeting of the district Housing Committee. Most sat on the stairs and landings, but a few stood near the door and against the walls, where they avoided the piles of dirty bedding and dishes Yagna had pushed in a corner. The women, dressed in drab skirts and worn blouses, grim-faced and tired, flicked their cigarette ashes to the grimy floor and greeted each other. The air was heavy, the sour smell of perspiration and cheap talcum powder rose to the upper landings.

Elvira Maria and Nadia sat on the stairs as two Party members, middle-aged women with clipboards, counted the attendees and called the meeting to order. Their voices were stern and determined. They read the minutes of the previous meeting that both Elvira Maria and Nadia had failed to attend. There had been a discussion about penalties for missing subsequent meetings, including the reduction of food rations. That was why there was a robust turnout this time.

Elvira Maria peered through the spindles in the railing. The women in the vestibule looked nervous. Next to her, Nadia bit a hangnail on her middle finger and jiggled her heel up and down.

The taller of the two Party members claimed the floor. "Our agenda will include critical issues we must address," she said. She waved a pesky fly from her cheek, held up a paper, and read the top priorities: safer streets, cleaner water, a neighborhood banya, and fuel for a large communal kitchen.

The second Party member cleared her throat. "We will vote to decide which of these we'll tackle first," she said, looking at her colleague for validation. The women near the door began to whisper to each other, and the Party member tapped her pen on her clipboard, calling for silence, and soldiered on.

Elvira Maria voted for the banya. If one could be built in the neighborhood it would improve their lives. She raised her voice so she could be heard, identified, counted, and recorded. Nadia followed her lead, voting for the banya and adding that Lydia voted for it too. Her daughter, she said, was almost an adult and although she wasn't at the meeting because she was upstairs minding the children, everyone needed to know that Lydia favored the banya. The Party members made note of it and agreed that younger voices advocating for sanitation improvements were essential to the soviet.

Yagna stepped to the center of the vestibule and unexpectedly requested that a new agenda item be added to the meeting. The Party members exchanged glances and hesitated. She was out of order. But Yagna pointed up the stairs and raised her voice. "Heddie Naryshkina is living il-legally on the third floor," she said. "She must be removed from this house." The room was suddenly quiet. Everyone stared at her. She jutted out her chin and snorted. "Heddie is a despicable woman. A whore who belongs in prison."

Elvira Maria stood up. "I object!" she said. She leaned over the railing. "Comrade Heddie is a kind woman. She doesn't bother anyone. You can't—"

"She's a health risk," Yagna shouted. "We must purge this house of riff-raff."

Nadia rose and flung a hand toward Yagna's soiled blankets and unwashed dishes stashed in the corner. "If you want to purge health risks," she said, "let's start right here!"

The women scanned the room, murmuring and shaking their heads. What about the banya? someone said. Weren't they supposed to be talking about that?

The Party women tapped on their clipboards and called for order. They declared that Yagna's unacceptable housekeeping and Heddie's presence in the tenement would be addressed at the next meeting. Both were a public nuisance.

Yagna cried she'd been unfairly singled out and abused.

While everyone complained about something, Nadia headed up to the landing, informally adjourning the meeting. After all, she said, her children needed her atten-tion and her husband expected his supper, such as it was.

The women, eager to leave, filed out the door. Yagna gathered up her dishes and shot Elvira Maria a nasty look.

Elvira Maria paced the attic. The events of the meeting rattled through her mind. Yagna was malicious. She called

Heddie a trollop behind her back and had laughed when, needing to use the outhouse, Heddie had found it locked. Elvira Maria wished that Heddie could stay, if not in the tenement, perhaps somewhere else in the city. But the danger from the Cheka and others, like Yagna, was too great. Now that the Housing Committee was involved Heddie had a new set of problems that wouldn't go away. She needed to leave for Paris before heavy boots climbed the stairs.

For now the boots climbing the stairs were Michail and Ana's. "You were wise to stay home," he said. Removing his cap, he wiped his sweaty forehead. He and Ana had been to a market hidden in an alley off Grecheskaya Street. "Shoppers were fighting over rotten potatoes and scraggly bunches of beets. Ana saved me from being trampled."

"I told two women to stop pushing," she said. "They were shoving an old man away from the onions. He was in line and it was his turn."

"Terrible." Michail placed the meager produce—two blighted potatoes, a soft beet, a piece of onion, and the bread he could hardly stomach—on the workbench. "The heat has added to everyone's desperation," he said. "And the wind. It's shaking loose everything that isn't tied down."

"We'll have to make that last," Elvira Maria said.

"Volodya was there, protecting his cabbage and doling out slices until a few belligerent women grabbed them all." He grimaced, remembering their meaty hands stuffing the slices into their pockets. "Poor man was there less than an hour. He must have been glad to leave."

"I'm sorry it was so unpleasant," Elvira Maria said. "If only I had a garden. Just a small patch, so we could grow some food, smell the earth." She smiled at Ana. "Remember the garden we had in Kos?"

"Can we have one here?" Ana asked. She kicked off her dusty shoes and pulled at the hole in her sock.

"I don't have any seeds, believe it or not." After all the years she had planted, her apron was empty.

Michail splashed water on his face at the basin and hung the towel by the grate. "They say the train is on its way."

Elvira Maria looked in his direction. Then shifted her gaze to Ana.

He took her hands. "It will arrive the day after tomorrow."

She thought about Sasha. His life sentence, printed in red ink, was posted on a bulletin board outside of the old city jail. He was an enemy of the state, and would join hundreds of other men and women destined for the labor camps. There would be no mercy. No judicial commander to listen to his story and understand the horror of that night. She was foolish to think a soldier would come to her door at the last minute with a reprieve. Once more her life would change overnight and forever without her consent. How would she live day to day knowing that Sasha was in chains, hungry and frightened, beyond her reach? What would she do when Heddie, now her constant friend, was gone? Would she ever sleep again, or always lie awake, worries and memories haunting her? She felt Michail's hands pressing hers as he tried to wrest her from her dark thoughts.

She pulled away. "I don't understand why I can't see him before they leave. How can the wardens deny him access to his mother?"

"The sentence is unjust," Michail said. "We must pray he's strong enough for the journey and what's to come."

"I want to go with him, to care for him the way some families do."

"I won't allow it, Elvira Maria. Ana needs you here and you've suffered enough. The state doesn't provide for families. Sasha will learn to manage."

"How long can prisoners survive in a labor camp?" she asked. Everyone knew about the conditions in the camps. Death rates from malnutrition, exhaustion, and disease were said to be higher there than anywhere else in Russia.

"I don't think it's like the Kara mines—" Michail stopped. Ana sat motionless on the floor, listening to their grim conversation. He could not allude to the brutal treatment the tsars inflicted on their prison labor. He changed his tone. "The Bolsheviks need people to work. I imagine he'll be logging trees, constructing barracks or digging canals, paving roads."

"But will he be fed? Will he be warm? The island's in the White Sea, isn't it? Near the Arctic Circle."

The shriveled pile of vegetables demanded her attention. She steadied her knife and chopped the spongy beetroot into tiny pieces. Trapped by grief and anger, she was close to panic. She looked at Ana, who now knew Sasha would not return. Ana had begun having nightmares in which street urchins with sticks and metal pipes chased her down dark tunnels.

Elvira Maria bit the inside of her cheek, trying to suppress her fury. She tossed the beets in the pot and added water. The red juice swirled. "God help him," she said to herself. "The demons are ruthless." Her troubled thoughts mounted and merged with memories of Lev's capture, and she knew that the men who held Sasha were cut from the same cloth as the soldiers who had killed Lev.

She crossed herself in haste and kissed her pendant, seeking protection from her vindictive thoughts. Michail took the knife. He sliced the onion. Hoisting the pot to the grate and adding wood for a small fire, he called Ana to come cook. He handed her the flint and she lit the kindling. Filled with sadness, he went to his puppets hanging on their wall pegs and examined Beauty and Baba Yaga. He took down Dedushka and hummed his folk song, hoping to change the oppressive atmosphere.

Ana stirred the red broth, the flames crackling. Though disconsolate, Elvira Maria joined her. She stroked her daughter's braids and retied her blue ribbons. "I will find Sasha a warm coat," she said, her voice certain. "They cannot deny him that if they want him to work in the bitter cold."

45

"THE WIND HAS CALMED DOWN," Michail said.

He and Boris sat on a bench near the sea wall over-looking the dockyards. The ink-colored water had grown unusually still. As twilight approached, cargo ships moored along the quays swayed on the dark water, their steel bows slapping softly against the rolling waves. The smoke from a nearby night shelter twined into the pink and violet sky spread out before them.

"Yes," Boris said. "It's the one time I wish it was still gusting. If it stays this quiet, the heat will continue. Not the best for train travel."

"For your sake, I hope everything leaves on time tomorrow. If you can get to Kyiv, passage might be easier from there."

"Michail, I haven't left this city in years," Boris said. "Thought I'd always stay here, wrangling with bureaucrats, herding girls around, shaking down tycoons who wouldn't pay." He laughed. "I was born in the Moldavanka right off Gospitalnaya Street." He pointed over his shoulder with his thumb. "I couldn't wait to leave. There were fifteen of us crammed in two rooms. We slept head to toe."

Michail whistled. "I had no idea."

"I joined Heddie's mother when I was sixteen. I had no intention of pushing a cart loaded with junk forever. I've lived the high life, right on the very edge. It's been glamorous, exciting, and—"

"—risky," Michail interjected. "And with Kotovsky's gang installed, the edge is thinner and sharper than ever before."

"True. But I'll miss the intrigue and the narrow escapes and outsmarting the goons." He paused to watch the sunset. The glimmer of an evening star appeared in the west. "I love living here," he said. "Odessa's my home and always will be. This city is alive day and night. I can't imagine anything better, not even Paris."

Michail looked at him, astonished by the claim.

"East and West meet here. One minute it's French champagne, the next, Bengali tea leaves or opium. Where else can you find poets on every street corner?" He stretched out a hand to the sea. "It's a port full of grand surprises— if you know what to look for, know what you want."

"I'm not so sure," Michail said. "It's still a port full of surprises, but they're not so grand anymore."

"Yes, I know," Boris said. "I'm just nostalgic for old times. I hate to leave them behind." He glanced toward the trees. "But I know danger when I see it. There's a sly, young fellow stalking me whenever I go out. He must be in the shadows right now, wondering when I'll go back to Fanconi's so he can go home and get some sleep. My time here is over and so is Heddie's."

"She'll be better off in Paris."

"The Cheka must have a file on us that's ten times thicker than the Manifesto."

They listened to a tram rumble along the boulevard and cross the intersection. Below, refugees and day workers at the dockyards disappeared into the shadows and shanties. The faint calls of sailors, rowing dories beyond the pier, echoed on the water.

A street lamp turned on, illuminating Boris's sober face. "Sasha's paying a terrible price for the Deputy's loathsome behavior."

"I fear he's headed for a difficult time," Michail said.

"Perhaps he'll fall in with some anarchists and find a bit of support. Political prisoners are sentenced to Solovki, aren't they?" Michail did not reply. Boris pushed on. "Or maybe he'll turn to the priests and monastics sent there. Must be more religious men in the camps than in all of Odessa these days."

"It will be a hard and unforgiving life," Michail said.

"At least he won't rot in a prison cell where sadistic guards will beat him every day."

"I've thought of that, too. It's not much consolation."

A group of women gathered at the bottom of the hill began to climb the Steps, their black dresses trailing behind them. They trudged up to the fifth landing where they claimed a corner of a stone slab and huddled together for the night beneath a cape.

"Boris," Michail said, "I couldn't protect the boy." Unable to further express his regret he stared blankly at the line of orange light that stretched across the horizon.

"I know," Boris said. "That was impossible."

46

HUNDREDS OF IMPATIENT PASSENGERS jammed the grand hall of the railway station. They shouted, pushed, and elbowed their way to the ticket counters where the orderly queues of the morning had long ago collapsed. Red Army soldiers, stationed beneath the arched entrance and in the hall, kept their eyes open. The passengers were impolite, but not unruly, at least not yet.

Boris, tickets in hand, struggled through the weary-looking crowd. Most were city slickers, dressed in shabby woolen suits and outdated summer skirts that were far too long by fashion's current standards. But there were also large numbers of peasant women in faded and patched sarafans, small children swaddled to their breasts. Their anxious eyes peered out from their colorful kerchiefs. They were stoic and maintained a dignity he admired. A street urchin tugged at his sleeve. He handed him a coin and dismissed another, whose pinched and grimy face did not inspire his sympathy. Someone at his side brushed against him for the third time. It was annoying, but pre-dictable. This was a pickpocket's promised land. He folded the tickets, finally stamped for departure, into his wallet and looked for an opening in the dense crowd. His eyes stung. The hall was thick with cigarette smoke. A blue-black haze hovered over everything, tinting the sunlight that beat down from the upper windows. The heavy after-noon heat suggested it was time for his siesta, a summer pleasure he'd enjoyed for years. Fighting fatigue, he made his way to Roza's tea stall, where Heddie stood with Elvira Maria.

Customers called out their orders, waving their hands for attention as they pressed toward the counter. The dented, polished brass samovars steamed beneath the pavilion where travelers, armed with bundles, baskets, and suitcases drank their tea and said their farewells.

"Your trunk is at the platform," Boris told Heddie. He pointed to the huge opened gates that led to the tracks. "I'm joining Michail. Please finish your tea and come along directly. This is not the time for chitchat."

"Yes, Boris," Heddie said. She took a final sip and handed her cup to Roza, who hastily beckoned Elena to join them.

Elena, clad in a dark linen apron, collected a coin from a babushka and hurried toward Heddie, ignoring her insistent customers. "Please, please send us a card from Paris," she said. "I shall miss you every day."

Heddie reached across the counter and kissed the sweaty cheeks of her former employees. She tucked a few rubles into Roza's hand and turned to leave, bumping into a young sailor determined to take her place. Elvira Maria pulled her forward, away from the hustle and bustle.

They pushed through the passengers on the platform. Already three hours late, the train was said to be approaching, but rumors of more delays and cancellations still trickled through the sunburnt and perspiring crowd. Exhausted from waiting all afternoon in the sweltering heat, some sat dull-faced on their luggage, waving-off persistent beggars, while others stood in family groups, shuffling from side to side on their tired feet.

"Mercy, I can't remember ever seeing so many people," Heddie said when they found Michail and Boris. She wiped her damp face with her handkerchief and shifted the fur-lined shuba in her arms.

"Give me your coat," Elvira Maria said. She held out a free hand. "I'll hold it for you."

"No, no, I'm fine," Heddie said. "It can't be long now. Besides, you've already got Sasha's."

The thick woolen coat Elvira Maria had bought the day before had been a rare find during a heat wave when peddlers preferred to roam the streets selling lighter summer wear. But here it was, lined with a patchwork of quilted cotton and trimmed with scruffy fur. Elvira Maria clung to it as she waited anxiously for the train.

"You might as well sit, ladies," Michail said. He dusted off the steamer trunk and made a sweeping gesture of invitation with his hands.

"At this rate we'll be in Kyiv by the end of the year," Boris said. He shoved his leather bag next to the trunk and searched his pockets for a cigarette. But he stopped when he saw a group of urchins running along the tracks, shouting and flinging their arms and caps in the air.

Elvira Maria grabbed Michail's arm. She stepped on top of the trunk and strained to see the excited herd of children. Ragged and covered with coal dust they ran barefoot over the sharp stones between the rails as they announced the train's arrival. The passengers stirred, collecting the parcels at their feet.

"Stay with me, Heddie," Boris said. The noise around them grew louder as the crowd awoke from its stupor. "We've both got to board carriage Number 9."

Heddie pulled Elvira Maria aside as two spindly boys in oversized railway uniforms came for her trunk. They hoisted it onto their bony shoulders and headed down the platform, weaving perilously among a throng of moving hats, shawls, and luggage.

Elvira Maria stood close to Michail, his protective arm around her shoulders. Together they moved forward with the crowd, finally reaching the line of soldiers positioned in front of the tracks. The soldiers ordered the agitated passengers to stand back, to keep a safe distance from the coming train. Elvira Maria searched the line for a commanding officer who might be willing to intercede on her behalf with the prison guards. All she needed was an ally, a kind soul perhaps with a boy of his own, to let her give the warm coat to her son. But the scowling soldiers, wielding bayonets and rifles, were far too busy controlling the disorderly passengers than to listen to her desperate request. She would not approach them until the commotion calmed down and she was certain the prisoners were on board the train.

The passengers waited, pressed against each other, their bodies tense and dripping with sweat. Elvira Maria watched the tracks, her heart pounding. She thought of Ana, playing at Nadia's with Heddie's parasol, a last-minute gift to reward Ana for obeying her mother and agreeing, although reluctantly, to stay home even if it meant never seeing her brother again. Elvira Maria couldn't bear the idea of bringing Ana to the station where she'd be surrounded by an aggressive crowd.

She took a deep breath to steady her nerves, but the thick smoke, now drifting through the hot and humid air, caught in her throat and made her cough. The taste was familiar, disturbing.

And then the long hours of waiting were over. The train was before her, the steam engine hissing and grinding loudly as it inched down the track, blasting black grit and cinders into the gray sky. One by one the empty carriages rolled in front of her until their screeching metal wheels stopped and locked in place. Passengers charged through the line of soldiers and swarmed the carriages, scrambling to claim seats.

"Let them go," Boris shouted. He grabbed Heddie's arm as she jostled against an elderly couple shoving her aside. "Our seats are assigned, the railway boys went ahead to claim them." He took Heddie's shuba and guided her along the platform. "Damn it, why can't these fools stop pushing?"

"Number 9 is the last carriage," Michail called out, "before the flatcars." He pointed ahead.

Boris scoffed at the passengers. They were running; their faces red and contorted, their arms overloaded with parcels, luggage, and crying children. A straw sun-hat whirled to the ground in front of a carriage and was crushed by the stampede of boots and leather shoes. He stole a glance at Heddie. Her chest was heaving, each breath forcing the next. The string of pearls that had escaped her blouse swung across her chest. He had to give her credit; she was keeping up with his long strides.

Winded, they reached the open door of Number 9. Boris presented their tickets to the conductor. "If anyone steals our seats," he said, "I'll demand their arrest."

"Yes, Comrade," the conductor said. He checked their tickets. "Better get yourselves settled."

Michail and Elvira Maria caught up to them. "How long is the wait?" Michail asked.

The conductor shrugged. "Might be an hour. Depends."

"On what?" Boris asked.

"On how many passengers we take up top." The conductor pointed to the men and boys climbing the ladders of the carriages. "Thirty's all I want on each, and I intend to count them. No accidents on my run."

"Good Lord," Heddie said. She scanned the carriage rooftops now teeming with seasoned railway urchins and wary passengers who clambered over their parcels and each other.

"Find your seats," Michail said. "Looks like they've oversold the tickets." Frantic people still streamed along the platform. They poked their heads in and out of the carriages, searching for a seat. "We'll be back shortly," he said. He glanced at the adjoining flatcars and turned to Elvira Maria. "Let's go. We haven't much time."

They hurried down the line to the first flatcar. It was filled with a large group of women and children accompanying the prisoners, their loved ones, to Solovki.

Surrounded by satchels, boxes, and assorted pieces of luggage and sitting on piles of blankets that covered the floorboards, they looked worn-out and hopeless. Two boys on board lifted a canvas tarp over the smaller children to shield them from the engine's grit and ash. Michail and Elvira Maria moved on.

They reached the next flatcar, loaded with the prisoners. The guard held out his hand to stop them. "Turn around, Comrades," he said. He squinted his wrinkled face, his bushy white eyebrows marking his age. "There's nothing for you here."

Undeterred, Michail greeted him and smiled heartily. "I thought I recognized you, Comrade. I'm the puppeteer. Remember the market last winter? I thought you'd never stop laughing."

"What are you talking about?" the guard said. He cocked his head and looked closely at Michail, suspicious of the unexpected and cordial encounter.

"I know it was you," Michail said. "*The Golden Reindeer*. It's my favorite show. You were there with your grand-son." He took the guard's forearm and shook his hand. "I can't forget a face like yours."

The guard stepped back. "What do you want? I'm on duty here. I can't be bothered with your nonsense."

"Forgive me, perhaps I've made a mistake."

"Damn right." Waving off Michail, the guard took notice of Elvira Maria, Sasha's coat in her arms. "What's this? What have you got there?"

"It's a winter coat for her son," Michail said. "He's one of your prisoners."

Elvira Maria ignored the guard and searched the

flatcar. Rows of enormous hay wheels were tied to each end, buffering the crush of at least fifty prisoners who sat on the floor in between them. She examined their grimy faces, her eyes traveling from ashen skin and worried brows, to a cross tattooed on a grizzled man's forehead. An old man with sunken cheeks rested his head on the shoulder of a younger prisoner who seemed healthier than the rest. An even younger prisoner twisted a long stem of grass between his teeth and watched her. There was a face streaked with dirt. And then, suddenly, Sasha's wide gray eyes, so like his father's, met her own.

He leaned forward, and without thinking, struggled to his feet. The men chained to him shifted and grumbled. He was dressed in the tunic and trousers he had on when she last saw him at the shophouse, but now they were ragged. Brown blood stains dotted his sleeves and the tops of his leather boots. He was thinner and lankier than she'd remembered. His beautiful flaxen hair was gone. There was nothing but stubble on his shaved head. He forced a weak smile and opened his empty hands to show her the pair of manacles that extended from his ankles to his wrists and prevented his movement. She stretched out a hand and stepped closer.

"Stand back," the guard said. "That's far enough." He pulled her away from the flatcar. "I've got my orders and they don't include visitors."

"I'm his mother," she said. "Comrade, I haven't seen him in months!" She wrenched her arm free.

Michail pointed to Sasha. "Look at him," he said to the guard. "He's got no clothes for this trip. He won't make it dressed like that."

"I can't help you," the guard said. "The warden should have issued him an outfit at the garrison where he came from. That coat is out of the question. Trims and lining aren't allowed." He flicked his stubby fingers against the scrappy fur collar, dismissing it. "It'll stir up rancor among the men." He looked up at Sasha and shook his head in disgust, irritated that he was so poorly dressed for such a difficult journey. "Move on. There's folks waiting for you." He gestured to Boris and Heddie, now standing at the end of the first flatcar, watching the encounter.

Elvira Maria thrust the coat in Michail's arms and ran to Heddie. "They won't allow it," she said. She'd begun to cry. "The guard claims the other prisoners will get jealous, give him a difficult time."

"Ask if he'll allow something else, something simpler," Heddie said. She could hardly look at Sasha. He was malnourished and pale, not the vibrant eleven-year-old boy she imagined he'd be. His clothes, torn and filthy, wouldn't last another week. She walked to the guard, Boris and Elvira Maria close at hand. "What about a tunic?" she asked. "Can she give him that?"

But the guard, now interrupted by a young Red Army officer, did not acknowledge her presence, and instead stood at attention, saluting his superior.

"Get them watered, Comrade," the officer said. "And get these bothersome people out of here. This isn't a garden party." He looked with contempt at the foursome, then glared at the guard. "Who do you think you're working for?" He clicked his heels together and moved down the platform, blowing a whistle to hail the conductor and stationmaster.

"I'm working for myself and my men," the guard said under his breath. He turned to leave.

"Wait," Boris said. He opened his leather bag and pulled out his gray winter tunic. "Put this on the boy. Don't worry, there's nothing wrapped in it. Check for yourself." He shook it to prove his point.

"That's exactly what he needs," Heddie said. "It's simple, nothing to scrap about, just a plain peasant garment. Take it, Comrade."

Elvira Maria recognized the tunic at once. Stunned, she looked from Heddie to Boris. Heddie nodded. Boris closed his bag and discreetly did the same.

The guard tossed the tunic over his shoulder and pulled out his heavy ring of keys. He called for his assistant to cover him as he climbed onto the flatcar. "Damned if I've ever seen such a fuss," he said. "Come here, boy, let's get this over with." He stood in front of Sasha and unlocked his wrist irons. "Put this on and be grateful." He glowered at the other prisoners. "No word about this or I'll starve you all for three days. Understand?" Sasha pulled the tunic over his head and tucked it under the chain that wrapped around his waist. The guard locked his manacles in place, slapped him on the cheek, and jumped down. "You got what you came for," he said to Michail. He straightened the visor of his cap and threw back his aging shoulders. "Now get going and leave me be."

Michail grabbed his hand and shook it in earnest. "Have a safe trip, my good man."

"I intend to."

"Will you go all the way to Solovki?"

"No," the guard said. "I only take them halfway. Nizhni Novgorod's my destination."

"Where the wild apples are sweet," Michail said, smiling.

"Yes Comrade, they surely are."

Michail gently pulled Elvira Maria away from the flatcar. She took a few steps, but unable to leave, stopped and turned. She looked at Sasha through her tears, memorizing his face. Dressed in Boris's gray tunic he looked like the other prisoners, yet still maintained his youthful grace and clear intelligent eyes. She removed her pendant and held it aloft for him to see. He bowed his head as she blessed him and prayed for Mother Theotokos to protect him.

The engine bell, clanging loudly, resounded through the station, signaling the train's imminent departure. Elvira Maria felt Heddie's arms around her, the scent of rose perfume next to her cheek.

"Goodbye, my dear, goodbye!"

"Oh, Heddie," Elvira Maria embraced her and cried. "I cannot believe that you and Boris gave Sasha—" She could not continue.

"It was the only way," Heddie said. "It was the best way."

"Do you think he'll find it?" Elvira Maria whispered.

"We have to believe he will." She wiped the tears from Elvira Maria's face and embraced her again.

"Come along," Boris said, taking Heddie's arm. "We cannot miss this train."

Elvira Maria, standing back from the rails with Michail, watched them hurry to their carriage. As the bell rang out insistently and they reached Number 9, Boris helped Heddie climb the steep steps. Together they stood in the doorway breathless and waving.

The bell clanged on and on. Steam and cinders heaved from the engine as the train moved forward. The wooden platform shook. Passengers, straining out the open windows, shouted to bystanders, their farewells lost in the deafening noise. Railway urchins and stowaways ran beside the carriages, and grabbing the railings and ladders, swung up onto the roof. The train gathered speed. The flatcars, grinding their wheels, rolled past Elvira Maria and Michail and then disappeared from sight in a heavy cloud of smoke.

THE END

CHRONOLOGY

This chronology is intended to aid the reader in better understanding the historical context of this novel. It is by no means complete, but highlights key events relevant to 1919–1920, the year in which *Night Train to Odessa* takes place.

1794   City of Odessa is founded by a decree from Russian Empress Catherine the Great.

1802   Approximately 9,000 residents live in Odessa.

1823–24   Alexander Pushkin, poet and publicist, in Odessa.

1830s   Large-scale Jewish immigration to Odessa begins.

1841   The "Odessa Steps," a large outdoor staircase, initially constructed of limestone, is completed. In 1955 the steps are renamed the "Potemkin Steps."

1861   Serfdom is abolished in Russia with Emperor
                Alexander II's *Emancipation Manifesto*. A wave
                of anti-Jewish pogroms follow.

1871, 1881   Anti-Jewish pogroms.

1890   Brussels Conference Act bans the slave trade
                of dhimmi boys (dancing boys often abused
                as sexual slaves), popular in the Ottoman
                Empire. The illegal training and trade of
                dhimmi boys continues underground.

1897   Imperial Census counts 403,800 residents
                living in Odessa. Jews comprise 34 percent of
                the seaport's population.

1905   Anti-Jewish pogrom breaks out in Odessa.
                Wide-spread violence continues for months,
                resulting in the injury of thousands, and the
                death of over 800 Jews, and countless other
                ordinary residents.

1914 – 18   First World War. Russia enters the war in
                August 1914 supporting the Serbs and their
                French and British Allies.

1914   Vladimir Vladimirovich Mayakovsky, known
                as the poet of the Great Russian Revolution,
                visits Odessa. He joins the Bolshevik cause,
                welcoming the Revolution of 1917. He
                also produces an astonishing number of
                revolutionary posters. Before his untimely
                death in 1930 he visits Odessa three more
                times.

1915   Orphans or abandoned children
        (besprizorniki) are left homeless on the
        streets, often the result of WWI, the Russian
        Revolution, and Civil War. Approximately
        seven million children, separated from their
        parents, wander homeless throughout the
        country following the Bolshevik victory.

1917   February Revolution in Russia. The first
        stage of the revolution takes place February
        24 – 28 (old style). The monarchy is
        overthrown and replaced by the Provisional
        Government.

1917   Tsar Nicholas II abdicates.

1917   October Revolution in Russia takes
        place October 24 – 25 (old style). Leftist
        revolutionaries, led by Bolshevik Party
        leader, Vladimir Lenin, carry out a coup
        d'état against the Duma's Provisional
        Government.

1917-1920   Ukrainians seek an independent Ukrainian
            state, the Ukrainian People's Republic (UPR),
            also called Ukrainian National Republic
            (UNR).

1917   Vladimir Lenin forms the Cheka, a Bolshevik
        security force and intelligence agency
        charged with combating counterrevolution
        and sabotage.

1918   Gregorian calendar is implemented in Russia.

1918   Alexander Alexandrovich Blok, lyric poet,
            writes his revolutionary poem, "The
            Scythians."

1918   Yuri Carlovich Oleysha attends the
            University of Novorossiya in Odessa where
            he establishes himself in the literary scene. A
            prolific writer, he publishes poems, satirical
            prose, plays, short stories, and novels. Later
            in life, he faces government censorship.

1918–20   Russian Civil War. Factions include the
            Red Army (fighting for Lenin's Bolshevik
            government) and the White Army, also
            referred to as the Whites' Volunteer Army
            (fighting for a large group of allied forces
            including monarchists, capitalists, and
            supporters of democratic socialism). Odessa
            is controlled in turn by French, Ukrainian,
            White, and Bolshevik troops.

1919   Red Army invades Ukraine at the beginning
            of the year.

1919   Solovki Camp, a forced labor prison camp,
            also known as Solovki Special Purpose Prison
            Camp (SLON) is established by Vladimir
            Lenin. The management of the camp is
            entrusted to the Cheka under the Gulag, the
            government agency in charge of forced labor
            camps at that time. Solovki, located in the
            archipelago of the White Sea, is the former
            site of the Russian Orthodox Solovetsky
            monastic complex.

1920   Red Army General, Grigory Ivanovich
            Kotovsky, and his Red Banner Brigade make
            a final entry into Odessa on February 7 and
            take the city. Tens of thousands of refugees
            are evacuated by Allied warships (supporting
            the Whites) in Odessa's harbor. After the
            departure of the Whites, fighting continues
            in the city.

1920   American anarchist, Emma Goldman, is
            deported to Russia December 19, 1919. She
            travels in Russia and finds corruption and
            rampant opportunism throughout the Soviet
            government. Visiting Odessa in 1920, she
            reports sabotaged utility stations, Ukrainians
            antagonistic to the Soviet regime, and
            residents fearful of a brutal Cheka.

1921   Isaac Babel's first short story in *Odessa Tales* is
            published by Maxim Gorky, leftist writer and
            editor.

1921–23   Povolzhye Famine. Food shortages increase,
            and famine sweeps across Russia. 1.5–2
            million people, many Ukrainian, die of
            starvation and accompanying epidemics.

1922   Soviet Union is established.

THE ANTI-JEWISH POGROM OF 1905

The origins of the anti-Jewish pogroms in Odessa, in particular the pogrom of 1905 referred to in Night Train to Odessa, are complex. An extensive analysis, beyond this one, is available in Odessa: Genius and Death in a City of Dreams, a fascinating, lyrical chronicle of the city written by Charles King (W. W. Norton & Company: New York & London, 2011).

The early Jewish settlers in Odessa were most notably from Galicia and Poland, regions where economic limitations and religious and cultural constraints circumscribed their lives. In Odessa, known for its welcoming and liberal atmosphere, they hoped to find progressive change and new opportunities.

In 1802 9,000 residents lived in the city, but in just twelve years that number tripled as not only Jews, but immigrants from other ethnic groups arrived by the tens of thousands. In 1816 Tsar Alexander II's Emancipation Manifesto freed over 23 million peasants in the Russian

Empire and gave rise to rapid migration. The Imperial Census of 1897 counted 403,800 residents living in the seaport city, with Jews comprising approximately one-quarter of the population.

Odessa was a vibrant place where residents, despite their cultural differences, thought of themselves as Odessans. Though Jews continued to speak Yiddish, Russian, the language of assimilation, was dominant. Writers escaping from the shtetl published in both languages, hoping to reach a larger audience. Periodicals, books, newspapers, musical scores, and librettos in Yiddish and Russian were available to a literate public in shops, reading rooms, and libraries. Throughout the nineteenth century Jews established synagogues, schools, a hospital, a burial society, and a Kehillah, a dedicated group in charge of community affairs. In Odessa, a city without a ghetto, they chose their place of residence according to their livelihoods and resources. Many lived in mixed ethnic neighborhoods in the city center with wide tree-lined streets, parks, and daily markets, poised above the Black Sea and a dockyards that boomed with business.

But as the city's population grew during late Imperial Russia (between 1890 and 1917), thousands of poor Jews crowded into the Moldavanka Suburb. Ethnic groups became more competitive than ever before and vied for living space, higher wages, and employment. Housing in working class suburbs became crowded, derelict, and crime-ridden. Brawls and riots between Christians and Jews became more frequent, with police deliberately ignoring the conflict. Tensions mounted, and those who blamed the Jews for their troubles remembered their deep-seated religious prejudice against them.

Though the city's economic life was largely dominated by Christians engaged in shipping and agricultural production, Jews played a significant and creative role in the public arena. Here they interacted with other immigrants as proprietors, merchants, traders, journalists, domestic servants, and the like, in positions that remained open to them by state-imposed laws and convention. Their visibility strengthened misperceptions of their economic influence, and fueled distrust and jealousy. In 1881 simmering hostilities erupted into three days of riots that targeted Jews. The following year, the state stripped away legal protections, making them second-class subjects under the tsar. In response, Jews organized defense leagues to protect themselves from violence and discrimination.

Animosities surfaced again in the wake of the 1905 uprising when Jews were accused of failing to support Tsar Nicholas II's reforms and of leading a socialist and radical agenda that encouraged the massive strikes and revolutionary activity seizing the country. In northeast Asia, where Japan and Russia waged war, the effects were disastrous for Odessa, a grain supplier to the Russian Far East. Japanese naval blockades kept Russian grain from the city's overseas markets, forcing the port in Odessa to close. Businesses shut down and credit dried up. Strikes supported by Jewish longshoremen angered their Russian and Ukrainian counterparts. A pogrom, the largest in Russian history thus far, swept through the city. Jewish homes and businesses were attacked by mobs, with armed defense leagues fighting back. Explosions, shoot-outs, raids, assassinations, and widespread violence continued for months. The great artistic and commercial city of southern Russia was at war with itself. The destruction, swift and brutal, resulted in extensive property damage, the injury of thousands, and the death of over 800 Jews and countless other residents.

Recovery was slow and painful. Many Jews fled the city, while others talked about Zionism and the promise of Palestine. Those who were determined to stay recognized that civic life had changed, that a revolution was inevitable, and that a Civil War would determine the direction and mood of their beloved Odessa.

ACKNOWLEDGMENTS

Though Night Train to Odessa is a work of fiction, it is inspired by events that took place in the life of my great-aunt, Tanta Elvina, a survivor of the Russian Revolution and Civil War. She was the matriarch of our small family and kept me close with a watchful eye and stern voice, knowing first-hand that children could disappear in a crowd and never be found again. Her heart-felt stories of the war, mixed with tears and regrets, impressed me greatly as a child and, years later, piqued my interest to write this novel. Elvira Maria's story, quite different in detail from yours, belongs to you, loving Tanta. I cannot thank you enough.

The Russian Civil War, a period of tremendous upheaval, is complicated, to say the least. Navigating the events, players, ideologies, and boots on the ground was a challenging and never-ending task. I am particularly indebted to the following historical works and superb researchers: Odessa: Genius and Death in a City of Dreams by Charles King; Odessa Recollected: The Port and the People by Patricia Herlihy; Odessa Memories edited by Nicolas V.

Iljine and Patricia Herlihy; *And Now My Soul is Hardened: Abandoned Children in Soviet Russia, 1918–1930* by Alan M. Ball; *The Akhmatova Journals* by Lydia Chukovskaya; *Born of the Storm: Civil War in the Ukraine* by Nikolai A. Ostrovsky; and *The Big Show in Bololand: The American Relief Expedition to Soviet Russia in the Famine of 1921* by Bertrand M. Patenaude. This list could continue for pages and also include the poems of Vladimir V. Mayakovsky and Alexander A. Blok, the short stories of Isaac Babel, and the essays of Maxim Gorky, Emma Goldman, John Reed, and so forth. I am grateful to each of you for your extraordinary scholarship.

Many people with valuable expertise helped me realize this book. Judith Claire Mitchell, whose encouragement and critical eye never wavered, deserves an honorable mention. Jane Katims, Jim Rutke, Judith Weber, Patricia A. McNair, Jane Guill, Kyle Cochrun, Michelle Mercer, Kim Weiss, and Kathleen Dexter provided comments, contacts, and technical and literary support. Thanks also go to Shake Rag Alley Center for the Arts in Mineral Point, Wisconsin. Their writing retreats and workshops provided the perfect place for me to explore new scenes and characters essential to this story. Though David Usitalo, a master puppeteer, is no longer with us, I am thankful to have toured with his summer theater. It was a joy to craft puppets and dance them on stage.

In Santa Fe, the house of painter and art educator, Randall Davey, provided inspiration for the exotic mural in Heddie Naryshkina's brothel. Anyone who has toured this house, now part of the Randall Davey Audubon Center and Sanctuary, cannot help but smile when they see the dressing room murals Davey painted for his wife. I could not resist paying tribute to them in this story.

Finally, I would like to acknowledge and thank the family members — Cheyene, Christina, and Grant Grow, and my sister, Phyllis E. Browne — who remained interested in my writing adventure, and the many friends who supported me with their extraordinary hospitality and affection: Winifred Batson, Christine Tharnstram, Michael Donovan, Tammy Teschner, Lyn Anglin, Al Miller, Richard La Belle, and Diane Michalski-Turner.

As for my husband, Jean-Marc Richel, who encouraged me to stay the course — I could not be more grateful. *Tu es une galaxie d'inspiration toujours.*

ABOUT THE AUTHOR

Mary L. Grow is a cultural anthropologist and former Fulbright-Hays research scholar. Her ethnographies of performance traditions have been published by Yale University, Smithsonian Institution, and University of Hawai'i Press, among others. An intrepid traveler, she has performed with puppet theater troupes in the United States and Southeast Asia. She lives in the countryside, north of Santa Fe, with her husband and several curious peacocks.

A reading guide and additional information, including author tours, visits to book clubs, and contact information, may be found on MaryLGrow.com.

A NOTE ON THE TYPE

Night Train to Odessa is set in Rialto Piccolo, a typeface designed by Venetian calligrapher Giovanni de Faccio and Austrian typographer Lui Karner as a bridge between calligraphy and typography, styled after the neohumanist types prevalent in the early twentieth century.

Printed by Amazon Italia Logistica S.r.l.
Torrazza Piemonte (TO), Italy

60078671R00199